PRAISE FOR *THE LAUGHING DEAD*

"Turn on the lights and check your locks before settling down with Jess Lourey's latest thriller. *The Laughing Dead* is a tense, twisty read that will grab you by the throat and won't let go until you race to the very last, spectacularly creepy page."

—Melinda Leigh, #1 *Wall Street Journal* bestselling author

"Writing from multiple perspectives, Lourey weaves an intricate tale of despair and hope, leading to an explosive and gripping climax that had my jaw dropping to the floor."

—Yasmin Angoe, author of the Nena Knight trilogy and *Not What She Seems*

PRAISE FOR *THE REAPING*

"Mystery and horror mix in a creepy novel whose suspenseful ending hints at a very special sequel."

—*Kirkus Reviews*

"*The Reaping* is so much more than a mere thriller. There are complex characters, unpredictable settings, and a mix of supernatural and mystery elements that drive this tale to a unique finale."

—Bookreporter

"There are just some books—or series—that grab you and don't let go, and this is one of those."

—*Madison Daily Leader*

Praise for *The Taken Ones*

Short-listed for the 2024 Edgar Award for
Best Paperback Original

"Setting the standard for top-notch thrillers, *The Taken Ones* is smart, compelling, and filled with utterly real characters. Lourey brings her formidable storytelling talent to the game and, on top of that, wows us with a deft stylistic touch. This is a one-sitting read!"

—Jeffery Deaver, author of *The Bone Collector* and *The Watchmaker's Hand*

"*The Taken Ones* has Jess Lourey's trademark of suspense all the way. A damaged and brave heroine, an equally damaged evildoer, and missing girls from long ago all combine to keep the reader rushing through to the explosive ending."

—Charlaine Harris, *New York Times* bestselling author

"Lourey is at the top of her game with *The Taken Ones*. A master of building tension while maintaining a riveting pace, Lourey is a hell of a writer on all fronts, but her greatest talent may be her characters."

—Danielle Girard, *USA Today* and Amazon #1 bestselling author of *Up Close*

Praise for *The Quarry Girls*

Winner of the 2023 Anthony Award for
Best Paperback Original

Winner of the 2023 Minnesota
Book Award for Genre Fiction

"Few authors can blend the genuine fear generated by a sordid tale of true crime with evocative, three-dimensional characters and mesmerizing prose like Jess Lourey. Her fictional stories feel rooted in a world we all know but also fear. *The Quarry Girls* is a story of secrets gone to seed, and Lourey gives readers her best novel yet—which is quite the accomplishment. Calling it: *The Quarry Girls* will be one of the best books of the year."

—Alex Segura, acclaimed author of
Secret Identity, *Star Wars Poe Dameron: Free Fall*, and *Miami Midnight*

"Lourey conveys the edgy, hungry restlessness of teen girls with a touch of Megan Abbott while steadily intensifying the claustrophobic atmosphere of a small 1977 Minnesota town where darkness snakes below the surface."

—Loreth Anne White, *Washington Post* and Amazon Charts
bestselling author of *The Patient's Secret*

"Jess Lourey is a master of the coming-of-age thriller, and *The Quarry Girls* may be her best yet—as dark, twisty, and full of secrets as the tunnels that lurk beneath Pantown's deceptively idyllic streets."

—Chris Holm, Anthony Award–winning author of *The Killing Kind*

Praise for *Bloodline*

Winner of the 2022 Anthony Award for
Best Paperback Original

Winner of the 2022 ITW Thriller Award for
Best Paperback Original

Short-listed for the 2021 Goodreads Choice Awards

"Fans of *Rosemary's Baby* will relish this."

—*Publishers Weekly*

"Based on a true story, this is a sinister, suspenseful thriller full of creeping horror."

—*Kirkus Reviews*

"Lourey ratchets up the fear in a novel that verges on horror."

—*Library Journal*

"In *Bloodline*, Jess Lourey blends elements of mystery, suspense, and horror to stunning effect."

—*BOLO Books*

"Inspired by a true story, it's a creepy page-turner that has me eager to read more of Ms. Lourey's works, especially if they're all as incisive as this thought-provoking novel."

—Criminal Element

"*Bloodline* by Jess Lourey is a psychological thriller that grabbed me from the beginning and didn't let go."

—*Mystery & Suspense Magazine*

"*Bloodline* blends page-turning storytelling with clever homages to such horror classics as *Rosemary's Baby*, *The Stepford Wives*, and *Harvest Home*."

—*Toronto Star*

"*Bloodline* is a terrific, creepy thriller, and Jess Lourey clearly knows how to get under your skin."

—Bookreporter

"[A] tightly coiled domestic thriller that slowly but persuasively builds the suspense."

—*South Florida Sun Sentinel*

"Set in an idyllic small town rooted in family history and horrific secrets, *Bloodline* is *Pleasantville* meets *Rosemary's Baby*. A deeply unsettling, darkly unnerving, and utterly compelling novel, this book chilled me to the core, and I loved every bit of it."

—Jennifer Hillier, author of *Little Secrets* and the award-winning *Jar of Hearts*

"Jess Lourey writes small-town Minnesota like Stephen King writes small-town Maine. *Bloodline* is a tremendous book with a heart and a hacksaw . . . and I loved every second of it."

—Rachel Howzell Hall, author of the critically acclaimed novels *And Now She's Gone* and *They All Fall Down*

Praise for *Unspeakable Things*

Winner of the 2021 Anthony Award for
Best Paperback Original

Short-listed for the 2021 Edgar Awards and
2020 Goodreads Choice Awards

"The suspense never wavers in this page-turner."

—*Publishers Weekly*

"The atmospheric suspense novel is haunting because it's narrated from the point of view of a thirteen-year-old, an age that should be more innocent but often isn't. Even more chilling, it's based on real-life incidents. Lourey may be known for comic capers (*March of Crimes*), but this tense novel combines the best of a coming-of-age story with suspense and an unforgettable young narrator."

—*Library Journal* (starred review)

"Part suspense, part coming-of-age, Jess Lourey's *Unspeakable Things* is a story of creeping dread, about childhood when you know the monster under your bed is real. A novel that clings to you long after the last page."

—Lori Rader-Day, Edgar Award–nominated author of *Under a Dark Sky*

"A noose of a novel that tightens by inches. The squirming tension comes from every direction—including the ones that are supposed to be safe. I felt complicit as I read, as if at any moment I stopped I would be abandoning Cassie, alone, in the dark, straining to listen and fearing to hear."

—Marcus Sakey, bestselling author of *Brilliance*

"*Unspeakable Things* is an absolutely riveting novel about the poisonous secrets buried deep in towns and families. Jess Lourey has created a story that will chill you to the bone and a main character who will break your heart wide open."

—Lou Berney, Edgar Award–winning author of *November Road*

"Inspired by a true story, *Unspeakable Things* crackles with authenticity, humanity, and humor. The novel reminded me of *To Kill a Mockingbird* and *The Marsh King's Daughter*. Highly recommended."

—Mark Sullivan, bestselling author of *Beneath a Scarlet Sky*

"Jess Lourey does a masterful job building tension and dread, but her greatest asset in *Unspeakable Things* is Cassie—an arresting narrator you identify with, root for, and desperately want to protect. This is a book that will stick with you long after you've torn through it."

—Rob Hart, author of *The Warehouse*

"With *Unspeakable Things*, Jess Lourey has managed the near-impossible, crafting a mystery as harrowing as it is tender, as gut-wrenching as it is lyrical. There is real darkness here, a creeping, inescapable dread that more than once had me looking over my own shoulder. But at its heart beats the irrepressible—and irresistible—spirit of its . . . heroine, a young woman so bright and vital and brave she kept even the fiercest monsters at bay. This is a book that will stay with me for a long time."

—Elizabeth Little, *Los Angeles Times* bestselling author of *Dear Daughter* and *Pretty as a Picture*

Praise for *Salem's Cipher*

"A fast-paced, sometimes brutal thriller reminiscent of Dan Brown's *The Da Vinci Code*."

—*Booklist* (starred review)

"A hair-raising thrill ride."

—*Library Journal* (starred review)

"The fascinating historical information combined with a storyline ripped from the headlines will hook conspiracy theorists and action addicts alike."

—*Kirkus Reviews*

"Fans of *The Da Vinci Code* are going to love this book . . . One of my favorite reads of 2016."

—*Crimespree Magazine*

"This suspenseful tale has something for absolutely everyone to enjoy."

—*Suspense Magazine*

Praise for *May Day*

"Jess Lourey writes about a small-town assistant librarian, but this is no genteel traditional mystery. Mira James . . . flees a dead-end job and a dead-end boyfriend in Minneapolis and ends up in Battle Lake, a little town with plenty of dirty secrets. The first-person narrative in *May Day* is fresh, the characters quirky. Minnesota has many fine crime writers, and Jess Lourey has just entered their ranks!"

—Ellen Hart, award-winning author of the Jane Lawless and Sophie Greenway series

"This trade paperback packed a punch . . . I loved it from the get-go!"
—*Tulsa World*

"What a romp this is! I found myself laughing out loud."
—*Crimespree Magazine*

"Mira digs up a closetful of dirty secrets, including sex parties, cross-dressing, and blackmail, on her way to exposing the killer. Lourey's debut has a likable heroine and surfeit of sass."
—*Kirkus Reviews*

Praise for *Rewrite Your Life: Discover Your Truth Through the Healing Power of Fiction*

"Interweaving practical advice with stories and insights garnered in her own writing journey, Jessica Lourey offers a step-by-step guide for writers struggling to create fiction from their life experiences. But this book isn't just about writing. It's also about the power of stories to transform those who write them. I know of no other guide that delivers on its promise with such honesty, simplicity, and beauty."
—William Kent Krueger, *New York Times* bestselling author of the Cork O'Connor series and *Ordinary Grace*

THE CRYING KILLER

OTHER TITLES BY JESS LOUREY

BLACKTHORN BOOKS

The Blackthorn Women

"Twice in a Blue Moon"

STEINBECK AND REED THRILLERS

"Catch Her in a Lie"

The Taken Ones

The Reaping

The Laughing Dead

MURDER BY MONTH MYSTERIES

May Day

June Bug

Knee High by the Fourth of July

August Moon

September Mourn

October Fest

November Hunt

December Dread

January Thaw

February Fever

March of Crimes

April Fools

THRILLERS

Unspeakable Things

Bloodline

Litani

The Quarry Girls

SALEM'S CIPHER THRILLERS

Salem's Cipher

Mercy's Chase

CHILDREN'S BOOKS

Leave My Book Alone! Starring Claudette, a Dragon with Control Issues

YOUNG ADULT

The Verdant Cage

NONFICTION

Rewrite Your Life: Discover Your Truth Through the Healing Power of Fiction

Better Than Gin: A Coloring Book for Writers

THE CRYING KILLER

JESS LOUREY

THOMAS & MERCER

This is a work of fiction. Names, characters, organizations, places, events, and incidents are either products of the author's imagination or are used fictitiously. Otherwise, any resemblance to actual persons, living or dead, is purely coincidental.

Published by Thomas & Mercer, Seattle

www.apub.com

EU product safety contact:
Amazon Media EU S. à r.l.
38, avenue John F. Kennedy, L-1855 Luxembourg
amazonpublishing-gpsr@amazon.com

ISBN-13: 9781662531491 (paperback)
ISBN-13: 9781662531484 (digital)

Cover design by Alicia Tatone
Cover image: © Jenny Woodworth / Shutterstock; © acilo / Getty Images

Printed in the United States of America

To the Longfellow group.
Beer, bourbon, and solidarity.
Who could ask for anything more?

AUTHOR'S NOTE

Serial killings have an outsize grip on the American imagination despite accounting for only 1 percent of homicides. Millions of us tune into podcasts like *Crime Junkie* and *Morbid*, binge documentaries like *Conversations with a Killer: The Ted Bundy Tapes*, devour books like Michelle McNamara's *I'll Be Gone in the Dark*.

I think there's an element of self-protection to the obsession. If we learn how the predators hunt, we might be able to keep ourselves safe. Plus, there's the timeless appeal of hearing a scary story while you yourself are safe. But those factors are universal, so I don't think they account for the uniquely *American* fascination with serial killers.

That, I think, is explained by ratios.

Specifically, the US has more documented serial killers than any other nation, over twenty times as many as England, which ranks second. If a population has a twentyfold difference in anything deadly—car accidents, earthquakes, salmonella outbreaks—it's going to rightfully invite attention.

On a per capita basis, the three states that consistently top the list for numbers of serial killings are Alaska, Montana, and Nevada, though my home state of Minnesota has recorded its share of repeat offenders. Paul Michael Stephani, otherwise known as the Weepy-Voiced Killer, is one of the most notorious. He earned his nickname due to his whining, anonymous phone calls to police after all but one of his gruesome crimes.

Stephani was born September 8, 1944, in Austin, Minnesota, to a devoutly Catholic mother. His father died when he was young, and his mother remarried a man who was reportedly abusive. Stephani, now part of a blended family of ten children, moved out of the house and to Saint Paul in the mid-'60s. There he held various low-wage jobs, including as a shipping clerk and janitor. He stayed mostly below the radar until December 31, 1980, when he viciously attacked twenty-year-old Karen Potack, beating her with a tire iron and leaving her for dead. In a span of two years, he would go on to murder three women and stab a fourth who—like Karen Potack—survived, bringing his total number of known victims to five.

Because of his childhood spent in a deeply religious family, it's possible that Stephani's high-pitched confessional calls after his attacks were not just theatrics but attempts at atonement, pathetic pleas for absolution that offered no comfort to his victims or their families. (For example, he complained, "I'll never make it into heaven!" when admitting to stabbing Barbara Simons, a nurse, over forty times. As with his other weeping phone calls, he left no identifying information.) His recorded confessions brought him wide attention, which in turn made him seem larger than life.

Like many—all?—serial killers Americans find themselves fascinated with, though, the myth of Paul Michael Stephani overshadowed the reality. Think Dennis Rader, the self-styled BTK ("bind, torture, kill") Killer, who lived for decades as a Boy Scout leader and church council president, all while concealing his monstrous double life. When caught, he was revealed to be less a criminal mastermind than a middle-aged narcissist. Or Ted Bundy, often romanticized for his charisma and intelligence, who was actually a deeply insecure man as well as a mediocre student with average intelligence. Richard Ramirez—the Night Stalker—left behind ample evidence, including fingerprints, and Joseph James DeAngelo, better known as the Golden State Killer, was described by his neighbors as aloof but unexceptional.

The list goes on.

Serial killers, once stripped of their fabricated mystique, are not the legends popular culture often makes them out to be. They're typically unremarkable men who benefit from institutional bias and imperfect police work.

Stephani was a prime example.

He struggled to maintain steady employment and was nearly caught multiple times. For the setting of his first attack, he chose the grounds of the manufacturing plant he'd been previously fired from. After his first known murder six months later, the June 1981 ice pick stabbing of recent high school graduate Kimberly Compton, police had witnesses and details connecting him to the scene, yet he wasn't charged. He was also identified as the last person seen leaving a bar with Barbara Simons, whose mutilated body was discovered the next day.

His bizarre, emotional phone calls also left a trail.

But Stephani was only—*finally*—arrested after attacking Denise Williams in late August 1982. Williams, an extraordinary nineteen-year-old, bit him, kicked him, and struck him with a glass bottle as he held her down and stabbed her over a dozen times with a screwdriver. He fled the scene. When he got home, he called for medical assistance due to the injuries she'd inflicted. That call linked him to the assault. Williams and the young man who'd come to her aid both identified Stephani, who was ultimately convicted in Williams's attempted murder as well as the murder of Barbara Simons three weeks earlier.

It wasn't until fifteen years later, when Stephani learned in prison that he had terminal cancer and confessed, that police were able to definitively tie him to his other crimes.

Despite his mediocrity, like many named serial killers, Stephani has become a grim celebrity. Stories about him focus on his melodramatic calls and his apparent religious guilt, painting him as a fascinating enigma rather than what he was: a man with a possible untreated mental illness, unable to regulate his emotions, who relied on luck and societal blind spots to elude capture. He's featured in blogs, podcasts, and TV shows, many of them examining his motivation and his crimes.

His victims, on the other hand?

At least historically, they were reduced to names: Karen Potack, Kimberly Compton, Kathleen Greening, Barbara Simons, and Denise Williams. Maybe a detail or two appeared—a student nurse, a bar patron, a woman attacked while walking home. Their lives, so full and intricate, were rarely explored beyond their brief intersection with Stephani's violence. It's a difficult balance for journalists to strike because on the one hand, the victims and their families deserve privacy. But also, once named, those who suffered should be presented as more than footnotes in their own lives.

Fortunately, some modern true-crime storytelling, especially the thoughtful approach taken by many podcasters as well as writers (Sarah Weinman's excellent essay collections are a prime example), has begun to center what too often was left in shadow: the victims. This approach demonstrates how they were more than their encounter with a killer, more than the day they were murdered. They are presented as whole people, with dreams and flaws, with relationships and stories worth telling. Attention is gradually turning from the perpetrators, frequently dull, one-note monsters, to the deep losses their actions created.

Fiction can also help to rebalance the scale.

This novel, inspired by the haunting crimes and confessions of Paul Michael Stephani, shifts the focus from him, instead concentrating on the communities and the families—including the murderer's own—that are forever altered by serial killings. I find the narratives shattered by the crimes much more compelling than the serial killers themselves, and I aim to stitch them together, piece by piece, placing them at the center of the story.

Where they belong.

Monday's child is fair of face,
Tuesday's child is full of grace.

—from "Monday's Child," traditional nursery rhyme

PROLOGUE

June 1986

The evening was velvet-dark, quiet save for the trailer's tin walls ticking as they held the day's heat. Nicholas Gajdusek, the Hendrickson girls' best friend since middle school, sat cross-legged on the green carpet. His eyes were pinned on newborn Julia like he still couldn't believe she was real. *Here.* The sisters sat apart. Tuesday Hendrickson, eighteen, was perched on the edge of the rust-colored couch holding a bottle, her long legs jiggling anxiously, her gaze flicking every so often toward the window. Sixteen-year-old Trixie Hendrickson sat nearest the baby, her body angled protectively, her whole world anchored to the infant's rise-and-fall breaths. She couldn't stop rubbing her fingertip over Julia's cloud fluff of hair. "Three Musketeers and a baby," Nick said, his voice painted with wonder.

"She's perfect," Trixie whispered. "Absolutely perfect."

"Here," Tuesday said, offering her little sister the bottle.

Trixie's sweatshirt pulled up as she leaned over the secondhand bassinet, exposing the ridged X carved into her lower back. She tugged the sweatshirt down, but not fast enough.

Tuesday's eyes narrowed. "You positive he doesn't know?"

Trixie swallowed, but she kept her attention on baby Julia. "I told you, there's no way. He left town last December. No one's seen him since."

Wariness tightened Nick's features. He didn't live with the Hendrickson girls, but given how often he was over, he might as well have. "Trixie—"

"He's gone," she snapped.

Julia made a startled noise. Trixie immediately softened, murmuring apologies to the tiny bundle as she adjusted the blue baby blanket.

Tuesday crossed her arms, the fresh high school graduate taking up her habitual role as protector. "And if he comes back? What then?"

"He won't." Trixie met Tuesday's gaze, steady and unflinching. In profile they were almost identical, with their strong noses and matching chins. "Why would he? He doesn't know about her." She touched her lips to baby Julia's cheek, inhaling deeply of the honey powder scent. "Nobody does, except us. And it's gonna stay that way."

Julia was Trixie's. Trixie's, Tuesday's, and Nicholas's, that's what they'd agreed.

The room fell quiet, the kind of quiet that made it hard to breathe. Nick ran a hand through his curls, his shoulders hunched.

It'd been Tuesday's idea to drive Trixie—who'd been screaming from labor pains—three towns over to the hospital in Willmar. They were less likely to be recognized there. She was also the one who insisted they swap names. Pregnant at eighteen bought you quiet sympathy; sixteen would trigger a barrelful of questions. The switch should be easy. They had the same eyes, same thin lips, same dirty-blond hair.

On the panicked ride to the hospital, Tuesday coached Trixie on how to talk to the nurses. If asked where the father is, say he's out of state. Someone wants to know what your plans for the future are? Tell them you're excited for college. They want to know any family genetic issues? Share that great-grandfather Hendrickson had epilepsy.

Tuesday lived by these words: *Always tell the truth, but never the whole truth.* In the end, nobody challenged them. The hospital staff treated Trixie like any other small-town girl too dumb to lock the barn door and too poor to afford health insurance. The birth was bloody and quick. The next day, the nurses bundled up Trixie and the baby and sent them all on their way. They'd stopped on the way home to pick up celebratory snacks, gummy bears and a splurge: Cool Ranch Doritos. Tuesday, Trixie, and Nick had been too stunned to open either. They still couldn't believe the hospital had allowed them to leave with a helpless little human.

Trixie glanced out the window, into the yawning dark beyond the glass. It was hot out there, one of those humid Minnesota summer nights that a fan couldn't touch. She grabbed for the bag of gummy bears but stopped when Julia's tiny hands clutched the air. She let her daughter grip one of her fingers, a tear sliding down her cheek.

"We're getting out of Lilydale tomorrow," Tuesday said firmly from the couch, the words seemingly directed as much at herself as them. "All four of us. *Together*. We'll go where he'll never find us, where Nick doesn't get ragged on every time the world spins sideways and"—here her gaze slid to Trixie—"somewhere we're not treated like dirt because we had the crap luck to be born a Hendrickson in this cornhole town."

She'd dragged herself to the back bedroom and crashed out. So what'd woken her just now? Was it whistling? She was so tired, the garage sale quilt holding her like a hug. She didn't want to get up. It'd been days—weeks?—since she'd slept deeply. There'd been so much worry with the baby coming. She was drifting away again when a noise in the next room startled her awake, fully this time.

The red numbers on the bedside clock said it was almost two a.m. Was someone talking out there? Yeah, someone was definitely getting into it in the living room. She didn't recognize the voice at first, low and smooth. Her sister responded, her words slurring like she was tired or . . . scared?

Then, a male voice, clear this time. "It's a nice match for the knife you put in my back," he said.

She was suddenly on her feet, all remnants of sleep vanishing as a razor-edged pulse split her veins. *She recognized that voice.* She lunged for the door but reality had turned to spider silk, and she couldn't fight her way through.

Julia's wail cut through the night, so pure it hurt.

And then, the gunshot.

It was quick. Loud.

Final.

CHAPTER 1

After
January 1, 1995

We're all saints the hour before dawn. That's double true on New Year's Day, with the fresh year spreading out like an altar cloth, set with hope and better choices, kindness and grace. *Maybe this is the year I'll start remembering birthdays, or turning down seconds on dessert.*

So much potential.

So many ways to screw it up.

I snorted and pressed my palm flat to the frosty window, the glass cold enough to burn. Outside, fat, wet snowflakes fell, giant moths fluttering to earth. Mom used to call that kind of snow God's dandruff. She wouldn't say it like a joke, either. Mom resented God and winter equally.

My heart cramped thinking of her. She hadn't recognized me the last few times I'd visited. It made each time harder. Harder to know if I should bring Julia, harder to linger at the facility. But I wouldn't abandon her. I knew how much that hurt.

She and Dad had taught us that.

The falling snow was mesmerizing, drifting lazily through the streetlight's glow. The city would keep those star-shaped garlands on the light poles through the first week of January.

The Victorian's ancient wood floor squawked beneath my feet as I turned away from the window to get breakfast ready. My kitchen used to be the second-story servants' quarters, before the giant house was cut up to make two apartments, one on each floor. The kitchen was huge, though the sloped ceilings made it feel cozy. I yanked open the Harvest Gold Frigidaire and pulled out ingredients for eggs Benedict, Julia's favorite. I'd even splurged to buy the name-brand Canadian bacon she loved, plus a package of bacon for Nic.

The routine of cooking soothed me. *Crack, whisk, simmer.* Everything in my kitchen felt orderly. The white walls, the Nordic-blue-trimmed windows with their red curtains, the cobalt countertops, all of it a Swedish dream.

I could almost convince myself that I lived a normal life, that I deserved this peace.

The radio played in the background, pop music and ads, white noise to drown out the memories. I had the bacon pop-crackling, the hollandaise ready to pour, and was mixing a cup of Suisse Mocha when the DJ's voice obliterated my domestic thoughts.

"Today marks eight years since the Crying Killer's final call," he said.

The kitchen swayed around me.

"For those of you too young to remember," he continued, "the Crying Killer was Minnesota's most famous serial murderer, calling in to this very radio station after each of his crimes, begging forgiveness."

The female DJ cut in. "He called to *apologize* after killing people? That might be the most Minnesotan thing I've ever heard."

The two of them chuckled merrily, like they were talking about a fumble at a football game. Me, I was fighting to get to the radio and shut it off. Too bad my legs were cast in lead.

The male DJ wound down his laugh. I could almost see him wiping his eyes. "Do you want to hear one of the recordings?"

"You betcha!" she chirped.

I moaned, my gut burning with acid.

They played a snippet of the call. Just sobs, then the words "I didn't mean to" in a breathy, high-pitched voice.

The female DJ snorted. "He doesn't sound like much. They caught him after that?"

"Oh, no, he went on to kill one more person."

Tears were streaming down my cheeks. My hand was almost at the radio, but I couldn't reach it fast enough.

"I thought you said it was the anniversary of his last killing?"

The guy made a tsking noise. "I said it was the anniversary of his last *call*. It took six more months to stop him. The cops shot him dead coming out of the trailer where he'd just killed his final victim."

If I had to hear the DJ say "Trixie Hendrickson" in that arrogant, careless voice, like she was a nobody, a fictional character or a game token, my heart would stop. With a groan, I broke free from my paralysis, finally able to stab the off button on the radio at the same time Nicolette walked into the kitchen.

Her eyebrows met in worry. "What's wrong, Tuesday?"

"Nothing," I lied, wiping my face and turning away. "Just hate reruns." She threw me a dubious look before grabbing the General Foods International Coffees tin, holding it close to her face. "If you say so. Can I try some?"

I stretched, trying to crack-pop the cortisol out of my joints. "You won't like it."

She took her coffee black, had since high school, back when she still went by Nicholas and her, Trixie, and me were the Three Musketeers. It was an affect then, alongside the unfiltered cigarettes, mohawk, and raccoon eyeliner. Now it was a conviction.

"If you say so." She set down the tin and strode out the opposite door to the bathroom.

"Julia up?" I asked her departing form.

A sweet, high voice from behind answered me. "Duh. Of course I'm up."

I turned to the arched entryway to see Julia was not only awake but bright-eyed, her blond hair scraped into pigtails held in place with tangerine-colored plastic balls. Like magic, the remaining awfulness of hearing that recording melted away. So the DJs were ghouls who made a spectacle out of other people's deepest trauma. That wasn't my problem. I had everything important to me right here, safe. My heart sang like it did every time I laid eyes on Julia, every time since the moment she was born. She was a miracle, though I'd never say it out loud. Eight-year-olds could smell sentiment a mile away.

"It's the last morning of Christmas break," I said neutrally. "I thought you'd sleep in."

She rolled her eyes so hard I worried she could see her brain. "I told you a *million* times!" Her tone reflected the suffering of the ages. "I'm going to the Mall of America with Sarah and her family."

I grabbed the counter, fighting to keep my emotions off my face. Letting her attend school was one thing. I'd grudgingly accepted that because I had no choice. But hanging out with friends outside of school? I wasn't ready. Sure, I'd okayed her plans for today, but then I'd promptly buried them in the No Thanks chest where I kept everything I didn't want to think about. I breathed deep, steadying myself. I'd made a promise as I'd cradled her tiny body in my arms, the acrid scent of gunpowder burning my nostrils. I'd sworn I'd give her the childhood she deserved, and that meant letting her leave the house without me.

"I didn't know you'd be leaving so early, is all." I forced my voice to remain even. "Does the mall even open before ten?"

"Double duh, Mom."

Mom.

The word lodged in my gut, honey laced with glass. Julia knew I'd had a wild-child younger sister named Trixie. She also knew Trixie had died a few days after Julia was born. What would it serve her to learn Trixie had been the one who'd given birth to her, or that she'd been brutally murdered trying to protect her baby girl? I raised Julia like she was mine, always had, always would. That's what mattered.

Julia continued. "We're going out for breakfast first." She smiled happily, oblivious to both my inner roller coaster and the expensive, time-consuming spread I'd hoped to surprise her with.

I stepped in front of the water bubbling for the poached eggs, the English muffins poised in the toaster, the fat slices of tomato already salted. "When're Sarah and her parents supposed to get here?"

A polite morning honk answered me. Julia's face lit up. "It's them!"

I flicked off all the burners and started toward the door. "I want to say hi."

I wished Nic would hurry up in the bathroom so she could witness me rolling with this. More than once, she'd called me "dangerously overprotective," whereas I saw myself as reasonably cautious, given what the three of us had survived. No need to rehash the corners we'd chosen, but me letting Julia leave without so much as a fuss was something she'd approve of.

"Remind me of Sarah's parents' names."

"Mr. and Mrs. Lennox," Julia replied without a hint of sarcasm.

I couldn't suppress the smile. It was difficult for an eight-year-old to imagine adults having a whole life that included hopes, dreams, and first names. I squeezed her shoulder. "Thanks, baby."

She grabbed her coat on the way, pulling it on over the Gap overalls she'd unwrapped Christmas morning, the outfit she'd begged for and that I'd had to pause my gym membership to afford.

Worth it.

I disabled the security system, a wall of chill hitting me when I opened the door at the top of the stairway. The Victorian was the only house we'd lived in since fleeing Lilydale. Coretta, the owner, occupied the floor below us. She preferred the house cold, one of the many things Nic disliked about the woman.

"Mom," Julia said, glancing worriedly at my feet, "you're barefoot."

"It's okay, Jules. This should only take a couple seconds."

I hurried down the stairs, where I entered a code into the panel at the bottom. Once the light turned from red to green, I opened the front door and waved at the white sedan blending in with the falling snow. Because its headlights were on, I couldn't make out the person behind the wheel. A familiar snake of worry slithered down my throat. Maybe I'd prematurely gloated about my ability to roll with this.

Julia tried to slip past, but I thrust out an arm. "Not until we meet."

"Moooommmm." The word hung there, long and tortured, but she knew the drill. She stood next to me, waving limply at the car.

After a few seconds of a standoff, Sarah popped out from the back seat at the same time a man opened the driver's side door. He was late twenties, Eddie Vedder hair tucked in a ponytail, his jacket far too thin for the weather.

"That Mr. Lennox?" I asked.

"Yeah," Julia grumbled.

"Morning, Mrs. Kenn!" Sarah called cheerily.

She didn't know I wasn't a Missus, certainly didn't know I wasn't even a Kenn. The name change had come with the move. I pitched my voice to carry. "Hi, Sarah. That your dad?"

He grinned. "Ethan," he said loudly, his voice deep. "Thanks for letting us hang out with Julia today."

"Tuesday," I replied, my bare feet keeping me from stepping past the threshold. "Pleased to meet you."

Julia glanced hopefully at me. I leaned down and tapped my cheek. She planted a kiss before scurrying across the porch and down the steps. I'd need to shovel them soon, before Coretta got up. Nic was useless on that front.

"Have her back for dinner?" I called out.

"Sure thing," Ethan said.

Nothing about him set off my radar.

Still, as I watched Julia climb into the car, I felt a coil of dread warning me that some sins couldn't be washed clean.

CHAPTER 2

The kitchen smelled like cold bacon when I returned. I strode directly to the pad of paper by the wall phone and scribbled down Ethan's license plate number even though I'd never forget it. I'd always had a photographic memory, at least for the important things.

I pressed the paper hard enough to tattoo.

Behind me, Nic cleared her throat, loud and deliberate. "Good work this morning. Does that mean you're going to stop the worrying and admit Julia's gonna be fine?"

She must've overheard the whole interaction. I shot her a look over my shoulder, but there was no heat in it. She had been my steady center since we were kids, a rare friend who didn't make me feel like I was constantly performing in a play where everyone knew the lines but me. She'd earned the right to nag.

I walked over to the stove, grabbed a rubbery piece of bacon, and bit into it, chewing slowly. The salt stung the corner of my mouth where my lip had split the week before during open sparring. I moved to the blue counter, carefully packing up the luxury breakfast. I could reheat it all tomorrow. It wouldn't be nearly as good, but I'd been hungry too often as a kid to ever throw away food. There'd been a particularly rough patch one of the times Dad disappeared and Mom wasn't well enough to get off the sofa for a week. Trixie and I made a single jar of Peter Pan peanut butter last as long as we could before we started eating the ketchup and mustard in the fridge door, the only other food in the house. Trixie mixed hers until it made orange, but I kept mine separate, red soup marbled with yellow.

The school finally sent someone out to check on us. Mom had pulled herself together enough to convince the officer that we were fine.

I could feel Nic studying me, could even predict her posture: leaned against the arched doorway, arms crossed, the flannel shirt she wore like a uniform hanging loose over a Henley, the sleeves frayed. She'd grown out her shoulder-length curls and gotten more skilled with her makeup. Other than that, she looked and acted the same as she had since high school, back when she, my sister, and I had been inseparable.

When I promised I'd give my life for the two of them.

I'm the oldest, I'd said. *It's my job.*

"I'm gonna hit the gym," I told Nic. "If I don't, I'll just sit around feeling like shit."

"It's good you let Julia go."

The softness in her voice surprised me. I guess I'd been gearing up for a fight.

"Thanks," I bit out. Poor kids hated compliments. It was just one of those things.

I risked a glance over my shoulder. I'd been right about her posture. She was studying me like she wanted to say something more, but then she just nodded before disappearing down the hall. Probably going to tunnel back into bed. She bartended six nights a week, rarely made it home before three in the morning. The smell of bacon must have called her out.

I waited until I heard her door close to climb up on the counter and open the cupboard above the refrigerator. Nic called it the "Cabinet of Lost Hope." More importantly, Julia couldn't reach it. I pushed aside the vases, a fondue set I'd picked up at a garage sale, a candle shaped like a giant green frog that was too cute to use and too ugly to display. There it was. The orange prescription bottle. The pills inside rattled like tiny dice, and my stomach tightened as I realized how low I was. The doctor would only give me a three-month supply before requiring a checkup. He wanted even more regular appointments than that, but we didn't always get what we wanted, did we?

I split one in half with a tooth and swallowed it dry, the bitter tang catching in my throat. Half was probably better anyhow. Nic got so mad when I took a whole one that she'd disappear for days. I dropped the other half back in the bottle and tucked it behind the rest of the junk. Then I climbed down and bagged up a leftover meal from last night's New Year's Eve dinner for my boss, Corn Stamoran, who'd given me my PI job.

Once everything in my kitchen was tucked away and the countertops were glistening, I headed to the bathroom to brush my teeth, wash my face, and give thanks to the pixie-cut gods for my low-maintenance hair. Studying my lipsticks, I selected a Revlon ColorStay in Raisin and spread it on thick, then inked a swoop of black at the corner of each eye. I was already wearing sweats and a sports bra, so all that was left to do was grab my winter gear and reset the security system.

I entered the code and was answered with three loud beeps, then a buzzing like an insect trapped in glass.

"Nice to be locked in like a prisoner!" Nic hollered from her bedroom.

I flipped her the middle finger without turning around, my mouth curving into a smile.

It'd taken her years to track down Julia and me after the horror of that night.

It was smart that she'd ditched Lilydale and lain low afterward. She'd never have gotten a fair shake if she'd stayed. Still, it'd been so hard to figure everything out without her. Life was just easier when Nic was around.

That's why I'd be forever grateful that she found us again, even if it sometimes felt like our friendship was held together with duct tape and secrets.

CHAPTER 3

The grand old houses that made up this corner of Saint Paul stood bundled against the Minnesota cold, their facades clinging to an elegance even though many—like mine—were now subdivided into apartments. Through bare windows I glimpsed tinseled Christmas trees and merry twinkle lights arranged in what once had been formal dining rooms. Most people had already shoveled their walks even though the snow hadn't stopped falling, though it was lighter now than it'd been at predawn.

A kid with a Walkman crossed the street in front of me, bopping his head to some unheard beat, his hands buried deep in his pockets. He was followed by a woman in a puffy teal jacket dragging a yapping terrier. I tensed automatically, but neither seemed to be a threat. The street was otherwise quiet, salt-crusted snow piled high along the sidewalks. I started my car and let it warm while I scraped the windows. Then I slid behind the wheel, telling myself that Julia was safe. She was with good people, in the daylight, doing fun things.

Safe safe safe

Still, I jumped when my tires cracked with cold at their first rotation, and it took until I reached the gym for my hands to unclench the steering wheel. Thank god for mixed martial arts. It was my refuge, one of the few things that kept me sane.

Or at least as sane as my past allowed.

I'd stumbled across MMA a couple years ago, after my career change from the police department to private investigation. I loved the way the gym smelled like sweat and disinfectant, blood and body funk. I loved the way my fists ached as they slammed into the bag, the rhythm steady and punishing, my own heartbeat turned metronome. I even loved open sparring the few times I'd participated. Ducking. Diving. Striking. With MMA, my muscles would burn, my ribs would heave, and for sixty minutes, the world narrowed to the satisfying *thud* of glove against flesh or leather.

I parked the car in the half-full gym lot, wound my scarf tight, and hopped out to penguin shuffle across the icy pavement. Even though I was barely keeping my feet under me, I set my shoulders and pointed my eyes forward. A woman's first weapon wasn't her fists, it was how she moved. How she carried herself like she belonged even when she wasn't sure she did.

It was an act—an exhausting one—that every girl learned young if she wanted to survive.

I'd begun mentally planning my workout when I recognized a form across the street. It was just a glimpse of a figure slipping into a coffee shop, but I'd have known him anywhere. My chest seized, muscle lifting from bone.

It was him.

My sister's killer.

CHAPTER 4

Before

Arsen Bauer sprawled across one end of the couch, his legs stretched out, bare feet on the coffee table. At twenty-two, he was the exact flavor of trouble that made teenage girls swoon and mothers clutch their pearls. Lean and electric, with hungry eyes and a wicked smile. Tonight he wore a faded black T-shirt with a leering image of Charles Manson on its front, threadbare at the collar. The Members Only jacket he never went in public without was draped over the back of the couch.

Too hot for leather.

Trixie nudged his leg with her knee. "Move over, you're hogging the whole couch." Her hair was pulled back in a messy ponytail, dark roots showing beneath peroxide blond. She swiped sweat off the back of her neck. The box fan perched on an end table did nothing but get the oven-cooked August air to them sooner.

"There's plenty of room," Arsen said, pulling her close and giving her a squeeze.

She smiled despite the heat, a secret smile known to any girl who's ever felt chosen.

"Microwave's busted again," Tuesday called from the kitchen. "No popcorn."

"Did you try hitting it?" Nicholas asked. He sat on the nubby green carpet, cross-legged in front of the television. He shuffled a deck of cards, the whisper-soft sound almost lost beneath the dialogue on-screen. "That's how my dad fixes everything."

"Yeah, well, that's how Mom *breaks* everything," Tuesday said, emerging with an open bag of generic potato chips—a rare score from the food shelf—and dropping into the vinyl chair next to Nick.

The TV glowed, casting its blue-green light across their faces. *Jaws 3-D* was playing, the cheesiest of the *Jaws* movies, but it was on network TV, and it was free, which meant they were watching it. The cramped trailer was their mom Pia's. No one mentioned her empty bedroom at the end of the hall, door closed since last Wednesday, when the station wagon from Rochester had come.

Nick was trying to do a magic trick, his tongue pressed between his teeth as he shuffled, watching Tuesday out of the corner of his eye. She caught him staring and shoved his shoulder with her foot. "Knock it off, weirdo."

He startled, fumbling the deck. "What?"

She rolled her eyes. She and Nick were a year apart. She was starting her senior year, Nick his junior, and Trixie her sophomore. Arsen had graduated four years earlier.

"You're looking at me like I'm gonna start levitating," she said.

Nick gathered the cards. In the television light, his features were delicate, almost porcelain—elegant nose, eyelashes that cast shadows. "Well, I wouldn't be surprised if you had some kind of freaky telekinesis. I saw what happened to Greg Parker in shop class."

Tuesday hooted and slapped the chair's arm. "That wasn't telekinesis! That was karma. And Greg Parker's fine. His eyebrows grew back."

Arsen chuckled. Trixie rested her head on his shoulder despite the sticky heat. She, Tuesday, and Nick called themselves the Three Musketeers, had since they'd caught the Gene Kelly and Lana Turner movie on TV.

Arsen was a new addition to the group.

The knock at the door startled everyone but him. "There's my beer!" he shouted, jumping to his feet. Arsen was about the same size as Nick, but he seemed to claim much more room, striding to the door like he owned the whole damn trailer park.

Mark Clamchik—Clam—stood on the stoop holding up a sweating six-pack of Hamm's. "Welcome to the land of sky-blue waters!" he crowed.

Clam was one of several high school kids who always seemed to be fighting for the role of Arsen's shadow. He was a skinny kid, held back so he was in Trixie's grade. His eyes had a habit of sliding sideways when he spoke.

"You're not old enough to have beer, Clam," Tuesday called from her chair, ever the responsible one. She looked like she wanted to pull the words back when Arsen glared at her, but she held her ground.

Arsen peeled a can from the six-pack Clam still held. It made a hiss when he opened it. He faced Trixie, Tuesday, and Nick like he was putting on a show, knocking his head back and swallowing the beer in one long pull, his throat working like a boa constrictor's. When he finished, he burped loudly and crushed the can.

"Gross," Trixie said.

Arsen's eyes flashed.

Tuesday stood quickly, putting herself between Trixie and Arsen. "You've gotta go, Clam," she said to the boy still standing on their stoop. Arsen might have four years on her, but he wasn't ever going to act like an adult, so that left only her. "We don't want the cops busting us."

Clam snickered. He cupped his free hand in front of his stomach like he had a beer belly. "No need to worry. Arsen's fat ol' police chief dad is up the river!"

Arsen spun, winding up a fist that he held in the air like a warning.

Clam jerked back. "Jesus, man, you make fun of him all the time." When Arsen kept his fist cocked, Clam scowled. "Fine. Here's your beers."

He dropped the remaining five on the porch along with an opened bag of gummy bears. "Sorry if the beers are popping. Oh, and enjoy your candy. I took the good ones out."

Arsen grabbed the gummy bears and the beer before shutting the door. He tossed the open bag of candy onto the coffee table and set the five cold ones next to it. "Go on," he said lazily, stretching back into the couch, eyes hooded but watchful. "Pick your poison."

Trixie was the first to move. She rummaged around in the bag. "Clam took all the pineapple, looks like," she said. "Suits me just fine." She removed the orange, holding one up. "As good as a vitamin," she said, grinning at her sister.

Tuesday shook her head but closed the bag of chips and reached for the yellows, her favorite, before handing the candy to Nick. He fished out the green ones, lining them up in a neat little row on the table edge before eating them one by one.

"That leaves red for me," Arsen said. "Sweet little bloody bears."

"Check it out," Nick said, pointing at the TV. A Breaking News banner scrolled across the bottom of the screen.

Trixie groaned. "Ugh, no. No news." She reached for the remote, but Arsen grabbed her arm.

"Wait," he said, eyes pinned on the TV.

A serious-looking anchor stared out at them, his blue tie blade sharp against his crisp white shirt. "We have a developing story. Authorities believe they have a serial killer on their hands after the second local murder in six months. The suspect has reportedly called emergency services after both crimes, confessing to the killings before hanging up. He didn't leave any identifying information in either case. Police urge residents to remain vigilant and report any suspicious activity immediately. And whatever you do, be sure to lock your doors."

The screen cut to a photo of a young woman, her smile tentative. Beneath, the caption: "Patricia Olson, 22, the second confirmed victim."

The room went quiet except for the fan's fruitless hum.

Tuesday glanced over at her sister. Trixie shifted, tucking her feet under her like the floor might open up. Arsen and Nick were locked on the screen, their expressions unreadable.

"I bet he's a priest," Nick said suddenly. "Or a cop." He sucked on his bottom lip. "Like your dad before he was arrested, Arsen. Those are the only kinds of people who feel bad enough to confess."

"Jesus, Nick," Trixie said, shooting a worried glance at Arsen.

"What?" Nick flipped a card between his fingers. "I'm just saying."

Arsen ignored him, stretching his arms behind his head, reassuming his relaxed posture. "Doesn't matter who he is," he said, voice light. "He'll get caught. They always do." He kicked at Nick, nearly catching him in the face. "Where were *you* last night, anyhow, Nicky? Up to some murder?"

Nick stared at Tuesday—she kept her eyes on her hands—and then glanced back at his cards.

The news flash cut off, and *Jaws 3-D* blared back on, louder and dumber than before, the shark attacking some poor schmuck at SeaWorld. No one moved. The trailer felt smaller, the shadows sharper.

Trixie suddenly sat up and grinned. "You know what?" she said. "I could take him."

"The shark?" Nick asked.

Trixie jutted out her chin. "The killer."

Tuesday snorted. "You can't even take on a wasp in the trailer without screaming."

Outside, the heat pressed on, thick and sticky.

None of them locked the door, despite the news anchor's warning.

CHAPTER 5

After

"Ma'am? You okay?"

It was some guy with a soul patch heading into the MMA gym, concern creasing his brow as I stood like a frozen statue in the parking lot, staring at the coffee shop across the street, heart thudding in my chest.

I hadn't just spotted the Crying Killer. *Couldn't* have. He died that night in a hail of bullets after he murdered my sister. Even so, I'd been seeing his ghost for years—in grocery stores, at gas stations, lurking in the shadows of parking garages. Nic called it survivor's guilt, but survivor's guilt didn't explain why my security system cost more than my car, or why I only slept in clothes I could fight in.

"I'm fine," I told the guy. "Thanks."

I strode into the gym, head down, pounded the bag until my knuckles burned beneath the wraps, each impact sending shock waves up my arms. Sweat rolled down my back, my ribs heaving. I needed it. Needed the burn, the ache, the steady, mindless shudder of impact. Anything to keep from thinking too hard.

CHAPTER 6

Cornell "Corn" ("Like the vegetable, but less husky," he'd tell people, then slap his knee like he hadn't shared that dorky joke a thousand times) Stamoran's office door creaked as I opened it, the coconut curry smells of the hallway giving way to a faint mildew odor. Before opening his PI office, he'd been a detective in Narcotics and Vice working out of the Saint Paul Police Central District. I'd been a beat cop, and we'd struck up a friendship.

After he retired, he opened his PI agency above an Indian restaurant called Curry Up and Wait. He knew I'd been going through a hard patch at the SPPD, and so once he'd established himself, he offered me the position as his number two. That'd been a couple years earlier. It hadn't been an easy choice—burning out wasn't as clean as it sounded, and I'd had to give up my pension—but in the end, I'd taken him up on it.

It was one of the best decisions of my life.

Here it was just the two of us. No chains of command, no office drama, just the work.

Corn glanced up from his desk. He was a bulky guy in his late sixties who'd never met a dad joke he didn't like. Gray threaded his *Magnum, P.I.* mustache like frost, though the hair on his head was still thick and dark. I assumed he dyed it. His face had settled into soft lines, but his eyes were a sharp bottle blue. He wore the same dark, rumpled blazer he always did, only the T-shirts beneath changing. Today's read I'M YOUR HUCKLEBERRY. The dude loved Westerns.

"Tuesday," he said, smiling. "You look like you've been hit by a truck."

He was used to seeing me come straight from the gym, so this was gentle teasing. I set the container of holiday food on his desk. He loved cold turkey, cold carrots, and cold mashed potatoes, the doofus.

"Not yet," I said. "Still time, though."

He cocked his head, studying me in that way he did, the way that made me wonder how much he'd heard about what'd happened on my last week on the force before I'd jumped ship to join him. As a courtesy, I'd told him that I'd lost my sister back in Lilydale the summer after graduating high school and that I'd had a different last name back then. Thankfully, he hadn't pressed for details. Corn understood boundaries better than anyone I'd ever met.

Another reason I liked him.

He gestured toward the chair opposite him. The cuffs of his blazer were rolled up, revealing forearms that were still muscular. "Sit," he said. "Got something interesting."

I dropped into the chair, not bothering to remove my coat. "Not another cheating spouse, I hope."

He snorted. "Nope. This one's different. A woman by the name of Melissa Hachette believes she's being stalked. Cops won't help her. They think she's imagining it."

I took the folder he offered. "What do you think?"

He shrugged. "I think you'll figure it out."

I flipped open the folder. A photo stared back at me, a woman in her mid-twenties, brown eyes a little close set, long brown hair, her look polished but not too much. The kind of lady you'd pass on the street and immediately forget.

"Can I work from home on this?" He didn't need to know I wanted to be close to the phone in case Julia called with an emergency while out with Sarah. She could reach me at work, but it might not be her first thought if she was really in trouble.

Corn handed me the floppy disk containing access credentials for his database. "Sure. Don't know why you're even coming in on a Sunday."

I slid the disk into the interior pocket of my coat. "Because I took most of the holidays off," I said, telling him what he already knew.

He grunted. "Do what you like. Me, I'm knee-deep in tax prep all day. Probably all week. Won't be much for company." He scowled at a stack of papers. "Why don't they just tell me how much I owe 'em and be done with it? Neither one of us wants to look at every single receipt." He tapped the tin-foiled food. "Thanks for the feast, anyhow. Should keep me going through these dark times."

"Sure thing." I started to stand, then froze. On the corner of his desk, half buried beneath a stack of papers, was a magazine. *Private Eye Monthly*, glossy and garish, the kind of rag that made the profession look like a bad TV show. But that wasn't what had stolen my breath. It was the photo on the lower left.

My photo.

"What the hell?" I asked, my voice suddenly sharp as an ice pick.

Corn tossed me a curious look and then followed my gaze. "Oh, that."

He reached for the magazine, but I was already there, snatching it off his desk. Beneath my face was a line that made my stomach twist: *Rising Star: Tuesday Kenn*. I opened to the article, skimmed it. There was a bigger version of the cover photo, plus some glowing BS about the types of cases I solved and how professional I was.

"Are you kidding me?" I said, tossing the magazine at him.

He raised his eyebrows at my outburst but kept his tone even. "I nominated you for an award," he said, like it was nothing that he'd forecast my face and name, like he was *proud* of himself, even. "Best up-and-comer. It'll bring us some business, especially anyone looking to work with a female detective. What's the big deal?"

"The big deal?" My voice rose until it was nearly a yell. "The big deal is that I don't want my picture in some dime-store detective magazine! Jesus Christ."

"Tuesday." He held up a hand. "First of all, the article has been out for a few months, so it ain't fresh. Second, you're good at what you do. You deserve to be recognized. No one's gonna—"

I didn't let him finish. I clutched the Hachette folder, feeling dizzy. I knew Corn meant well. Heck, I could even agree it was a smart business move. But if I stayed, I was going to start a fight with him just to have something solid to hang on to, so I stormed out, slamming the door behind me. My pulse was pounding, and not just from anger.

Corn had said it didn't matter, but he didn't know.

Didn't know that the nightmare of shots ringing out still woke me up some nights, my heart slamming my chest as I choked back sobs. Didn't know how gunpowder and human blood smelled like fireworks in a butcher shop.

I'd bundled up Julia and fled to a Thrifty Scot Motel on the edge of the Twin Cities within a week of my sister's murder. I don't remember how I got to it, just that I couldn't drive anymore and there it was on the side of the road. We were given room 118, with its murky green carpets that smelled like cigarettes and swamp, where the walls were so thin I could hear the couple in the next room argue over a lottery ticket at two in the morning.

Julia was just six days old. I barely slept. Every sound had me jerking upright, heart jackhammering. The crack of a car backfiring outside? The killer. The scrape of a shoe in the hallway? The killer. The flickering neon outside our window? Him, watching me. Waiting.

With my sister slaughtered and Nick disappeared, I was lost.

One night, I swore I heard the killer outside our door. I gathered Julia from her makeshift crib—a drawer lined with towels—and locked us in the bathroom, perched on the edge of the tub with a pair of scissors clutched in my trembling hand. I stayed like that until dawn broke, listening to the water drip from the faucet, counting each drop like a second hand, waiting for the door to splinter open. But no one came. The manager told me later it must have been the ice machine cycling on, the vibrations traveling through the paper-thin walls. I nodded but had him move us to a room on the other side of the building anyway.

The police said the killer was dead, but they didn't know what it felt like to be helpless as your sister was gunned down, knowing that you should have been the one to take the bullet. Didn't know that shame like that grew legs and followed you for the rest of your life.

He watched Her stomp out of the detective agency from the café across the street. She always did have to make an exit.

He hated Her.

He loved Her.

But mostly, he resented Her, because no matter everything She'd been through, She still moved like She held the world in her hand, shoulders squared against the January cold. Strutting down the damn sidewalk like She owned it. That's what got under his skin—how She walked around like She didn't answer to anybody. Talked without checking if people liked what She said. Took up space like it was Hers for the claiming.

Just the sort of girl who needed to be slammed down a notch.

She'd disappeared into Her car and torn away.

Didn't matter. He knew where She lived, and he'd always been patient.

Long game.

CHAPTER 7

I woke up in the middle of the night with the disorienting sensation of being in the Lilydale trailer park, yanked back in time, my sister about to be murdered. My eyes flew open, my pulse banging in my veins. Had I heard whistling? Was that what'd woken me? My gaze darted to the corners of my bedroom, bulging, straining to see *behind the chair in the closet under the bed.*

When I caught his ragged breathing, my heart jumped into my mouth.

Except it wasn't his breath. It was mine.

I tried to calm myself but I was struggling, panicked air caught in a trap between my nose and my throat. I was losing it, my lizard brain running the show, when something unexpected pulled me out of the tailspin. It was a whiff of perfume. Pineapple, sage, hyacinth.

Benetton perfume.

My perfume. *Today.*

I could never have afforded it back in 1986. Heck, I could barely afford it now. But grasping on to something current, something real, was grounding. My gaze slowed. Less ricochet, more recognition. My nerves were still buzzing, so my eyes touched the familiar, like fingers on rosary beads. I was in my bedroom in the converted Victorian. A cheap plastic-framed full-length mirror nailed to the back of the door reflected the single window across from it, a dark new moon peering inside. I'd bought the mirror for fifty cents at a garage sale. It came with a Ziploc bag of jeweled plastic hooks taped to its back. My dresser matched my bed, both constructed of heavy, scuffed oak and already residents of this room when I'd moved in eight years earlier, back when Julia and I slept in here together, Julia in her hand-me-down crib.

But now Julia had her own room.

We had the whole top floor, Julia, Nic, and me.

Julia.

Her name, finally, pierced my paralysis. I lurched into a sitting position, green waves of nausea telling me to slow down. I wasn't fully out of the past yet, and I knew better than to rush the process. I'd woken to too many nightmares, ended up curled on the ground too many times. But I couldn't stay still. I needed to check on my girl, so I flexed my hands and slid my feet to the floor, forcing myself to cross my bedroom, open the door.

Except I was still walking through time, part of me unable to escape the trailer.

CHAPTER 8

Before

The Three Musketeers had been bone-tired when they got back from the hospital, but none of them wanted to close their eyes and miss a second with the new baby. Finally, though, they started crashing. She was the first Musketeer down, crawling to the back bedroom to grab a few winks, promising Nick and her sister that she'd take the next shift. The sound of their voices through the wall soothed her as she drifted off—warm murmurs, laughter, probably fussing over Julia. Her whole world was right, and the warmth of the blankets wrapped around her like a second skin, pulling her down into sleep.

She was soon out cold.

A noise woke her. Just a whisper at first, or a whistle. She fell back asleep again until her eyes snapped open for the second time, the hairs on the back of her neck rising. Through the thin walls, she heard a new voice in the other room, an argument building. She jolted out of bed. Seconds passed—she didn't know how many—before the gunshot cracked through the night.

Julia!

That was her first thought. Her sister came second, one of the many shames from that evening that would later hang around her neck like stones. She charged toward the bedroom door, ripping it open. Heat zoomed past her cheek, the bullet passing through the doorjamb and raining down splinters. Instinctively, she dropped to her knees, cowering beneath her hands as three more bullets came her way, shredding the trailer walls like a can opener cutting through metal.

Fortuitously, two officers were already at the trailer park dealing with a domestic dispute. They were only five hundred yards away when they heard the first shot. They called for backup, then hurried toward Pia's trailer in time to witness the Crying Killer stumble out, covered in blood. They fired at him before he fell back inside, returning their shots. Then they showered the entire trailer with bullets, not even considering who else might be caught in the cross fire.

Nick ran past her down the hallway. She saw the flash of his shoes, heard the thunder of footsteps beneath the symphony of lead piercing the walls. Then another figure rushed past, or maybe it was just the echo of gunshots playing tricks on her mind. She tried to get to her feet, but her legs refused to support her.

The police finally stopped shooting. Their trailer looked like smoking Swiss cheese.

Reinforcements had arrived by then. When they burst through the trailer door with weapons drawn, they discovered her still curled in a fetal position in the bedroom doorway, her limbs folded against each other as if glued in place. A single thought looped through her mind: *If you move, it'll make all this real. If you sit up, you have to face what's in the living room.*

Were they dead? Her sister? Julia?

A cop grabbed her, tugging her to her feet. Suddenly she heard it—an infant's cry piercing through the chaos.

Julia was alive. *Alive.*

A noise escaped her throat then, raw and guttural. Someone shoved the baby into her arms, a wriggling bundle of powder and blankets speckled with blood, none of it Julia's own. They led her out of the trailer, her legs unsteady beneath her, trying to shield her eyes as they ushered her past the wreckage.

But she saw it all.

Her sister draped across the cradle, lifeless, peonies of blood blooming across the back of her T-shirt, vivid against the pale fabric.

The first shot hadn't killed her. She'd had enough life left in her to save the baby.

Just inside the front door lay the second mutilated body, a grotesque imitation of a man, his leather Members Only jacket full of holes and glistening with blood. A bullet had destroyed his face, but the wallet in his back pocket confirmed what the jacket he was never without had already suggested: This was Arsen Bauer, son of former police chief Aramis Bauer.

Two of the cops were clustered around the corpse, trading theories in low voices.

"Damn," the cop nearest the body said. "His dad ain't gonna like this."

"You think?" the second officer said. He at least had the decency to look a little green around the gills. "You *think* the former chief of police who's doing his own jail time might not want to find out his son is the pansy-assed crybaby killer?"

"The hell?" the first officer said.

The second officer sat back on his heels. "You hadn't heard? The task force out of Saint Cloud pegged Arsen for the murders. Who knows when. They don't tell us jack. I guess they have witnesses who put him in the area, friends he bragged to, everything. Only problem was he'd fled the state." He prodded Arsen's leg with his boot. The body was already starting to go stiff. "If he'd never come back to town, who knows if we'd have caught the Crying Killer?"

She bit back a scream, still clutching Julia to her chest. She'd known Arsen was out here. She'd heard his voice. But that Arsen Bauer was the same man who'd called a local radio station to whine his anonymous confessions after he'd murdered four women? Not in a million years had the Three Musketeers suspected it. Sure, he had a short temper, and he was the kind of guy who always believed he was the victim, even when he was the one swinging fists, but a *serial killer*? She tried thinking back to how he'd reacted to that newsbreak about the Crying Killer, anything he'd ever said about the murders, desperate for a clue, but her mind was unraveling. She couldn't hold a thought.

The autopsy would later show that Arsen's own bullet—to his face—was likely the one that killed him, so the police said he must have guessed what was coming. But she didn't know that as she stood over the body clad in the leather jacket, staring into the meat inside his skull, her sister's corpse only feet away. All she knew was that this couldn't be happening because it was splitting her brain in two.

That's when she picked up on something about the body that was supposed to be Arsen. She'd sat on the raggedy sofa with him a hundred times, talked with him, laughed with him, shared meals, and she was suddenly certain this wasn't him. It wasn't in the face, which was gone. It was the hands. They were long-fingered, nearly hairless. Arsen had a working man's hands.

That's when she started screaming.

Arsen slipped out the back, she yelled, *like Nick.* This body was one of his friends, it must be. Maybe Clam, maybe someone else, wearing Arsen's jacket.

This. Isn't. Arsen.

She kept screaming as they led her outside, where a circle of neighbors had gathered. When people she'd lived next to for years started staring at her the same way they did her mom in one of her spells, she shut her trap.

That's when she realized Julia was shrieking, too.

Trembling, she started to sing to her, desperately, to kiss her face, to do everything she could think of to calm the baby down. She allowed herself to be guided into the back of a police car. She told herself she'd never again say she thought Arsen was still alive, or they'd put her away just like they had her mom.

CHAPTER 9

After

Julia's door was just ahead. Closed.

The girl had been on cloud nine when she'd returned from her Mall of America day with Sarah, but she'd also been crabby from too much sugar. I'd sent her to bed early, hit my own mattress not long after, exhausted from worrying about her all day and then realizing I was no longer anonymous, that if Arsen happened to see a copy of that PI magazine, he'd not only know what last name I was using but also what city we lived in and where I worked. Arsen Bauer, who—before he inserted himself into my family and murdered my sister—had been stalking and killing other women.

No wonder I'd had the nightmare followed by a flashback, the second in a month.

Suddenly, my legs spasmed, pumping with lactic acid, my body's delayed promise that it would have fought for me if we'd really needed it. I twirled my feet, pushing through the knot in each calf. I was grateful for the pain. It reminded me that I was alive. I gripped the frigid doorknob to Julia's bedroom. Victorian houses were nice to look at but didn't heat for balls in a Minnesota winter, especially with Coretta's predilection for cold. I turned the knob, listened for a moment, ahead and behind. The house was sighing in the January wind, nothing unusual. I stepped inside.

Julia was snoring softly, a little wheeze-honk.

My shoulders finally unclenched.

I padded silently over to her, witnessing her chest rising and falling. Her *Animaniacs* quilt was bunched around her feet. She'd always slept hot. I kissed her cheek, savoring the smell of her breath, minty and sour with sleep. She murmured and turned from her back to her side, away from me, her tangle of blond hair showing up as white fuzz in the moonlight. She reminded me of a sleeping dandelion.

I loved her so much it felt like dying.

I left her room to grab what I'd need and then returned to bundle her in her quilt and bring her downstairs to Coretta's. Coretta, who'd discovered the trick to getting Julia back to sleep when she was a colicky baby, who was there when Julia took her first steps, who to this day cared for Julia when I had to work late. She was a handful, one of those hyper-religious older ladies who lived inside a mirror-lined bubble, but she loved Julia. Plus, she hadn't raised the rent in all the years we'd lived here, not even once, and she was the one who'd introduced me to AA, which I'd desperately needed after I'd lost my sister and then gone looking for her in a bottle.

Best of all? Coretta knew how to take care of herself, I had a key to her apartment, and when I had to go out at night, she didn't ask questions.

CHAPTER 10

Believe me when I tell you that I knew it mostly wasn't strangers who attacked women. That it wasn't usually some shadowy dude who dragged you from a parking lot. It was more often your dad, or your husband, or your doctor, or the guy who'd been sitting next to you in economics class for the past two months, that kid who thought you owed him something because one time he shared a bag of chips with you.

But sometimes, it *was* the stranger who offered to buy you a drink and then wouldn't take no for an answer.

That was the kind of guy I went out at night looking for. I'd been unable to save my sister from being slaughtered. I couldn't bring her back, but I could tip the scales for other women.

I hadn't planned it the first time. I was walking to my car, lost in thought, when I spotted a lady maybe my age, maybe a little younger, walking briskly down the sidewalk. A guy trailed her fifty yards behind. The second I laid eyes on him, my blood grew too thick for my veins. I wasn't sure what set me off. Maybe it was the focused way he followed, or how she kept glancing over her shoulder like she already knew what was coming.

Either way, I wasn't about to let it happen like I had with Trixie.

I glided forward, moving between cars until I intersected with the pair at the same time he lunged for her—her purse, her body, I'd never know. I tackled him at the knees and punched him senseless. It felt like breathing lightning, and it burned away the guilt for a few precious moments.

That'd been a hot summer night three years earlier. The sensation was the only antidote on the nights I woke to flashbacks.

The nights like tonight.

I let myself into Coretta's apartment, tucked a still-sleeping Julia into the single bed set aside for her, triple-checked the security system I'd outfitted Coretta's with, and hit the road. I drove to a cluster of dive bars on the run-down edge of Macalester College, my latest hunting ground.

It was ripe for the kind of behavior I was seeking.

I followed my routine of parking two blocks away before making my way back on foot. It was important I never be identified on scene. I found a spot outside the dingiest of the bars, the Gopher Hole, managing to melt into the shadows just as a basket of college boys stumbled out wearing puffer jackets and overpriced sneakers, their faces flushed from drink. I could hear them arguing, some idiot debate about whether *Reservoir Dogs* or *Pulp Fiction* was the better Tarantino vehicle.

I stayed motionless, the cold creeping into my gut as they passed by. Over the next hour, up to and past bar close, I studied patrons streaming out in fits and bursts, watching for it. Most nights I went home without engaging. Maybe this would be one of them. But I couldn't leave yet. There might be one straggler who didn't notice the quiet threat brushing past her.

She would need me.

You'd be a fool to leave women's justice to the laws of men.

I first learned that growing up in Lilydale, Minnesota, infamous in the '60s for a cult it'd produced and then again in the '80s for a string of abductions of boys ending in murder, all that before what happened with the Crying Killer. If Lilydale were a smile, it'd be warm and wide with just one too many teeth. It was tricky like that.

Exhibit A: Rammy Bauer, Arsen's dad, was the chief of police tasked with cracking the '80s cases. Unfortunately, he'd been too distracted committing his own crimes. That's what Lilydale did, fooled you into believing somebody out there was on your team, that justice would take care of itself, that things were as they seemed.

Same way it tricked me into not understanding how dangerous Arsen was.

He'd been one of those guys you couldn't look away from. He was a human magnet, but beneath his charm, there was something off. I knew it, my sister knew it, *everyone* knew it, but Trixie was drawn to him. Made sense. Any Psych 101 book would have told you that, given how we'd been raised, what kind of dad we'd had. That ricochet dance happened a lot in a small town. Happened in a big city, too, but in a small town it felt personal. Heck, Arsen even looked a little like our dad.

Once Trixie started dating him, he slotted in with our group pretty quick. Nick, Trixie, and me were still the Three Musketeers, but when Trixie brought Arsen around, he fit in okay. I was surprised he wanted to. Macho guys had a strong reaction to Nick, like him dressing and acting how he wanted called them out for living their lives too small. But Arsen and Nick hit it off out of the gate, and we had some good laughs.

Maybe that's why I didn't pay enough attention when Arsen's dark side leaked out, why I didn't make too big a deal when he confessed how much he loved Charles Manson. It seemed like a phase every small-town guy went through, mistaking cruelty for charisma, swagger for strength. Even our own dad had referred to Manson admiringly on occasion.

"The dude's a god," Arsen said once.

I'd studied his face to see if he was joking. "Didn't he hide in a cupboard the first time the cops came for him?"

My comment made Arsen so mad we didn't see him for days, which was fine by me. Next time he showed up, he was carrying a copy of *Helter Skelter* that he began quoting like it was the Bible. He so believed in Manson's mission that he'd cut an X—the same sign Manson had etched low on his forehead before turning it into a swastika—on Trixie's back the October before she broke up with him.

I wouldn't learn until I started working for the SPPD that the man the press had dubbed the Crying Killer had carved identical markings on all four of his victims and splayed their bodies out in the same shape, wouldn't know until I got my hands on that official file that the Lilydale cops who'd said Arsen Bauer was a serial killer had been right.

About that part, at least.

I saw Trixie's X by accident, charging into the bathroom to grab my curling iron, not realizing she was stepping out of the shower. She'd been so mad that she'd screamed at me, told me no way could I understand a love like her and Arsen's. Big surprise, it wasn't long until he started hitting her, just like our pops used to do to our mom. Dad was at his worst after bar close. We'd hear the front door open, and I'd crawl over to Trixie's bed and hold her. Some nights, it was fine. Dad would pass out on the couch, or he'd stumble into their bedroom and have loud sex with Mom.

But other nights, terrible nights, he'd come through that door whistling "The House of the Rising Sun," and that's when we knew it was coming. He swore it was his favorite song, but he only ever whistled it when he was about to smack Mom bloody. The whole tune was wild and spooky. It scared Trixie so much that it worked terrible magic on her forever after that, freezing her in place like the world's best-trained dog.

Nick was the one who let that secret slip to Arsen, by the way.

Told him one night when we were all high that if a person ever wanted to see a neat trick, all they had to do was whistle that old Animals tune around Trixie. The only reason he told was because he was feeling dumb and ugly that day and wanted Arsen's attention, his approval—at least, that's what he confessed later. Arsen tried whistling the song then and there, but of course it didn't work. Trixie was expecting it. He had to get her when she was already afraid. Or sleeping.

I could imagine him whistling it when he etched that X into her back. That thought gnawed at me to this day. It was one of many dark memories I settled with my own kind of justice.

Or at least tried to. Most nights, like tonight, I got nothing. I was shivering with cold, and the bars had all emptied out. The nearest parking lot was down to four cars, probably belonging to employees. I was just about to leave my shadowed spot and head home when a woman stumbled out of the Blackhearted Loon across the street, an American Legion–esque hole-in-the-wall that was deeper than it was wide.

My breath grew shallow.

She was unsteady on her feet, swaying slightly. Her heeled suede boots clicked with each step—too fast, too uneven. She was tipsy if not outright drunk. She was also by herself, her face down, hands shoved in her pockets.

And I wasn't the only one watching her.

My heart bumped up against my throat.

The man who'd tailed her out of the bar was all wrong, his movements predatory. He stayed just far enough back so he wouldn't be noticed, but she must've sensed him. When she quickened her pace, my blood gave a hot burst. The night was dark and quiet, all the other customers gone home. I'm sure he thought he had her to himself.

It took only moments before he lunged, smooth as a shark, and dragged her into the nearest alley.

I was already halfway across the street.

Her muffled protest barely registered, drowned out by the sound of my pulse shredding my ears. I hoped I could make it to them before he did any damage. I'd been lax, just about ready to call it a night.

The alley he'd dragged her into was between a record store and a café. I expected to round the corner and see him shoving her against the brick or kneeling over her or worse. Instead, I burst ahead and saw . . . no one.

The alley was empty.

I glanced around in disbelief, the world tilting beneath me. The guy had been subtle when he'd pulled her into the dark, keeping his movements smooth and quiet so that a casual observer wouldn't have looked twice, but he was no magician, no wizard. He couldn't make them both go *poof.* I thought of the pills in the orange bottle, of how stress played kickball with my brain. But no, I hadn't been hallucinating. He'd *definitely* pulled that woman into this alleyway.

But all I could see now were dumpsters and ice.

I was trying to draw a full breath when a scream tore through the air, but not from the alley. I whipped around. It'd come from the direction of the Gopher Hole. For a terrible suspended moment, I was back in the trailer, being led past my dead sister and the man the cops swore was Arsen. But it wasn't that night. It was now, and someone was in trouble.

I skidded toward the scream, fighting for balance. A woman crouched beneath the Gopher Hole's neon sign, wailing as the name flashed red and green above her like a drunk Christmas decoration.

My gut kicked.

She was the same woman I had thought I'd just seen dragged into the alley, the one wearing suede heeled boots. She was on her knees, shrieking, and there was something—some*one*—sprawled out on the ground in front of her.

I ran forward, stopping a few feet short, my chest heaving, heart pounding against my ribs. The body on the ground was also a woman. Her arms were outstretched, palms up, like she'd been posed in the shape of an X.

Crying Killer–style.

CHAPTER 11

Before

The Crying Killer's first victim, a twenty-one-year-old college student named Mary Lenzen, was discovered on the outskirts of Willmar. She'd been walking home from her shift at a diner, likely in a hurry to escape the December chill. They found her lying in a snowbank, arms and legs stretched wide, forming a grotesque human X. The stab wounds—all thirty-nine of them—had been contained to her chest.

That night, a man called a radio station, whimpering, choking out the words, "I'm so sorry. I couldn't help myself."

He told the DJ where to find the body.

The second murder, the one they heard on the breaking news while watching *Jaws 3-D*, came six months later. Patricia Olson, twenty-two, stabbed to death with an ice pick in her Willmar home, her body splayed like an X. Another confessional call.

Trixie, Tuesday, and Nick put it out of their heads as only teenagers could, until the third killing happened in New London, a town halfway between Willmar and Lilydale. Sylvia Schwab was a mother of three, had been walking to her car after church choir practice. It was dark, and her keys were still in her hand when he struck.

She was found posed the same way, her arms and legs forming that sickening shape.

Arsen had been over the day after Schwab's murder. Trixie, Tuesday, and him were crammed onto the sagging couch, Nick perched in the armchair, still practicing magic tricks. The TV was on. Nick and Arsen were both drinking the Schlitz that Arsen had brought, and the four of them were trying to figure out if they wanted to go to the movies or just hang when the news started, the lead story grabbing their attention.

"Good evening. I'm reporting with an update on the brutal murder of Sylvia Schwab, found dead last night. Authorities say the crime bears similarities to two previous killings in the area. We're about to play an audio recording of a call made to our station earlier today that we believe is related to Ms. Schwab's murder. We want to warn our viewers that the content may be disturbing."

The recording crackled to life: "I killed her . . . I had to kill her . . . She wouldn't stop screaming . . . Oh god, what have I done? I can't stop crying . . . I can't stop . . . She was so kind. I didn't want to."

Tuesday and Trixie made eye contact, both of them thinking the same thing: how whiny the caller sounded, how pitiful.

Their dad had taught them that only losers showed weakness. They got a lesson in that one day when he was showing them how to throw punches at the heavy bag he'd hung from the oak tree behind their house. He said they couldn't quit until they'd landed twenty clean hits. When Trixie started crying after her third swing, he grew angry. She tried apologizing, but he wasn't having it.

"Strong people don't cry, don't say they're sorry," he'd said, wrapping her hands in old, torn sheets to protect them from the coarse bag. His touch was tender, even if his words weren't. He'd always gone easier on Trixie than Tuesday. "A strong person just does better."

Trixie nodded, desperate to demonstrate she understood. She almost apologized again but bit it back. Tuesday went at the bag like an animal. She didn't know if she was doing it to distract her father from Trixie or just because it felt so good to hit something.

The newscaster continued, and Tuesday and Trixie focused back on the TV. "The serial murderer is being called 'the Crying Killer,' based on this and previous confession calls where the suspect can clearly be heard weeping."

When those words hit the air, Arsen sat straight up, slamming his beer on the coffee table. "Doesn't even make sense they call him that," he muttered, his eyes darting to Nick. "The man isn't crying. He's *confessing*. What he's doing must be tearing him up."

Nick didn't answer.

And the killing didn't stop.

The winter after Sylvia Schwab's death, a fourth body was discovered at Lake Koronis. Brenda Checkers had been hitchhiking near Lilydale, a single woman like the other three. The rest of the pattern also repeated. The same pose, the same tear-soaked calls to 911, his guilt as much a signature as the violence itself.

The headlines screamed about those calls, covering his remorse like it was a curiosity, like it was proof he was special, somehow more decent than the other monsters out there hunting at night.

But Trixie and Tuesday believed it made him worse, his weeping into the void he carved.

CHAPTER 12

After

I stood, frozen, still a few feet away from the body on the ground.

The door to the Gopher Hole opened. A man poked his head out. "Everything okay out here?"

The woman I'd seen dragged into the alley gasped, staring up at him then me like she'd just noticed us both. She took off running. The guy—likely a bartender—caught sight of the body on the ground, swore under his breath, and ducked back inside, I hoped to call the cops.

I studied the body on the ground. She wore no coat. Blood bloomed across the front of her white T-shirt, dark and glistening, soaking into the ice beneath her. Her chest looked lumpy, like pudding. *Multiple stab wounds.* But that wasn't what made my breath catch in my throat.

It was her face.

She was a dead ringer for my sister.

The same strong jaw, the same sharp cheekbones, even the same dirty-blond hair, arrayed around her like a halo.

Which meant she looked like me, too.

Panic and something worse crawled up my spine. I leaned forward to take her pulse. She was still warm, but she was dead.

I felt my knees lock as I tried to search everywhere all at once. This wasn't random. It couldn't be. I forced myself to study the scene, trying to see what *wasn't* there. The woman's arms, the angle—they were just like the Crying Killer's other victims, all of them except Trixie. She'd been different. Special. I fought the pull to turn this woman over, to check her lower back for the X.

The sound of a siren shattered the night, red and blue lights reflecting off the sky. It was too early for them to be here even if the bartender had gone straight to the phone, which meant someone had called it in before it'd happened.

This had been a setup.

I hurried toward the parking lot, the cold biting through my coat. There was no longer a question. Arsen had found us.

Hadn't he?

The memory came unbidden. It was while I was still on the Saint Paul force, a week before the anniversary of Trixie's murder. My partner, Shawn, and I'd been called out on a routine domestic. Just another rainy Saint Paul night in the squad car, watching him take statements while I checked the perimeter.

That's when I spotted Arsen Bauer for the first time since my sister's murder.

A clean version of the leather Members Only jacket he always wore. The rolling swagger, like he owned whatever ground his feet touched. For a second I couldn't breathe, my lungs seizing up like they had that night in the trailer. But this time I moved. My hand found my gun and I was out of the car before conscious thought kicked in. The guy must have felt me coming. He turned, and in the sodium glow of the streetlamp, I saw Arsen's face.

A face I'd known since high school.

"Police! Don't move, Arsen!" My voice sounded strange, stretched thin.

Of course he ran.

I chased him down, my boots slapping against wet pavement. He was fast but I was faster, riding a wave of a half decade of rage. When I tackled him, we went down hard, leaving a pound of flesh. I had my knee in his back, cuffs out, heart thundering in my throat.

"Tuesday?" Shawn's voice, coming up behind me. "What the hell?"

"It's him," I said, though my certainty was already starting to fray. "It's Arsen Bauer. The guy who shot my sister."

Shawn crouched beside me, shining his flashlight on the suspect's face. He was crying, pleading innocence. He was young and scared, probably not even eighteen years old. It wasn't Arsen, just some random dude in a leather jacket with features that had seemed so familiar in the dark but now looked nothing like my sister's killer's.

I released him, hands shaking.

Shawn helped him up, apologizing, while the guy bled and watched me like I was some sort of wild animal. Shawn wanted to cover for me, told me he'd look the other way about the whole deal, but I reported myself to my superior that night.

In the end, nothing came of it. I was the only one who seemed to care what I'd done.

That was the week that Nic—God bless Nic—showed up, slipping back into my life like she'd never been gone. She'd finally become herself, and her timing couldn't have been better. She saved me, which meant she saved Julia. She was always good for that, her voice calm and firm, like she could hold the pieces of me together by sheer force of will.

And if Nic were standing next to me now, in this frozen night, she'd tell me this wasn't the Crying Killer's work outside the Gopher Hole.

It couldn't be.

I was hurrying back to my car, sticking to the shadows, when the first wave of cops arrived on scene. They were uniforms, none I recognized, but it was only moments before a detective pulled up, stepping onto the icy pavement with the kind of ease that suggested she didn't know how to slip. I paused behind a tree, covered in inky dark, to study her. The suit beneath her open coat was tailored, expensive, the lines clean. I bet it felt like armor, wearing clothes like that.

She scanned the perimeter, her gaze sharp and calculating. Her eyes seemed to pause on the spot where I was hiding before sweeping to my right and, finally, landing back on the body.

That was my signal to leave. I kept to the shadows, wondering if I was finally, once and for all, losing my mind.

Couldn't believe his damn luck the first time, three weeks back, when he saw Her sneak out. He'd been outside that drafty old house, watching like always, planning his next move, when out the front door She marched.

He had a choice between testing Her fancy-dancy security system and following Her.

He went after Her.

She drove straight to some dive bars near Macalester College. He couldn't guess what She was up to until midnight or so, when a guy and a gal stumbled out of some hole-in-the-wall, both of them in a loud argument. The guy pulled back like he was gonna smack the chick and—boom—Little Miss Hero jumped out of an alley and punched him in the kidneys.

Guy dropped like a sack of potatoes.

Made him laugh, honest to god.

But the laugh burned out quick. Crazy bitch thought She was some kinda savior. Thought She was better than everyone else. Always had.

That's when the idea hit him, clear as day. He'd pay a couple lowlifes to put on a show for Her. Fake attack, quick and dirty. Girl goes one way, guy goes the other, just long enough to make the princess doubt what She's seeing. Then He'd step in, finish the job for real.

Took a few tries to line up the help. Drunks were unreliable as hell. But it all came together tonight.

He watched Her when it all went down. The shock, the confusion. She was for sure thinking She was losing it, like Her crazy mama up in that hospital.

He almost laughed again, had to bite it back. Didn't wanna draw looks.

She wasn't strutting around proud anymore. Not after this, *no way*. He'd put the fear back in Her, good and deep.

World was starting to feel right again.

CHAPTER 13

I parked in front of the Victorian and flew out of my car, my boots crunching against the snow. The air felt brittle, like if I breathed too deeply, it might crack my lungs. I spotted movement inside the foyer, a figure swishing back and forth in front of the door's side windows. My heart leaped into my mouth before I recognized the form.

Coretta.

I disarmed the security system and stepped inside, the stifling smell of wood polish hitting me. Coretta was whacking the wall above her door with the brush end of her broom, her face twisted in concentration. She wore a flannel robe over a pair of jeans, its hem trailing the floor.

She didn't glance my way. "Julia's fine," she said. "Sleeping still."

I melted with relief, fighting the urge to hug Coretta. She wasn't a fan of physical affection. I'd witnessed her intimidate many a person, but they hadn't seen her tenderly clean Julia's skinned knees, braid her tangled hair, teach her how to roll perfect pie crusts on a Sunday afternoon. Coretta's tongue might be thorns and vinegar, but underneath was a heart that could warm the whole damn street if she cared to.

Plus, I knew she'd fight to protect Julia just as hard as I would.

"You're up early," I told her, trying to get a grip on my breathing.

"Am I?" she shot back. "Maybe that's because someone snuck their child into my apartment in the middle of the night, and these noises in the walls have been keeping me up ever since." She jabbed the broom upward again. "Blasted squirrels. Sounds like a pack of wild dogs running around up there."

I tilted my head. "I don't hear anything."

She stopped long enough to glare at me. Coretta was small and wiry, with a head of tight gray curls and an expression like she'd been chewing lemons since birth. "Don't patronize me, Tuesday Kenn," she said. "You think I don't know what squirrels sound like? I've owned this house longer than you've been alive."

"And it's still standing," I said, trying a joke. "Guess that's thanks to you."

Her eyes narrowed. "You want to be helpful, go up those attic stairs and scare them out yourself. At least peek up through that access panel in your bedroom ceiling, see what you can see. I'm guessing there's a whole colony."

"I'll get to it," I promised, though I didn't have the faintest idea what I'd do with a squirrel if I found one.

Coretta muttered under her breath, gave the wall one more whack, and stomped off through her front door. The broom scraped the floor behind her.

Seeing her in top form lowered my blood pressure even more. In fact, the farther I got from the crime scene, the more ridiculous it was that I'd thought it could have been the Crying Killer. So the woman had fallen in a fashion similar to the way he'd posed his victims. So it looked like she'd been stabbed multiple times in the chest, exactly as Arsen had done to his four victims before my sister. It didn't mean anything except that it wasn't safe to be a woman in this world, which wasn't exactly a news flash.

I bundled up a sleeping Julia, pausing so Coretta could kiss her forehead. Then I climbed the stairs, balancing the child on my hip so I could enter the security code. The system's answering beeps reassured me. I entered and listened. The hallway was quiet, the only noise the wooden floor creaking under my weight. I rearmed the security system and carried Julia to her room. Her door was cracked exactly as I'd left it. I opened it with my foot, padded across the floor, and tucked her in. She snuffled sweetly before curling into a ball, her face slack with sleep.

She looked so peaceful. I lingered, studying her as a memory of my sister and me emerged. I was like a rat pushing a lever for these lately. This particular memory had made it into the Lilydale newspaper's local gossip column, "Heard Around Town," alongside stories about lawn mowers driven to church and prize marigolds devoured by runaway goats. Our parents had not been pleased.

> Local daredevil Trixie Hendrickson took quite the tumble this week while climbing an old oak near the creek. Seems she convinced her sister, Tuesday, to join her on a quest for "fairy luck" (we're not making this up, folks!), but when her sister wisely declined, young Trixie went ahead solo. Witnesses report she was laughing all the way up—right until that rotten branch gave way with a snap heard clear across the creek. Down she went, collecting scratches like trading cards on her way. Her quick-thinking sister jumped into the water to help her. Lucky for Trixie, she escaped with nothing worse than some scrapes and what we imagine is a whopper of a story. The oak tree, meanwhile, remains undefeated.
>
> *Remember, kids: Fairy luck doesn't include a parachute.*

The old guy we'd seen fishing in the creek must have called it in.

I still remembered the sound those breaking branches made, like bones breaking. If I'd written that "Heard Around Town" story, this is what I would have added:

> When Tuesday hauled her sister to shore, the girl had the nerve to laugh about the whole ordeal. Busted out with giggles like she'd just won a prize instead of

> nearly killing herself. Tuesday, showing more restraint than most would credit a child with, didn't yell.
>
> Instead, she held Trixie on the creek bank until the laughter turned to tears and Trixie started shivering like a scared rabbit. Tuesday loved her sister more than anything in the world, and she knew Trixie needed to believe she was wild and untouchable, like lightning crackling across the sky. Tuesday played the tether, steady and sure, always reeling her back from the edge. Back then, they had no idea that even the strongest rope eventually frays.

I closed Julia's door quietly and leaned against the wall, my chest tight.

CHAPTER 14

Before

The spring Tuesday was seven and Trixie five, Pia began wearing her hair in a high ponytail, secured with a paisley silk scarf. The style made her look younger than her thirty-two years, more like a teenager from the beach movies she adored watching on Saturday afternoons. She had high cheekbones, lips always painted cherry red, and eyes the color of summer skies after a storm. Her blond hair had started to darken at the roots, but she fought it with Lady Clairol.

"A woman's hair is her crowning glory," Pia would say, studying her reflection in the mirror while her daughters sat cross-legged on the bed. She teased the front sections with a rat-tail comb until they achieved the perfect height, then sprayed it all into submission with Aqua Net. The sharp scent mingled with her Charlie perfume, creating that distinctly Pia fragrance that clung to her clothes, her bedsheets, the air around her.

Pia favored fitted sweater sets in soft pastels, paired with flowing skirts or tailored pants. Other neighborhood mothers wore polyester housedresses from Sears and practical shoes. Not Pia. She sewed her own outfits, paired them with delicate kitten heels, even to run to the grocery store. They might have been poor, but she always looked put together, at least before the illness fully sank its claws into her.

To Tuesday and Trixie, their mother was a bird out of place, exotic and bright against Lilydale's gray backdrop. They trailed after her at the five-and-dime, watching male clerks stumble over themselves to serve her.

"That woman thinks she's Jackie Kennedy," Mrs. Peterson once whispered to Mrs. Miller at church, and both had laughed.

They didn't know Pia had stitched that skirt by the glow of the moon after their electricity had been cut. They didn't know she was too worn down from working to make clothes for her daughters, dismissing it with the excuse that children grew too fast.

One spring afternoon, Pia picked the girls up from school on their lunch break and loaded them into the beat-up station wagon that smelled of cigarettes and sun-warmed vinyl. She called it "the chariot," and when they laughed, she said, "Well, it gets us where we're going, doesn't it?"

That day she dressed differently—bell-bottom jeans and a loose white blouse with embroidered flowers, a blouse she usually saved for home. She said it made her feel like a hippie, like she was free. Neither daughter asked free from what.

She drove them to Lake Koronis park, spread a blanket on the grass, and pulled sandwiches from a brown paper bag. "Eat up, girls," she said, handing Trixie a PB&J and Tuesday a bologna and cheese. "You're going to need your strength."

"For what?" Tuesday had asked.

"For skipping rocks." Pia smiled, a true grin that lit her face and made her look ten years younger.

The lake mirrored the sky, a perfect blue for a Minnesota spring. Pia picked up a smooth stone, turned it over in her hand, and flicked her wrist. The rock skipped five times before sinking.

"That's how you do it," she said, her body loose in a way it rarely was. "It's all in the wrist."

Trixie's first rock sank at once. Pia laughed, bright and unguarded, and wrapped her arms around her youngest daughter. "Try again, sweetheart. Like this." Together they threw, and when the rock skipped three times, Pia's cheer echoed across the lake.

When Tuesday's turn came, her mother guided her in the same way, hands warm and steady. Tuesday's rock skipped twice.

It had been one of the good days, the calm between spells.

Neither Trixie nor Tuesday had told their mother that that day mattered, that *she* mattered. It'd never even crossed their mind, but that was okay.

Pia Hendrickson was not the sort of woman who let sentimentality in.

She lived her life in fragments.

CHAPTER 15

After

When I woke up, the sun was scratching the horizon, the snow blushing with the first pink of light. Both Julia and Nic were still asleep. I headed straight downstairs for the newspaper. It was waiting for me on the front porch, tucked tight against the January wind, the corners outside the plastic smudged with salt. I yanked it open with stiff fingers and scanned it right there on the stoop.

Last night's murder in front of the Gopher Hole was covered in the Metro section, but there was no mention of a phone call confession. I went weak with relief. I hadn't believed that poor woman had been killed by Arsen, not really, not once I'd gotten far enough away from the scene, but it was nice to have it confirmed, not to mention to be assured that I *had* really witnessed a dead body.

I must've been mistaken about the woman being pulled in the alleyway, was all.

The article was brief, the kind of piece they ran for crimes that happened right before the paper went to press. A woman stabbed multiple times in the chest and left on the icy sidewalk.

Victim's identity withheld pending notification of next of kin.

It was a terrible tragedy, but it had nothing to do with me. I folded the paper and made my way back upstairs to the little nook off the living room where I'd set up my makeshift office. My trusty IBM tower sat below the desk, its beige casing scuffed. I reached down to press the chunky power button. The machine hummed to life. A few moments later, the monitor flickered and glowed, the start-up screen filling the dark-green display. I waited for the hard drive to stop its noisy clicks before inserting the floppy disk Corn had given me.

I should have gone straight to the Hachette case I'd begun background research on yesterday, but on impulse, I navigated to my personal files, the ones I'd saved under a generic folder name so Julia wouldn't stumble across them.

When I opened it, the Crying Killer's victims stared back at me in black-and-white photographs I'd gazed at a thousand times. Five women. The first in 1985, the last, according to the police—Trixie—in 1986. All five had passing similarities. Blond hair, strong features, a kind of defiance in their posture, single.

After Trixie's murder, I'd become an expert on serial killers. I was eighteen, with no internet to scroll through and no documentaries to binge. Instead, it was microfiche—newspaper and magazines—and books from the library, dog-eared paperbacks about Bundy and Dahmer and Gacy. My understanding of killers came together in fits and starts, like assembling a puzzle without the box.

I was desperate to learn where Arsen Bauer fit in.

It wasn't until the Crying Killer's third victim—Sylvia Schwab—that the news played one of his calls. He'd pitched his voice unnaturally high, almost childlike, as he confessed to his crimes, but never to who he was. Once I was told it had been Arsen making the calls, I decided I recognized his voice, but before? It could have been anyone.

The details of the killings were kept hidden from the public, but I'd accessed them after I became a cop. The first four victims, all of them living within thirty miles of Lilydale, were stabbed in the chest with a screwdriver or an ice pick between eighteen and sixty-one times, then he sliced an X in their lower back after they were dead. With two of them, he'd carved so deep he nicked bone.

Trixie's murder had been an aberration. A shooting, not a stabbing, the X carved into her back already well healed.

She and Arsen had started dating late winter of Trixie's freshman year. He'd been out of high school a few years at that point, which should have been a red flag if we'd acknowledged things like that back then. Arsen was cute, and he could be funny, and his dad had been a cop, albeit a twisted one. That was a lot to recommend a guy in 1980s Lilydale.

By that time, the Crying Killer had already murdered his first two victims.

I stared at the photo of Trixie longer than I meant to. Her smile was frozen, her head tipped sideways.

The creak of the floor pulled me back. I whipped around to see Nic standing behind me, her eyes trained on the computer.

"You went out last night?" she asked.

I searched for judgment but heard only concern. I tried to change the subject. "Coretta's hearing noise in the walls, thinks it's squirrels. Do you know anything about that?"

Nic refused to be distracted. "If you went out, that means you're having flashbacks again," she pressed. "Tuesday—"

"I'm fine." I jabbed the off button on the computer and stood.

"Let me in," Nic pleaded. "You're running. You always run."

She was a fine one to talk. I didn't have the energy for this conversation, so I pushed past her, heading to Julia's room. She was still crashed when I nudged her awake, her hair sticking up in soft tufts.

"Come on, Jules," I said, smoothing her hair. "I'll make you breakfast."

She stretched like a cat, smiling sleepily. "Oatmeal?"

My jaw unknotted, her beautiful face working its magic. "Of course. Extra brown sugar."

The rest of the morning was peace and love in my blue, white, and red kitchen as I got her ready for school. Nic thankfully stayed out of my way. Julia and I talked homework and sledding and squirrels, oh my. When I dropped her off outside Highland Park Elementary, she waved from the steps, her purple mittens flashing. I waved back, my chest tightening with a familiar ache.

It wasn't until she was safely inside the school that the thought I'd been holding at bay dropped into place: *I need to go into the room in the attic.*

I'd started filling it with things I didn't want to think about shortly after moving into Coretta's.

I'd been a high school graduate for less than three months.

I'd felt utterly alone in the world. Dad had skipped town a couple years earlier, and Mom was institutionalized on and off. The local police didn't want me to leave town after my sister's murder, but what was there to stay for? I answered all their questions, attended her burial, then packed a suitcase, buckled Julia into her car seat, and drove us toward the Cities, vowing never to return to Lilydale, a cursed town if ever there was one. I had a full scholarship to Metro State in Saint Paul, but that seemed meaningless in this new, terrible version of my life.

The one spot of luck was that, thanks to swapping names at the hospital, Julia's birth certificate had me down as her mother.

For all that the world—other than Trixie and Nick—knew, I was.

My sister is dead Nick ran my sister is dead Nick ran my sister is dead

I ate up my meager savings staying in that Thrifty Scot in Brooklyn Center for a few weeks, a total wreck who couldn't do much more than care for Julia and eat gas station burritos. I probably would've never gotten it together if I hadn't lucked onto an ad for cheap rent on the top floor of Coretta's place. Once Coretta realized I was the sister of the girl who'd been murdered over in Lilydale, she insisted on watching Julia during the day so I could start college. I didn't see a choice if I was to make a better life for Julia and me. We barely had time to settle into the Victorian before classes started.

To hold it all together, I claimed a room in the attic, a space Coretta didn't need, and I began to collect all the information I could find on Arsen and the Crying Killer. This was before I had a computer. I was hoping to make sense of that awful night, to understand how I could have missed how dangerous Arsen was.

When Nick, who was now Nic, finally tracked us down a couple of years ago, she filled in the blanks from the night of my sister's murder. She confirmed that Arsen had shown up, said they'd argued. Arsen had found out about baby Julia and thought she was his, even though he and Trixie had broken up the previous December. Nic swore to him that she wasn't, that Julia was the child of some guy he didn't even know, started getting in Arsen's face. She said everything happened pretty quick after that. Shooting, Arsen running out the front and then back in, bleeding from a bullet wound.

When I asked her who else had shown up with Arsen at the trailer that night, she gave me a strange look and refused to help me figure out who could have been planted to look like Arsen. When she found out about everything I'd collected up in the attic room, she demanded I give her the key and never go back to it. So I hadn't been up there for a couple years, not since that dark period when I'd hallucinated Arsen while on patrol.

Instead, I'd focused on protecting Julia as best as I could, and holding my breath, always expecting Arsen Bauer to return, because he'd been right about one thing.

Julia was his daughter, and like Arsen always used to say, you didn't leave family behind.

CHAPTER 16

I stepped over a patch of ice, cursing winter under my breath. January in Saint Paul meant the air had teeth. The downtown neighborhood surrounding Corn's office hummed with life despite the cold, bundled figures scurrying along the sidewalks, heads down, shoulders hunched.

My oversize suit coat flapped against my thighs, the wool doing its best to keep the wind at bay as my shoes tried to grip the ground. My pixie cut was styled neatly, the ends gelled to perfection, and my makeup was solid: lips done in Revlon Blackberry, smudged purple eyeliner, pale cheeks. It was a look I'd modeled after Winona Ryder. It worked for her, and—despite my dirty-blond hair—seemed to work for me.

The office was warm when I strode in. Corn was already at his desk, bent over a file. He looked up as the door jingled shut behind me.

"Nice of you to join me," he said, raising an eyebrow. Today's T-shirt beneath his blazer read DYIN' AIN'T MUCH OF A LIVIN', BOY.

"Traffic slowed me down," I said, dropping my bag onto my desk. I held up a foot. "Ever try driving in Doc Martens?"

"I leave that to you," he said, gesturing to his sturdy loafers. "Though I'd kill to see you wear white tennies one day. Just to prove you're Midwestern." Corn always knew how to draw out a smile, even when I didn't want to give him one. He let me hold it for a second before he coughed uncomfortably. "Hey, sorry about your photo in the PI mag. I should've asked first."

My skin blazed. Not only did poor kids—at least the ones raised by a drunk—not accept compliments well, but we weren't sure what to do with sincere apologies, either. But that was Corn for you, out there acting like a grown-up. I'd liked him since the first time I met him, when I was assigned as his ride-along. Corn Stamoran had been a legend in Vice, a guy with an exceptional clearance rate who seemed to get along with everyone. I expected he'd either rib me or ignore me, like all the other detectives did. It was nothing personal, just how they treated beat cops, particularly when they were female.

Instead, Corn'd given me a once-over before saying, "Women make the best detectives, you know." He'd smiled easily, like he was sharing a fact about the weather rather than something that could get him laughed out of the Saint Paul Police Department. He leaned back on his heels and crossed his arms before continuing, his voice deceptively casual. "You don't grow up hunted and not learn to smell a predator. You don't walk around in danger of getting grabbed most of your life without learning what a man looks like just before he strikes. Give me a lady partner any day of the week."

And then he'd walked out to his car.

I'd stood there—a stupid grin on my face—for a full ten seconds before racing to follow.

That'd been the first of many good days working with Corn, one of my closest friends despite his uncomfortable habit of almost always taking responsibility for his behavior.

Like he had just now by apologizing for the magazine article.

"It's fine," I grumbled. "Just don't do it again. I like to lay low."

He nodded, but his gaze lingered. "You sleep okay?" He laced his fingers together to crack his knuckles. If I didn't know better, I'd say he was genuinely relaxed rather than picking up on my mood and gently probing to see what was behind it.

I hesitated, but what was the point? "Saw something last night. A murder over by Macalester. It's in the paper."

"I haven't read it yet," he said carefully. "You call it in?"

I shook my head. "The cops were already there." *Always tell the truth, never the whole truth.*

He studied me for a few beats longer, stroking his mustache. "You know, you can tell me if you're going through a hard time. Seeing a murder victim takes a toll."

"I'm fine," I said, my voice steadier than I expected. "Really."

He didn't push, just gave me a long look before a brusque nod. "All right. But you tell me if that changes."

"Will do."

He indicated my empty hands. "How's the Hachette case going?"

"I plan to interview her, but I wanted to touch base with you first."

"It's been touched, now go talk to her." He gestured to a file on the edge of his desk. "While you're out, drop this off at the Western District HQ. It belongs to Detective Smith in Homicide. You familiar?"

"Vaguely," I lied. The names at the PD blurred together since I left. I was sure I'd known a Smith at some point. "What's in the file?"

Corn's eyes flashed, the expression so quick I might have imagined it. "Just something the PD asked me to look into, off the record. A little information sharing between an old cop and a new one." He pointed at the door, dismissing me. "Drive carefully. It's icy out there."

Corn hated winter almost as much as my mother. He'd actually planned to retire on Isla Mujeres, a pretty little island off the coast of Cancún. When the time came, he'd spent all of a month there before realizing he couldn't afford a good view. "On an *island*," he'd said to me when he returned, shaking his head in disbelief. "You have to strive to fail that hard."

I grabbed the file he was holding out to me. "Such a worrywart. I always drive careful."

He grunted.

Summit Avenue was a straight shot of old money, massive mansions sitting like overstuffed armchairs behind iron fences. I didn't belong here, where the huge houses were allowed to stay whole rather than cut into apartments, but I liked driving it anyway, chose it every time I got a chance, enjoyed the way the past felt so close you could almost smell it.

Cedar and mothballs.

Melissa Hachette lived on the other end of town, near the University of St. Thomas. It made sense to drop off the file at the Western District on the way to her place, but I was in no hurry to visit the cop shop.

I glanced at the manila folder on the seat next to me. So benign. It wasn't unusual for Corn to share info with the Saint Paul Police. He'd been on the force forever, and he still had good relationships with many of the guys there. Plus, he could uncover things in his line of work that they might have trouble justifying. I considered peeking at what was inside but then decided there'd be no point. Corn would let me know if it was something I needed to care about.

I was turning off Summit when I spotted a man holding a ladder, a rope of Christmas tree lights wound around his shoulder. I felt a jolt of ice.

He was a dead ringer for my dad.

CHAPTER 17

Before

It was the summer before Tuesday, the oldest of them, would enter high school. They were as close to innocence as the three of them could get, given the families they'd been born into. Cicadas whined in the trees, almost loud enough to drown out the highway a mile away. Heat pressed through the rental house's thin walls, sticky and close.

Tuesday sat cross-legged on the carpet, the deck of cards fanned in her hand. Nick waited for her play, fingers drumming on his knee.

"You're staring again," Tuesday said without looking up.

Nick's cheeks flushed pink. "Am not."

"Are too," Trixie called from the couch. She was painting her toenails with a bottle of Wet n Wild polish, the chemical tang overriding the faint scent of garbage coming from the kitchen. She leaned back, wiggling her toes so the cherry-red polish caught the light. "You've got hearts in your eyes, Nicky."

Trixie used to be jealous of the extra attention Nick gave Tuesday, until Tuesday pointed out that their father liked Trixie better, and wasn't that an improvement over having an annoying boy always gawping at her?

"Shut up," Nick told Trixie. He bent over his hand, shoulders tense.

Tuesday laid down a straight and grinned. Nick may have taught them how to play poker, but Tuesday usually won. "That's two in a row."

Nick muttered something under his breath and gathered the cards too fast. Trixie laughed, but she didn't look up from her toes.

That's when the back door rattled open.

All three froze.

Keys jangled, heavy and deliberate. Then the slam of the door. Daryl Hendrickson's boots struck the linoleum, an ominous drumbeat they all knew too well. He didn't stop in the kitchen to wash his hands, like usual. His steps angled toward the hallway.

Tuesday's gaze darted to Trixie. Her sister had gone rigid on the couch, nail polish brush hovering in the air. They heard the scrape of a key sliding into the hall closet lock. A metallic click. Hinges groaning. Their father visited that closet frequently, always after going out with his friends. Friends that he never brought home.

The closet door banged closed. The key twisted again, snicking, final. Boots climbed the stairs. Floorboards creaked above. Then silence.

Nick whispered, "What's in that closet?"

Tuesday and Trixie swallowed hard. They'd broken into it a few weeks ago. It'd been Trixie's idea—everything dangerous was. They'd both immediately regretted it when they saw what was inside. A smear of something on a tarp. A chain looped on a hook, heavy enough to blister the drywall. A glass jar with something cloudy floating in it, and tucked in the corner, a Styrofoam cooler sealed with tape. They never asked their dad what it all was, and he never explained. The lock on that door was enough of an answer.

"Nothing," Tuesday said too quickly.

Trixie gave a nervous laugh, thin as paper. "Nothing good, anyhow." She capped the polish, shoved it into the cushion beside her.

Nick leaned closer, eyes searching Tuesday's. "You know."

She looked back at him, steady. "I don't." It was a lie, or half of one. She felt it catch and hold in her chest, but she didn't flinch.

Nick lifted his chin. "You're good at that."

"At what?"

"Not saying the whole thing." His voice was soft, almost admiring.

She didn't know how to answer that, and she didn't have to. She was the oldest, after all.

Trixie swung her legs off the couch, nail polish forgotten. "We should get out of here," she said. Her eyes were too bright, the way they always got when she was scared. "Go down to the river. Anywhere but here."

For a moment, none of them moved. Upstairs, a floorboard creaked again.

They hurried outside, into the purifying sunlight.

CHAPTER 18

After

When I blinked, I realized the man hauling Christmas lights down Summit Avenue didn't look like my father, not really. But something in the way he moved, that loose-limbed swagger, the tilt of his head . . . it was pure Daryl Hendrickson, a ghost in broad daylight. Probably a family hangover from the holidays making me raw, peeling back the years until I felt like a kid again, all nerve endings and need.

The car ahead crawled to a stop, and I tapped my brakes, watching the Dad-guy drop the lights into the back of a pickup truck. He must have been hired to remove holiday decorations. Just the sort of job my jack-of-all-trades, master of none father would have done.

My mind skittered back to the golden days of my childhood before he ditched.

Sure, he was a drunk, and he once beat Mom so hard she permanently lost hearing in her left ear, but all of us looked for the good in our parents, no matter how bad they were. It was survival. And Dad, when he was sober, had a way of spinning our shabby reality into something magical. Our two-story rental with its groaning refrigerator and curling wallpaper wasn't just some run-down house. It was our kingdom. That's what he called it, and back then, we believed him.

"Every queen starts small," he'd say, his Southern drawl stretching the words like molasses. "You girls'll learn."

Mornings were the best. If he wasn't hungover, he'd shuffle into the kitchen wearing a ratty T-shirt and flannel PJ pants, talking a mile a minute, telling us stories about his own family, who we'd never met, each one of them worse than the last with only him coming out on top. He had this dish he loved to cook when he told us his family stories. Hot brown with eggs, like some kind of diner special. He'd layer the bread just so, topping it with turkey, tomato slices, and bacon before pouring neon-orange melted Velveeta over the works. Made the whole house smell sharp and rich. My sister and I'd sit at the table, legs swinging, watching him work like we were seeing a magic trick.

And maybe we were, because Dad shopped at the excuse store more often than he cooked.

Mom already knew what kind of man he was by the time we came into the picture; we could tell by the way she sharpened her words on him. It took Trixie and me longer to figure out the truth of him, and even after we did, we still didn't want to look straight at it.

"Don't have the rent money this month," he'd say when it was late again. "I'll cover it next time."

Next time never came. Mom worked several jobs, back when she could keep her worlds straight. I'm not sure what Dad did, other than teach us how to fix things—lawn mowers, leaky sinks, the washing machine that rattled like a train about to derail. He had a knack for breaking and mending in equal measure.

Even now, the smell of a two-stroke engine made me nostalgic for him. It was funny how many skills he taught my sister and me, given how much he hated independent women. Three drinks in, that was his favorite group to rail against.

The car behind me honked, dragging me back to the present. The guy taking down Christmas lights had disappeared into a yard. I eased my foot off the brake and drove to Melissa Hachette's.

She lived in a quadplex that resembled a wooden box the color of dishwater.

I crunched up the frozen walk, climbing the porch stairs to the four black mailboxes. My breath clouded as I squinted at them, finding her last name in a barely legible scratch beneath the second one. I jabbed the appropriate doorbell. The sound vibrated faintly, like a wasp nest in the walls. I waited, shifting from foot to foot as the chill January air worked its way inside my coat.

Nothing. No footsteps, no shadows moving behind the door's frosted glass pane.

The research I'd done on Hachette after Corn handed me her file hadn't revealed anything that altered the case. She had no criminal record, not even an unpaid parking ticket. She worked at a retail shop on Grand Avenue. She was single as far as I could tell, and active in two internet relay chat rooms, one on true crime and the other devoted to Janet Jackson. She was mostly a lurker in the first and a gushing fan in the second.

The most notable thing I knew about her was that she alleged she was being stalked and the police didn't care. I wanted to see her face the first time we spoke so I could get a feel for her relationship with the truth. I had no trouble believing she was in danger and wasn't getting the help she deserved. What I needed to see was whether she knew the guy and had failed to share that info with Corn. Society put forth a real effort to make women feel responsible for the behavior of the guys in their life, and shame made a person do stupid things.

I gave it another two minutes before reaching into my bag and pulling out two cards from a silver holder that I'd scored at a garage sale. One card went into her mailbox, the other I wedged carefully into the door handle. The phone number on them was the landline back at the office. More and more people walked around with their eyes glued to pagers these days. I figured it was only a matter of time until everyone carried them like a colostomy bag, and I wanted no part of that. My work messages could stay at work, where they belonged.

I turned and headed back to the car, the frozen air augering my nostrils. A quick stop at the station to drop off the folder, and then I'd pop into the office, finish up the stack of reports I had left to write, and see what other work had come in. We always received a steady stream of insurance fraud and missing person cases on top of an occasional request to dig up dirt on an employee or a politician, but a whole tsunami of secrets overtook people around the holidays. Christmas lights had a way of illuminating shadows people spent all year ignoring. Do I have a sister? Is my husband cheating? Where's our money going?

Bad for one's faith in humanity, good for the pocketbook, I thought as I parked in front of the Western District HQ of the SPPD. I'd done plenty of these runs for Corn and figured I'd be in and out in under a minute.

I'd never visited this branch, but I was unsurprised to see the interior looked like every other police department I'd ever set foot in—flickering fluorescent lights, nearly colorless walls, bulletin boards covered in grimy posters about workplace safety.

I approached the front desk, a high counter with a pane of scratched Plexiglas separating the civilian side from the inner workings. Behind it sat a woman with her hair wrenched into a bun so tight it pulled her eyes back. She wore a sharp, practiced scowl, glancing up at me over the rim of her glasses as I leaned in.

"Detective Smith around?" I asked, sliding the folder onto the counter.

She jabbed her thumb over her shoulder. "You're in luck. She's right there."

My brain took a second to catch up. Smith was a woman? That shouldn't have thrown me off but it did, until I looked where the desk worker had indicated and the real punch landed.

It was *her*.

The elegant detective from last night's murder scene.

She stood by a desk, talking to another plainclothes officer, her head tilted slightly, smoke curling upward from the cigarette she held with easy confidence. She was still dressed sharp as a blade, wearing a gray wool coat and tailored slacks like a Black Marlene Dietrich straight out of a noir film.

My pulse stuttered. My first thought was *Corn set me up.* The notion hit like ice water, but I immediately discarded it as ridiculous. He didn't know I'd witnessed Smith arrive at the scene last night, hadn't even known there'd been a murder before I told him.

Still, my skin prickled. I slid the folder the rest of the way forward. "Just hand this off to her, okay?"

Before the desk worker could respond, I turned on my heel and strode out fast enough to seem guilty. The cold air didn't do much to cool the heat spreading under my collar. I glanced back at the building, half expecting to see Smith at the door, watching me with those assessing eyes that didn't seem like they missed a trick.

But there was nothing, just the faint glow of the lobby lights bleeding into the gray January morning. I told myself to breathe.

I'd worked too hard to build this life to let it be thrown off course.

CHAPTER 19

Julia was waiting when I pulled up to her school. She stood near the gate clutching her backpack. I never let her take the bus. Too many things could go wrong. When she climbed into the car, I kissed the top of her head, inhaling the green-apple scent of her shampoo.

"Guess what, Mom?" she said, her voice bubbling with excitement.

"What?" I asked, pulling away from the curb.

"I got the math star today! My new teacher said I'm the fastest in the whole class at times tables." She beamed.

"That's amazing, baby." I reached over to squeeze her hand. Her fingers wrapped around mine, small and trusting. I was holding on to something fragile, something the world would love to break if it got the chance.

"Mom?" she said suddenly, her voice soft and curious.

"Yeah?"

"You think if I practice enough, I'll get the reading star, too?"

"Of course," I said. "You can do anything."

◈

I helped Julia with her homework and fed her a tomato soup and grilled cheese dinner before driving her to Corn's. This had been our routine on AA nights since I'd started attending. Coretta couldn't watch her because she'd be at the same meeting, and Nic worked her shift at the bar. I'd hated asking Corn to babysit the first time, right when I'd started working for him, but it turned out he loved spending time with Julia, and I knew she'd be safe with him.

Sure enough, he already had the popcorn buttered and the VCR fired up when we knocked. I bet he'd have her topped off with hot chocolate with whipped cream before I reached my car. I wouldn't have minded hanging out with them, but like MMA, I needed AA if I was going to stay healthy for my girl.

I'd started drinking in college, which . . . a lot of people did. But I'd really leaned into it around the same time I left the police force. I'd be forever grateful to Coretta for realizing where I was headed before I did, dragging me to my first meeting and refusing to let me quit.

She was already in the church basement when I arrived, her sharp voice cutting across the room as she chastised someone for bringing store-bought cookies.

"I've always loved Oreos," I said, making my way to the table and ignoring Coretta's glare. I grabbed a cookie and filled a Styrofoam cup with coffee-colored sludge before claiming a chair in the circle. Once everyone was settled, we started the familiar litany that began every meeting, the structure and words providing comfort. My bones began to warm. I recognized all the faces except one, a new guy a couple years older than me. He wore thick black-rimmed glasses and kept glancing at his watch and then the floor. Not unusual. Everyone was nervous their first time.

After the formalities were out of the way, we went around the circle and each shared how our week had been. The weight in my chest grew heavier until it was my turn. I'd known what I had to say since I'd mistakenly believed I'd seen that woman dragged into the alley. It was something I should have confessed to during my first meeting, but knowing what you should do and deciding to do it were two completely different animals.

"My name is Tuesday," I said, mouth so dry that my lips stuck to my teeth even though I'd said these words a hundred times. "And I'm an alcoholic."

The group murmured their acknowledgment. I stared down at the slick surface of my coffee, feeling the lingering heat in my palms. I was desperate to steady myself, but I was floating above my body. It was now or never.

"I'm . . . I've been thinking about my sister. About what happened . . . the night she was murdered. I've never said this out loud, but . . . it was my fault. She died because of me."

CHAPTER 20

Before

Nick might have told Arsen about "The House of the Rising Sun" paralyzing Trixie, but he wasn't the reason Arsen discovered he had a daughter. He and Trixie had broken up the December before Julia was born. He would've had no idea Trixie was even pregnant if not for a terrible moment of ego.

She hadn't meant for it to happen.

That night the three of them were all back from the hospital with Julia, planning to skip town the next day? Arsen called. It was bad luck that she was in the kitchen when the phone rang, that she was the one who picked up. As far as the three of them knew, Arsen was clear across the country, had been for months. Still, she waited until he confirmed he was living in Florida to let him know he was a stain in the shape of their father.

She should have stopped there, but the Hendrickson sisters had never been real smart when it came to men. High on . . . what? Love for Julia? Joy at the thought of being free, at the hope of a fresh start for all of them outside of Lilydale? It didn't matter. Whatever was bubbling in her veins convinced her to keep going.

"We're about to skip town, too," she said. "Me, Nick, my sister. You should know you lost out on the best woman you were ever gonna get. You'll never see her again."

For a second, she felt puffed up and strong. But when Julia cried in the background, fear shivered through her.

He was quiet for a moment, then: "Whose baby is that?" His voice was cold and low. "If it's mine, you know nothing's gonna keep me from claiming what belongs to me."

She hung up quick, her insides scraped clean.

◈

Arsen Bauer showed up a few hours later—he *had* been living in Florida, they would later find out, but was no longer—coming for a child he wouldn't have known about if she'd kept her stupid mouth shut.

She was the reason he came to the trailer that night.

She'd summoned the devil.

CHAPTER 21

After

The new AA guy with the black-rimmed glasses was staring at me with an intensity that was startling as I confessed to being the reason my sister had been murdered. Why did he seem more interested in my revelation than anyone else here? It set up my hackles. I realized he was attractive, his features chiseled and his lips full, but something about him made my belly twist. The way his eyes narrowed, the sudden tension in his shoulders. I looked away to focus on myself. There was relief in saying the truth out loud, and I wanted to feel it.

After circle, I slipped out before the cookies and the small talk, pulling my coat tight against the cold. As I headed for my car, footsteps sounded behind me, the same warning noise every woman I tried to protect heard just before she was attacked.

My pulse pounded as I spun around.

It was the new guy.

Justin, Jason. Something with a *J*. In the circle he'd said he was a teacher with a drinking problem, talked about how he'd swapped the whiskey for Tae Bo, but his eyes had been locked on me the whole time. Now he was asking if I wanted coffee, leaning into my space with that recovery-guy fervor.

"We're not supposed to date in group," I said, tasting metal on my tongue. "First-year rule."

He smiled. Expensive dental work for a teacher. "It wouldn't be a date. Just coffee."

"Pass." I left him standing there, making a point of walking slowly to my car so he didn't think I was afraid. I kept my hands out of my pockets, though, so I could do the most damage if he jumped me.

By the time I slid behind the wheel, he was long gone.

I realized I needed to see Nic immediately.

CHAPTER 22

I parked on the street and strode into O'Gara's, remembering the first time my sister and I met Nicholas Gajdusek.

The Hendricksons bopped around the Lilydale area a lot, getting kicked out of one rental and moving to the next, Dad selling it as an adventure and Mom stone-faced. Most of the places were run-down houses, but there was one glorious summer when we got to stay in the Purple Saucer, a motel that'd been converted to shoebox apartments. It was like living in a Barbie Dreamhouse—at least that's how Trixie and I saw it: tiny fridge, tiny stove, four plates and sets of silverware. Two beds, side by side.

But Nicholas was the best part of the whole deal. He'd lived at the Purple Saucer his whole life. He was small for his age, in the grade between my sister and me. We clicked the moment we met, and we hadn't unclicked since.

"You two living in the old Dahl place?" he'd asked, pointing at the unit right next to his. His blue eyes were wide and long lashed. He wore his hair in a ponytail, which made sense. It was hot out.

We nodded.

He scratched his nose, tipped his head as if deciding whether to tell us a secret. He landed on yes. "It's haunted, you know," he said, leaning in. "But there's a special flower down by the creek that'll get rid of the spirits. Want me to show you?"

We most definitely did.

He led us down to the Crow River—it meandered all through central Minnesota, and kids did as they pleased back then, particularly WIC kids—and we splashed and played hide-and-seek and shared our deepest secrets. Nick understood having a dad who drank, and the way you had to hold your head extra high like you didn't care what people thought about your hand-me-down clothes.

The magic plant he showed us turned out to be plain ol' milkweed, but it must have worked because we never saw a ghost. And rarely a day followed where we didn't hang out with Nick, even after we moved out of the motel. In fact, the time after Trixie was killed was the longest we'd been apart since that day we'd met at the Purple Saucer.

It was a gift Nic was back in my life, that I could stop by her job at O'Gara's whenever I felt low.

Like tonight.

She was swamped, darting between tables with her tray held high. On particularly busy nights, she had to work the floor instead of tending bar. She didn't see me at first, so I slid onto a stool and ordered a club soda, my ritual post-meeting drink. It was nice to be inside a bar rather than trolling for pervs outside one, to carve out a precious few moments where I didn't run the risk of seeing ghosts from my past. I watched Nic work as I waited to talk to her—those deliberate movements, the way her hands gripped the tray like it might fight back. Her makeup was straight out of a Max Factor ad: matte-brown lipstick, smoky liner smudged into oblivion.

She'd always been good at drawing stares.

Back in high school, Nick wore eyeliner so thick it looked like goggles and showed up to class in band tees shredded at the hem and collar. The jocks never missed a chance to punish him for standing out from the crowd. I remember one afternoon in sophomore year, he came to school wearing fishnet gloves. Someone scrawled "fag" in Sharpie on the back of his notebook, the only one he owned. He cut school shortly after. When he reappeared the next day, his wrists were raw, like he'd scrubbed himself clean of something. I hadn't asked him what. But now? Nic *owned* the clothes, the makeup, the stares, the whole damn vibe.

She caught my eye across the bar and gave me a quick wink, but there wasn't time for more than that, so I nursed my club soda, watching the weekday crowd surge and ebb.

Nic had dreamed of working—and performing—at O'Gara's, a Saint Paul bar famous for the open mic magic nights it'd been hosting since the '80s, since high school. It drew an eclectic crowd. A businessman near the door kept glancing my way until I fixed him with a dead-eyed stare. He found the overhead TV—it was playing a *Bosom Buddies* rerun—fascinating after that. I was tense and itchy, which made me think of Chad, my most recent poke-and-roll. We'd met at the gym. He had his appeal: tattooed hands, a studio apartment that smelled like sandalwood incense, the way he never asked questions. But that path led nowhere good. Neither did the little orange bottle above the fridge, though my brain kept suggesting otherwise.

I sighed. Best I go pick up Julia from Corn's. This was going to be a hardworking week to make up for the holiday time I'd taken off, especially with the slew of new cases Corn had gotten. I'd be bringing work home, trolling chat rooms, tracing handles, trying to unearth dirt.

Nic was still across the room taking an order. I'd talk to her tomorrow. I slid off the stool and was almost at the door when a hand grabbed me. It was the businessman in his ill-fitting suit. His eyes were glossy. I wondered how many drinks he'd had.

"Hey," he said, his words slurred, nodding at the TV. "What do you call a man who turns into a woman?"

I looked over at Nic, who had her head thrown back in laughter.

"Magic," I said, shaking the guy loose.

He watched Her leave the bar. He liked messing with Her. Fooling Her. But he'd have to quit that soon.

Waste of time, wasn't it?

His father's voice rose up like bile. "You some kind of idiot? Sitting around with your thumb up your ass?" Then he'd drink until his face went purple and chuck him down the stairs.

He used to think his mama was better. A good Christian woman, she'd say. She'd hold her crying boy, rub his hair, whisper that it'd be all right. But she never left her husband, did she? Kept setting supper for the beast. Kept servin' her boy up to him like it was the Lord's will.

Then the beast finally left.

And damned if he didn't become a better man than his father ever was.

Least, that's what he told himself.

Except sometimes he still wanted to cry. Booze helped. Women did, too.

The first one just sort of happened. She'd been walking alone, and he'd followed her because the anger in him needed somewhere to go, and she was there. When she turned to look at him, she had his mother's eyes, that same empty, frightened stare.

His hand found the screwdriver in his jacket pocket.

Afterward, he'd raced to a pay phone and dialed with bloody fingers that wouldn't stop shaking. The tears flowed before he even picked up the receiver. He called the radio station because it was the only number he knew by heart. Because he didn't know what else to do. Because the weight of what he'd just done was crushing and he needed to set it down somewhere.

"I didn't mean to," he'd sobbed into the phone, and it was true. He hadn't *meant* to. It'd just *happened*.

But here was the thing he discovered: After he confessed, weeping into the phone and telling them where to find her, something lifted. Not the guilt. That was always on his back. But the terrible *aloneness* of it was gone. Someone knew now. Someone had heard his pain. He wasn't invisible anymore.

The second time was easier. And the third. And by the fourth, he understood what he was doing: He was making women witness what they'd allowed. Every woman he carved the symbol into was his mother, who'd looked away while the beast raged. And every call afterward was that crying boy at the bottom of the stairs, still begging someone to acknowledge what'd been done to him.

He stared at the door She'd walked through. She thought She was so much better than everyone else, didn't She? Running around playing hero, saving women from men like him, raising that little girl on Her own.

He smiled.

Soon, he'd set Her right.

Soon, She'd understand that the most important thing in this world was family, even if it took you a few tries to find the right one.

After all, family had made him what he was.

CHAPTER 23

The week passed uneventfully. I worked like a dog, as did Nic. I hardly saw her. Julia and I joined Coretta for dinner one night. She couldn't stop talking about her troublemaker of a son, about how she thought he'd be coming home for a visit soon. When Saturday rolled around, Julia had another get-together with Sarah, this time at Sarah's house. I imagined they'd spend the day parked on a couch watching *Power Rangers* and eating the kind of sugary cereal I never bought.

"We should invite Sarah and her parents over sometime," I told Nic when I came in from driving Julia.

Nic was half watching the local Saturday morning news, puffing on her signature Gauloises Blondes, her chosen brand ever since she'd heard that's what David Bowie smoked. "We really should."

We both knew it'd never happen, but it felt good to pretend.

Because I'd been buried under work all week, my housekeeping had slid. I planned to spend today doing a deep clean. I went to the kitchen to fill a bucket with hot water and cleaner, the Pine-Sol scent sharp in my nose. Then I came into the living room and went after the dusty baseboards. "I'm thinking of visiting Mom," I told Nic as I cleaned.

She made a noncommittal noise.

"And maybe drop by Lilydale," I said, watching her out of the corner of my eye.

Her head swiveled, her mouth popping open with shock. "What in the hell for?"

I doubled down on my scrubbing, going at it so hard I was removing varnish. "Never said you needed to come with."

She was silent for a few beats. I was scared to look at her. Finally, she spoke, her voice threaded with something like wonder. "If you do, I *will* go with you," she said softly.

I felt an unexpected weight lift. Nic was the only person who knew the whole story. That meant she was the only one in the world I could be completely honest with, even though she had yet to tell me where she disappeared to after Trixie died. Years of silence, then she showed up at my door like no time had passed. But she'd always been my compass, pointing true north when I got lost. I kept scrubbing.

I could feel Nic studying me. Finally, she said, "You know nobody's coming to inspect your work, right? No white glove test happening here, auntie-mom."

"Stop," I snapped, my good cheer erased in a flash. "Don't *ever* call me that. I don't care if Julia isn't here."

"Sorry, doll." She appeared to mean it. "I get it. Some things shouldn't get teased about."

I was about to lie and tell her it was okay when a local update came on over the radio.

"In today's news: There was an assault last night near the University of St. Thomas in Saint Paul. The female victim is in the hospital in stable condition. Sources say an X was carved into her back. Police are investigating possible connections to a recent similar attack and telling women across the city to stay safe. More details at the top of the hour."

CHAPTER 24

My old precinct looked exactly like I remembered except for the plastic Christmas decorations drooping between cubicles and the slightly deflated Mylar Santa someone had stuck to the bulletin board. The whole place smelled like burned coffee and wet wool.

Shawn, my old partner and the guy who'd been present when I mistook that kid for Arsen, was at his desk. He was broader than I remembered, his uniform stretched across shoulders built more for football than police work. He'd grown a beard and mustache since I'd last seen him, keeping both close shaven in a way that reminded me of Ron Perlman's Vincent in *Beauty and the Beast.*

I didn't love it, but I didn't hate it.

His eyes narrowed when he caught sight of me. "Well, if it isn't Tuesday Kenn." He leaned back, chair creaking.

"Hey, Shawn." I forced a smile. "Long time."

"Come to finally clear out your desk?" he asked. "Think there's still half a protein bar in there from '92."

I kept my face as serene as I could play it. I needed his help.

I was desperate to talk to the woman who'd been attacked. That meant I had to uncover her name and which hospital she'd been taken to. Corn had friends at the station he could ask, but if I went to him for help, I'd have to explain what I thought was really going on, which was that the X carved into that poor woman's back could only mean one thing, right? That information had never been made public, so if it was happening again, it proved Arsen *hadn't* died that night, that he'd simply shot off his friend's face and then put his jacket and wallet on him so he could walk free. And the fact that he was hunting in the Cities, first the woman in front of the Gopher Hole and then the second one near the college I'd just driven by? His message couldn't be clearer: He knew my movements, and he was coming for his daughter. I had a bone-deep certainty Julia was in danger, same way I knew that if I said any of that out loud, even to Corn, they'd lock me up alongside my mother.

With Corn out of the picture, that left one person in the whole Saint Paul Police Department who might help me. We'd been partners and eventually lovers, for a bit. We hadn't parted on the best of terms, but beggars couldn't be choosers.

"That desk isn't mine anymore." I kept my voice neutral, professional.

"Right," he said. "You left because Corn offered you an 'ideal job.'" He made air quotes with thick fingers. "That's what the official report says, anyway. Not the part about you spending the two weeks after you kneecapped that poor kid convinced that everyone in your unit here was being replaced by duplicates."

Heat crawled up my neck. He shouldn't have been allowed to read that report, the one documenting exactly what *else* happened in the days after I'd mistakenly attacked that guy, leading up to the rest of the reason I needed to leave the force. *Tell the truth, just not the whole truth.* If Shawn hadn't been out sick the night it reached a head, he would've had a front-row seat to my breakdown. I certainly had no intention of talking about it now. It was a low point, and it was behind me. I cleared my throat. "Anyhow, I need a favor."

He seemed about to push back but instead he stood, moving into my space like he used to back when we were dating. "You look good, Tue. Better than I remember."

I ignored the bait, forcing myself to hold his gaze. "The woman who was assaulted last night. The one with the X in her back. What's her name, and what hospital's she in?"

He crossed his arms and snorted. “Glad to see you’re still as chill as ever.”

“Can you help me or not?”

“You know I can’t just—”

“Cut the crap. I know how you operate. You’ve been dying to tell someone since it happened. Might as well be me.”

His jaw worked for a moment, then he scratched the back of his neck. “What do I get out of this?”

My eyebrows shot up. “Seriously?”

He laughed. It took five years off his face and turned him from a meathead to the kind of guy you’d wished had asked you to prom back in high school.

“Relax, I’m kidding. Mostly.” He shifted, weighing options that only he could see. And then: “She’s at Regions. Her name’s Hannah Wheaton. Twenty-six.” He paused, eyes searching my face. “You want to grab coffee sometime? Talk about old times?”

“Thanks for the info.” I turned to leave, but his voice followed me.

“Tuesday? Whatever you think you’re onto here, be careful. You weren’t wrong about everything back then.” He lowered his voice. “Just most things.”

Story of my life.

CHAPTER 25

Before

Fluorescent lights hummed above the hospital waiting room, their glow flattening everyone into shades of gray. Tuesday pressed her back against the plastic chair, its cracked vinyl cold through her thin jacket. Trixie sat beside her, picking at a hangnail until it bled. They'd both been quiet since they'd gotten the call at school from Mrs. Palmer next door.

Another fall, Mrs. Palmer had said over the phone. *Just like last time.*

They were finally called back to the room. Their sneakers squeaked on the polished floor. Pia lay in a narrow bed, skin sallow against the pillowcase, a bandage wrapping her ear. Her hair was dull, but her eyes sparked with restless energy.

"Girls," she rasped, trying for lightness. "Don't you look like trouble."

"Are you okay?" Trixie whispered, clutching the rail.

Pia waved her off, talking too loud. "It's nothing. Just clumsy me again. Should've watched those stairs."

Tuesday's throat burned. She leaned closer, voice sharp. "That's not what happened."

Trixie frowned at her sister. "Mrs. Palmer said—"

"Mrs. Palmer's covering. This wasn't a fall." Tuesday's gaze stayed on their mother, her ruined ear, the fading bruises along her jaw. "Dad hit her. Hard. Why don't you tell the cops the truth, Mom?"

The air tightened. Pia's eyes slid away, wet at the edges. "The world's already got its opinion about us Hendricksons. No one needs mine."

Tuesday's pulse pounded. She wanted to shake her mother.

Trixie saw it all written across her sister's face, the rage, the helplessness. But Trixie knew a side of her father that no one else did. He could be so gentle, reading her stories, sneaking her candy. Sure, he had a temper, but it wasn't always his fault.

A nurse breezed in with discharge papers, relief painted across her face. "The doctor said you can leave. You'll want to watch your step moving forward, Mrs. Hendrickson."

Pia didn't even bother nodding.

Tuesday and Trixie eased their mother from the bed. She was lighter than she should have been, her body folding in on itself. They guided her through the cold, sterile corridor.

Their father waited in the car, fingers drumming the steering wheel. He didn't get out.

CHAPTER 26

After

Regions Hospital in Saint Paul reeked of antiseptic, just like every other hospital I'd ever visited. A janitor pushed his mop bucket down a hallway, wheels creaking over linoleum that'd gone yellow sometime during the Eisenhower administration.

Hannah Wheaton's room was at the end of a first-floor hall, just past the nurses' station. She lay behind a blue curtain, propped up against thin pillows, right arm in a cast. Her face was swollen on one side, a bruise creeping from her jaw to her temple. Her stringy blond hair clung to her cheeks like she'd just come in from the rain.

For a moment, I was pulled back in time, seeing my mother lying in Hannah's place.

Her eyes flickered with confusion, then wariness. "Who're you?" she asked, her voice scratchy and small.

"Ms. Wheaton?" I tried to keep my posture relaxed, but my brain had been bouncing around the cage of my skull since I'd heard about her attack. "I'm Tuesday Kenn. I'd like to ask you a few questions about what happened."

"The police already came," she said, her wariness deepening. Good. She'd need those instincts.

"I know. I'm former Saint Paul PD, now working as a private investigator. I'm following a different angle." I offered her a business card, and while she read it, I pulled the plastic visitor's chair closer, its legs scraping against the floor. Up close, the ugly red-black bruises on her face told a story: Her assailant hadn't just tried to hurt her, he'd wanted to humiliate her. I swallowed hard. "What can you tell me about who attacked you?"

She frowned. "I don't remember anything," she said abruptly, handing my card back.

"Nothing at all?" I pressed. "No face, no voice, not even . . . a feeling?"

She shook her head, wincing at the movement. "I was walking home from work. I teach at . . . I teach at a Montessori school. I heard footsteps. That's it. Then, lights out. Woke up here. They tell me a couple women were walking by and saw me being whooped. They yelled, and the guy attacking me ran off."

I nodded, glancing at her cast. "Your arm?"

"Broken." Her voice hitched, and she rubbed her free hand over the cast like she was trying to start a fire. "Doctor says it's clean, like someone knew what they were doing."

"Would you be willing to show me your back?"

Something hardened behind her eyes. Slowly, she leaned forward, letting me lift her gown. A clean square of gauze, two by two inches, was taped in the lower right of her back. She pulled a corner off to reveal a perfect X, each line an inch long, carved with surgical precision.

My heart skip-thudded. The current cops must not have yet connected this case to the Crying Killer or they'd never have released this detail to the public.

Hannah sighed. "They said it wasn't deep. Didn't even need stitches." She taped the gauze down and rolled tenderly over onto her back.

I tried to mask my reaction, but it was too late. Her expression grew miserable, somewhere between hope and suspicion. "You know something," she said.

I took a deep breath. "Is there someone who can be here with you?"

She shook her head, wincing again. "My parents are on a cruise. The police haven't been able to get ahold of them."

"Friends?" I asked.

"No need to bother them." Shame burned up her cheeks. It was upsetting to see. Not her reaction, which I understood too well. It was the inevitability of it, a woman assaulted feeling like not only was it her fault, but also that she had to spare others the burden of sharing her pain.

"They'll understand," I said softly. "I know it doesn't feel like it, but they will."

A tear rolled down her cheek, and anger flared in my gut. Anger for her, for the violence she'd endured, for whatever sick game was unfolding. That body outside the Gopher Hole had just been the start, Hannah's attack the follow-up. Arsen was coming for us, and Julia would be the end if I didn't stop him.

My nails dug into my palms. "You're going to be okay," I said, talking to both of us.

She didn't respond, just stared at me with tired eyes.

A voice outside—sounded like it was coming from the nurses' station—pulled my attention. "She's in with Hannah Wheaton?" It was a woman speaking, her tone sharp but controlled.

The skin over my skull tightened. I peeked around the edge of the curtain with a good guess as to who was out there.

Yup. Detective Smith.

She stood ten feet away, at an angle. If I hadn't recognized her from the murder scene two nights ago or the drop-off at the station yesterday, I would've known she was a cop from the way she carried herself—shoulders back, head high—as well as the telltale bulge under her jacket, the unmistakable outline of a concealed weapon.

Our eyes met. For a moment, neither of us blinked.

CHAPTER 27

She waved me into the beige hallway outside Wheaton's room, offering dramatic contrast to the institutional walls in her tailored charcoal pant-suit and cream silk blouse, gold hoops catching the light. Her winter jacket was draped over her arm.

"Detective Tayari Smith," she said, offering a hand. Her handshake was firm, her grip strong enough to tell me she'd cracked more than a few egos in her time. The whiskey warmth in her eyes didn't quite match her polished exterior. "I've been looking for you."

Should I be more worried that she knew who I was or that she'd expected to find me here?

"Oh?" I kept my tone light. A cart rattled past, the squeaking wheel setting my teeth on edge. This place needed to be dipped in WD-40.

She smiled faintly, a flash of white. "What do you know about the murder over by the Gopher Hole?"

The air suddenly felt stifling. She couldn't have known I was there. But she knew *something*, didn't she? "The one a couple nights ago? Just what I read in the paper." I suddenly felt like Rodney Dangerfield about to grab his own collar. "A stabbing, if I remember right."

She tilted her head, studying me like I was a riddle she was trying to solve. I tried to keep still, but my cheek twitched, betraying me. Her eyes narrowed. "What was kept out of the paper was its similarities to the Crying Killer case from the '80s," she said. "The positioning of the body, certain . . . markers."

I liked that she didn't waste my time with background, didn't insult my intelligence by reminding me who the Crying Killer was, how I was connected to him.

"Copycat, you think?" It felt like the sanest response. I certainly couldn't tell her that Arsen was back from the dead.

Smith paused a few beats. "Can I take you out for coffee?"

"Not today," I said, too quickly. "I have to be home. My daughter is getting dropped off."

She nodded. "Julia."

The way she said it, like she was trying either the name or the relationship on for size, ignited a blaze of defensiveness up my spine. "You've researched me. May I ask why?"

She tucked in her chin. "For the exact same reason you came to this hospital to check on Hannah Wheaton once you heard about the X." She glanced in both directions down the hallway. "Which, by the way, was never supposed to be leaked to the news. We now have two women, both assaulted, one dead."

"Both with the X?"

Rather than answer, she pulled a notepad from the interior pocket of her blazer. "We're looking for Nicholas Gajdusek. When was the last time you spoke with him?"

That was quite the left turn. I almost laughed. It was always the same with cops, looking to pin the crime on whoever stuck out. Never mind the statistics showing people like Nic were dramatically more likely to be victims than perpetrators or the fact that Nic was the gentlest soul I knew. Back in high school, Nick was the kid who stepped in when someone was getting picked on, even when it meant putting his own neck on the chopping block. His go-to was a magic trick or a joke to distract the bully, which could go one of two ways: They'd either laugh, or they'd transfer the bull's-eye onto his back.

Don't even get me started on how he'd share his school lunch with the hungry kids—usually me and Trixie—sliding half his peanut butter and jelly sandwich or a couple of cookies across the table, acting like it was no big deal that he preferred to be a little hungry than watch anyone else starve.

The Lilydale police had been rabid to nail him for something the whole time we lived there, even tried to float it that he and Arsen had been working together just because the two of them were over at our trailer a lot. Guess the more things changed, the more they stayed the same.

"I haven't talked to Nicholas since high school," I said. *Always tell the truth, never the whole truth.* "And I need to go." The hospital walls seemed to be closing in, the smell of rubbing alcohol burning my nose. "If I hear from him, you'll be my first call," I said, walking away.

Smith's voice stopped me before I'd gone five feet. "Hey."

I turned, half expecting another round of questions. Instead, her expression had softened, just enough to catch me off guard. "There's help out there, you know. For people dealing with this kind of thing. PTSD, trauma, all of it. You don't have to carry it alone." She waved at Hannah Wheaton's door. "You wouldn't be here if you weren't feeling it."

I stared, unsure if she was referring to Trixie's murder, the fact that the Crying Killer was back on the prowl, or my monumental breakdown when I was still on the force. Either way, she didn't know the half of it.

And she never would.

"Thanks for the tip," I said, my voice brittle.

I pushed through the double doors at the end of the hallway, striding through the waiting room and out into the biting winter air. Detective Smith was going to dig, and I didn't have the energy to stop her. I had only one goal, only one thing I could focus on. I needed to get to my girl, to hold her close and breathe in the sweet green-apple scent of her hair, to remind myself that some things were worth saving.

And then I had to kill Arsen before he reached her.

CHAPTER 28

Before

Trixie sat cross-legged on the sagging couch, picking at the hem of her stonewashed jeans while Arsen sprawled beside her, one arm draped possessively across her shoulders. At the other end of the couch, Nick half-lay sideways, eyes on *Family Ties*, the glow from the TV bleaching his face pale. He kept the volume low, the laugh track a thin background hum.

Tuesday stood in the kitchen doorway, arms crossed, watching all three with barely concealed irritation. A pan of ground beef was browning on the stovetop behind her, waiting for the Hamburger Helper to be added.

"You should stay," Trixie said to Arsen, her voice carrying that pleading note Tuesday had come to hate. "We're having dinner. It's nothing fancy, but—"

"I told you, babe, I can't." Arsen's fingers played with a strand of Trixie's hair, twirling it. "Family thing."

Nick snorted without looking away from the screen.

Arsen's head turned slowly. The smile he gave wasn't friendly. "Nothing more important than family, Nicky."

Nick held up both hands. "No argument from me." He pretended to refocus on the TV, but Tuesday saw the muscle in his jaw jump.

"You sure you have to go?" Trixie wheedled.

"Sorry, babe," Arsen said.

Tuesday watched the disappointment flicker across her sister's face and felt her own jaw tighten. Dating Arsen had transformed her sister from the wild girl who didn't care what anyone thought into someone who waited by the phone.

"But I'll be back," Arsen went on. "Fathers, friends, half this town'll leave ya. But I stay. I stay because I actually know what love means." He tilted his head, looking up at the ceiling like he could see through it. "Once I love someone—really love them—I never let them go. Even God can't come between us."

Nick's laughter came out thin. "That's . . . romantic, man."

Arsen sat up straighter. "You think I'm kidding?"

Nick's eyes flicked to Tuesday. Her fingernails dug into her palms. "Trixie, can you help me with something in the kitchen?"

"In a minute," Trixie said. "I wanna stay with Arsen as long as he's here."

Arsen laughed and pulled her tighter against his chest, turning his gaze to Tuesday. "We used to be friends, Tues. You don't seem to like me much anymore."

"Tuesday doesn't like anybody," Trixie said quickly, shooting her sister an apologetic glance.

"That's not true," Tuesday said evenly. "I just think—"

"See, here's something else you should know," Arsen interrupted, still looking at Tuesday but speaking to Trixie. "Family means keeping your nose where it belongs." He squeezed Trixie's shoulder. "Your sister and me, we're building something here. Something permanent. Right, babe?"

"Right," Trixie breathed.

Nick shifted again, muttering low. "Permanent's a long time."

"Sure is." Arsen stood, stretching, his Def Leppard T-shirt riding up to show a strip of pale stomach. "I gotta roll. But I'll see you tomorrow, yeah, Trixie? Maybe we can pick up Nick, drive around."

Nick rolled his eyes. "Can't wait."

Arsen bent to kiss Trixie. Tuesday looked away, focusing on the tinfoil-covered window, the water-stained ceiling—anywhere but them. When she looked back, Arsen was watching her over Trixie's head, his expression unreadable.

"You can come with, too," he said.

"Thanks," Tuesday replied, voice flat.

After he left, the trailer sagged into silence except for the canned applause from *Family Ties*. Nick muted it with a jab of the remote. Trixie sat hugging herself, staring at the door.

"Trix," Tuesday started, but her sister held up a hand.

"Don't. Just don't, okay?"

"He's—"

"He loves me," Trixie said quickly. "It's nice to have someone who won't leave me, you know?"

Nick scowled. "Sometimes the ones who swear they'll never leave are the ones you should run from."

Trixie glared. "You don't know him like I do."

Nick shrugged and unmuted the TV.

Tuesday moved to sit beside her sister, close enough that their knees touched. "I don't like the way he talks about it, about never letting family go—"

"You wouldn't understand." Trixie's voice cracked. "You've got your college applications, your perfect grades, your whole future. I've got him."

Tuesday wrapped an arm around Trixie's shoulders, feeling her sister's bones through the thin fabric of her off-the-shoulder sweatshirt.

"You've got me, too," she whispered. "Always."

When the sisters finally drifted off to their bedrooms, the trailer settled into its usual creaks and sighs. Nick stayed where he was, trying to decide whether to go home or crash on the couch. The TV screen had gone blue, humming softly in the dark. He reached for his lighter, flicked it open, shut it again. Out the window, the porch light buzzed once, then steadied.

There was a shape out there by the elm. Maybe only a shadow, maybe not. Nick froze, breath shallow. A long moment passed, but the shape didn't move.

Nick swallowed hard, forcing himself to look away. "Permanent's a long time," he whispered again, to no one.

CHAPTER 29

After

I snapped at everyone that night. Nic was breathing too loud. Even Julia sounded shrill, starting with when she was dropped off from her playdate in full tantrum mode, mad because I wouldn't let her stay up to watch *The X Files*.

"You're mean!" she hollered, her face flushed. Her hair was a messy halo of static electricity, the dark circles under her eyes telling me she wasn't getting enough sleep. "Sarah's mom lets her watch it!"

"Sarah's mom isn't me," I barked back. Her wounded expression hooked me right under the ribs, but even so, if Nic hadn't been there to lay a gentle hand on my arm, I would have dug in deeper.

It wasn't like me. I was the calm sister, the mature one, the one who figured things out. Fighting had been Trixie's default, not mine. But Trixie wasn't here, never would be again, and everything was getting too hard.

"Your chill pills running low?" Nic asked later, after I'd tucked Julia in for the night. "Time to make another appointment?"

When *Nic* suggested medication, I knew I was visibly fraying. "I'll think about it," I promised her.

And I was. I was thinking about it all the way to the attic. After everything else that'd happened today, I could no longer keep thoughts of my little room at bay.

Coretta had given me the excuse, cornering me in the foyer the minute I got home from the hospital, her steel-gray curls quivering with indignation as she ranted again about the squirrels. "I swear they're having a damn block party up there," she'd said, jabbing her finger at the ceiling with such force that the cross at her neck flew up. "You check on that, Tuesday. I'm too old to be dealing with rodents."

See? Once Julia was in bed and Nic left for work, I had no choice but to go to the ghost gallery that I hadn't visited since I'd left the police force. Still, I waited until only night sounds remained: the wheeze of the apartment's old radiators, the wind gnawing at loose shingles, Coretta's TV humming faintly through the floor below. Then I pulled on an extra sweater and walked out into the second floor's shared landing. Just off the hall was a narrow stairway to the attic, hidden behind a tall, skinny door that looked like it'd been built for Jack Skellington. The steps were steep and creaky, the kind you had to lean into to climb, so my breath was puffing by the time I reached the unheated top level.

Most of the attic was devoted to rows and rows of clutter—a BowFlex still in its box, a set of weights Nic swore she'd use again, storage crates labeled in Coretta's tight handwriting, Julia's childhood clothes and toys all packaged up.

I didn't stop at any of it.

I didn't check out the walls like I told Corretta I would, either. I wasn't up here hunting squirrels. Instead, I threaded the path to the rear, to the glorified closet that had once been a darkroom belonging to Coretta's son. It was locked, and Nic had the key, had insisted on keeping it the day I'd been put on mandatory leave and she learned what I'd been doing up here.

A healthy person would have simply asked her for the key back, but it was a spring latch door, and I was hoping that a credit card would do the job just fine. Where there's a will (to avoid a difficult conversation), a Minnesotan will find a way.

I angled the card between the door and frame, pushing against the latch. After about thirty seconds of wiggling and bending the card, the latch popped, and I stepped inside the room.

It was black and cold.

I drew a breath and turned on the light.

The mosaic of horror was a jolt to my system, like a shot of poison. The walls were blanketed with photos and clippings pinned in precise rows, maps marked with red ink, notes scrawled on paper yellowed from the attic's heat extremes. The photos were of victims and dead-eyed killers, the headlines screaming about butchery and depravity. The filing cabinet in the corner bulged with folders, the drawers barely shutting. Stacks of books leaned precariously on the particleboard desk I'd scored at a garage sale and hauled all the way up here myself, their titles a grim catalog of human wickedness. In the center of the room, a punching bag hung like a dead thing.

I kept the tame file on my computer.

Up here was where I stored my *real* work.

I'd been collecting data on serial killers since 1986, back when people still thought men like Ted Bundy and the Green River Killer were an aberration. They didn't understand that serial killers were everywhere. Usually, they were white males in their twenties or thirties. Usually, they targeted women, though some, like Wayne Williams, suspected of the 1979–1981 Atlanta murders, branched out to children. And usually, they got away with it for years because nobody wanted to believe that the nice man next door—or in their bed—could be a monster.

I reached for an old pair of boxing gloves I had stashed up here (I'd made the mistake of hitting the bag without them, and the state of my hands had terrified Julia) and threw a few punches, letting the impact travel up my arms. On the wall, Charles Manson's wild eyes stared out from a magazine clipping. Next to him was Arsen's high school photo, his hair so clean-cut, his smile so normal it made my stomach churn.

When he'd first shown us his copy of *Helter Skelter*, I'd rolled my eyes and told him he probably liked the book because of the short sentences. He'd laughed along with us, pretended to be someone who could handle teasing. The familiar drip of shame soured my gut. I'd never forgive myself for missing the signs of sociopathy.

That's why I'd built this room. I had to educate myself to protect Julia.

Arsen might have turned out differently if he hadn't been raised in Lilydale, hadn't sunk his roots deep into that poisoned soil. His childhood hadn't been that remarkable, at least for our part of the world. He had a Catholic mother who likely prayed the rosary every day, a father who doled out discipline with his fists, and was a mediocre student who grew up to work a mediocre job.

I stepped closer to Arsen's photo. "Where are you?"

He didn't answer. But I knew someone who might be able to. His sister, Liz. I remembered her from school as one of those girls who disappeared in every room she entered.

She was my best lead. Last I heard she lived in Saint Cloud, seventy miles up Highway 94.

My eyes drifted to the wooden box in the corner, the one I never opened. I took a step toward it, but it suddenly felt like someone was sitting on my chest. I tugged off my gloves and hurried out the door, locking it behind me.

Inside that box was everything I couldn't face.

Yet.

CHAPTER 30

When I tiptoed into Julia's room the next morning, she was curled in a tight ball. For a moment I hesitated, watching how peaceful she looked. Her mouth was slightly open, her little heart face unguarded. I wanted to let her sleep forever, to be safe and in my sight. But that wasn't the world we lived in. I shook her shoulder gently. Her eyelids fluttered, and she blinked up at me, confused.

"What's wrong?" she murmured, her voice thick with sleep.

"Time to get up, kiddo," I said softly, brushing a stray lock from her forehead. "School."

Her face scrunched up in that way that told me she was already annoyed. "Mom," she said, sitting up and rubbing her eyes. "It's a teacher in-service day. No classes."

The horror of forgetting hit me like a wave. I was the one who'd stuck the notification the school sent out to the fridge. I must have glanced at it a dozen times. I'd even reminded Julia yesterday that there was no school today. But last night, I'd taken half a pill to calm my racing thoughts.

Then I'd taken another half when the first didn't work.

It'd been a long time since I'd swallowed a whole pill, and I was remembering why. It left me fogged over, sluggish. "Of course it is. I was thinking . . ." I forced brightness into my voice, looking for some excuse. "We should visit Grandma Pia."

Julia tilted her head at me, skeptical. "I thought you had work."

"I'll go in tomorrow and work twice as hard," I said, trying to sound upbeat. She didn't need to know how badly I'd dropped the ball.

"All right," she said, her expression tentative, then growing bright as she warmed to the idea of playing hooky with me.

The Minnesota Psychiatric Hospital sat like a brick fortress on Rochester's outskirts. Mom had first been sent here back in '85, about the same time Trixie and Arsen started dating. That'd been a brief stay. She wasn't permanently institutionalized until after Trixie's death.

Her diagnosis? Severe and treatment-resistant schizophrenia.

As much as I tried to concentrate on memories of the good times on the drives to visit her, they were the seasoning of my childhood rather than the stew. A handful of days, Mom'd be vibrant like the time she took us to Lake Koronis to skip rocks, but most of the time, she was so far down the well that her eyes looked like empty rooms.

And then there were the violent outbursts, followed by the disappearances.

She'd vanish without warning, leaving us to fend for ourselves until a neighbor called it in or someone at school noticed. It was my idea to stop telling people she'd run off again after Dad left for good in '84. All reporting did was get us sent to foster homes, sometimes separately, each one colder and harder than the last. At least at home we could pretend she'd come back to us whole, that the woman who sometimes made us heart-shaped pancakes was still out there somewhere, just waiting for the right moment to resurface.

When her disability checks came to the trailer, the bank let me cash them, one of the few perks of living in a small town. My sister and I learned to make that money stretch, to buy only the staples, to keep ourselves presentable so as not to draw attention, and to lie.

All skills I used to this day.

As Julia and I approached the psychiatric hospital's front desk and went through the check-in process—signing forms, showing ID—I felt the familiar discomfort creeping along my skin like an itchy sweater that was sewn on. I held Julia's hand as we were waved on to the common room. I hoped Mom was in a good mood today. I was already coming up with a plan to shield Julia if she wasn't.

"Ready?" I asked her outside the common room.

She nodded, but her face looked pinched.

I squeezed her hand and opened the door, spotting Mom immediately. She was sitting in a chair near the window, her blond-gray hair flowing past her shoulders like a girl's. When she saw us, she stood and hurried over, greeting us with a wide smile.

"There's my babies! Tuesday," she said brightly, wrapping me in a fragile hug as the dozen or so other patients in the room glanced over. She knelt so she could look Julia in the eye. "And Trixie! Look at you, so beautiful."

"Mom, that's Julia, your granddaughter," I said gently. "Not Trixie."

She blinked, her smile faltering. "Of course. Because *you're* Trixie."

I exhaled slowly, putting my arm around Julia. She was used to Mom's condition, but I wanted to protect her from the worst of it. "No, Mom. I'm Tuesday. Your older daughter. This is *my* daughter, Julia. Your granddaughter. Remember?"

"Right, right," she said, brushing it off. Then she leaned forward conspiratorially. "I'm learning to play a new card game here. Gin rummy. Have you heard of it?"

"I like gin rummy!" Julia said.

"Of course you do, dear. You always have." Mom smiled absently and pulled a deck of cards out of her sweater pocket. It was the gray cardigan I'd gotten her for Christmas. It'd come from Goodwill, but it was new, with tags. The color brought out the lovely flecks of gold in her blue eyes.

"Are we going to play now?" Julia asked, delighted.

Mom turned to me as if Julia hadn't even spoken. "Have you heard from that nice boy Nicholas? Are you still dating him?"

"Mom, we're not—" I stopped myself. There was no point. I wasn't going to untangle her versions of reality. I handed Julia some quarters. "Go grab a snack from that vending machine we passed, sweetheart," I told her. Given the security required to get past the lobby, this was one of the few places I felt comfortable letting her out of my sight. "Get anything you like."

She hesitated, looking from Pia to me, then nodded, giving my waist a quick hug before darting off.

"I need to ask you something, Mom," I said, leading Pia back to her chair by the window. Someone across the room was whistling a tune that made my skull feel too tight, but I couldn't place it.

"All right," she said worriedly, "but you know your father handles the money."

My heart hurt. "It's not about Dad." She sat in the chair, and I leaned against the windowsill across from her. "It's about Arsen Bauer. Do you remember him?"

Something flickered behind her eyes. It looked like pain. "Arsen's mother loved her church," she said slowly. "Prayed every day, you know. But his father . . . he was a terrible man. Police Chief Aramis Bauer." She leaned forward to place a hand on my knee. "You remember. Him and Donny McDowell, they were up to no good out at the farm. Worse than selling drugs, I think. Maybe things like your father used to do."

A chill crept up my spine. "What kind of things?"

But Pia just shook her head, her expression clouding over. "I'm so tired today," she murmured, leaning back in the chair and closing her eyes.

"How are your other symptoms?"

She rattled off a list of symptoms—the voices, the shadows at the edge of her vision, the heavy blanket of dread that never lifted. I had them committed to memory for my own doctor's appointment later by the time Julia returned with two bags of pretzels, which she shared.

Mom had always loved pretzels. I watched her suck off the salt before taking a bite, just like she used to. Julia and I sat on the deep windowsill as Mom told us about her crafts, her doctor, her friends here. She said she was happy, and she seemed to mean it. When it was time to go, she gave us each a peck on the cheek.

It'd been a remarkably good visit.

Guilt gnawed at me on the way out, though, like it always did when I left her behind. I knew I couldn't take care of her and raise Julia at the same time, but it didn't mean it felt any better to leave her with strangers.

On the drive home, Julia had all sorts of questions—what had Mom been like when I was younger, did I think she missed Trixie, did Trixie or did I look more like Mom? I answered them as best as I could, but my mind was elsewhere. Julia must have picked up on it because she eventually stopped talking and cracked open the Baby-Sitters Club book she'd brought along. She and Sarah had been tearing through those. I hoped she wouldn't get it in her head to babysit when she got older. People who thought war was scary should try being eleven years old and responsible for someone else's children at night in a strange house with only *The Twilight Zone* on TV.

"Do you mind if we stop by Corn's on the way home?" I asked when the Saint Paul skyline came into view.

She bounced in her seat. "Can I watch movies with him?"

"No, baby. It's just to pick up a file." I felt guilty for not showing up to the office today. That on top of feeling bad about my mom was too much. Something had to give, and it was taking the shape of bringing work home.

"Wait in the car, hon," I told Julia in front of Curry Up and Wait. I felt a zing of worry at the thought of leaving her alone, even for sixty seconds, but reminded myself I didn't want my worry to become hers. A normal mother would simply run inside and then out, wouldn't she? Still. "And keep the doors locked. I'll be down in two shakes of a lamb's tail."

She nodded, happily immersed in her book.

I found Corn behind his desk, his reading glasses perched on his nose, his face creasing with tension when I walked in. I could only see part of his T-shirt, but I think it read IT'S A HELL OF A THING, KILLING A MAN.

"Don't say it," I said, holding up a hand. "I know I should have called to say I wasn't coming in. But Julia had a day off from school." It was the truth. "We drove down to visit Mom. You can't be mad about that, can you? I just dropped by to pick up some files to go over tonight, and I'll work twice as hard tomorrow. Promise."

"Tuesday," he said, his tone careful.

I had just a moment to acknowledge how uncharacteristically stiffly he was holding himself before the sound of the bathroom door opening made me turn.

Detective Smith stepped out, dark hair pulled back into a sleek ponytail, her blazer crisp, her expression unreadable.

CHAPTER 31

The skin along my spine turned cold.

Detective Smith tipped her head. "Just the woman I was looking for."

Corn remained behind his desk, his expression pained. "This should only take a minute," he said to me.

It was hard to focus over the alarm shrilling in my head. What was this about? What was she doing here? What had she discovered? "Julia's waiting in the car."

Corn stood, coming around the desk with his hands raised like I was some kind of skittish animal. "Relax. Tayari's on our side."

"Our side?" I shot him a look. "What the hell does that mean?"

Smith stepped closer, her heels clicking softly on the linoleum. "I think we can help each other," she said. "Why don't you sit down."

"I'm not staying," I said, my voice shaking now. "I just came by to tell Corn I'm finishing some work at home tonight and that I'm gonna try talking to Hachette again tomorrow." I didn't wait for permission. I backed out the door, my pulse roaring in my ears, my last view of Corn and Smith sharing a concerned glance.

The complex smells of curry grew stronger as I raced down the stairs past the restaurant's kitchen vent, but it barely registered. All I could think about was Smith and the way she'd looked at me, like she already knew everything. Like she was just waiting for me to confirm it. Had Corn told her I was at the Gopher Hole murder scene? I bet he had. *Bastard.*

Julia glanced over when I slid into the driver's seat. "Everything okay?" she asked.

"Fine," I lied, starting the engine. The car filled with the sound of tires chewing gravel as I squealed out, not daring to look back. I could feel their eyes staring down on me through the second-story window, could easily imagine them whispering, their voices low and urgent. Talking about *me*.

About what I'd done, back when I'd been a police officer, after I'd attacked that poor kid I mistook for Arsen. After everything unraveled.

By the time I got home, my skin was buzzing, my thoughts racing too fast to catch. Julia ran ahead, already asking about snacks and TV, her mood mercifully light. Ah, to have the attention span of an eight-year-old. I followed her inside, locking the door behind me and rearming the security system.

Safe. For now.

In the kitchen, I hopped onto the counter so I could reach the cabinet where I kept the pills. There was only one left, and I stared at it for a long moment before breaking it in half. Half was better than none, I told myself, swallowing it dry.

But god, I wanted the whole thing.

Knowing relief was on the way dulled the edges, barely. Just enough to think straight, to admit that I needed to make an appointment with the doctor.

There was no putting it off any longer.

I glanced down the hall to make sure Nic wasn't home and Julia was still in her room. Then I left a hushed message with the doctor's office, listing Mom's symptoms as I remembered them. The paranoia, the racing thoughts, the darkness that seemed to swallow her whole sometimes. Like mother, like daughter? The idea made my hands shake worse. *No, I'm just under a lot of pressure. This has happened before, and it's gone away. I just have to ride it out.* I hung up the phone.

"Can we play a game?" Julia called out.

By the time I joined her in the living room, she was already pulling out the cards, her little fingers shuffling them adeptly. Coretta played a lot of cards with her.

"Sure," I said, dropping onto the floor across from her, the coffee table between us. She dealt, and we played two hands of gin rummy before she circled back to questions about Mom. I thought she'd gotten them all out of her system.

"Why does Grandma have to stay there?" she asked, her eyes on the cards but her tone too serious for an eight-year-old. "She's not old."

"She's not well," I said, forcing my voice to stay pleasant. We'd had the conversation before, but Mom's psychiatrist said that often, kids needed to hear it several times to feel secure. "Sometimes people need someone caring for them all the time."

"But what's wrong with her?"

I opened my mouth, then closed it. How could I explain schizophrenia to a kid? How could I describe the screaming episodes, the paranoia, the threats Mom would make, the way she'd stare through me and my sister like we were strangers, interspersed with periods of calm and love and light that had us certain we were the luckiest girls in the world?

"It's complicated," I said finally. "But the doctors are taking good care of her. She's got friends there, and she enjoys her crafts. I think she's as happy as she can be."

Julia nodded, her face thoughtful, and then: "Can I watch TV instead of playing cards?"

"Sure," I said, too restless to argue.

She scrambled off the floor and onto the couch. She flipped on the TV, landing on a *Full House* rerun. The canned laughter grated against my nerves, but at least she was distracted. I went over to my office nook under the eaves, fired up my computer, and logged into AOL. Might as well get some work done.

One of the new cases Corn had assigned to me required that I dig up dirt on some guy, a husband suspected of cheating. I was trawling chat rooms and forums for leads. Usually it was easy work, if gross. But tonight, I couldn't focus. My fingers hovered over the keys before I stopped fighting it and logged onto IRC, the Wild West of the internet where people said the quiet things out loud. I'd spent time there recently following Hachette's online footprint, and before that, for my own personal research.

Returning to familiar ground, I typed /join #serialkillers.

I began scanning posts for any mention of the Crying Killer. There were no new tips, just the same old chatter, half conspiracy theories, half urban legends. I skimmed nearly everything and was about to give up until one message caught my eye, buried in a thread from several weeks earlier:

> Trixie Hendrickson. Crying Killer's last victim?

My breath hitched. I clicked the message, and there it was—the same story I'd spent nearly a decade trying to forget.

> Alright, folks, we all know the Crying Killer legend, don't we? The guy's infamous—five Minnesota women dead at his hand. And the kicker? He'd pick up the phone and sob a confession after. Like, real tears.
>
> But here's where it gets wild. His girlfriend? Trixie Hendrickson. Yep, her. Everyone thinks she was his fifth and last victim—shot right in the back. But I don't think she was his last victim. All five killings that we know about were done within 30 miles of Lilydale, and all four women plus Trixie had an X marked on their back (which not everyone knows about but it's true). So what about the woman killed that same summer, three weeks after Trixie died, in

> St. Cloud, which is only forty-five minutes from Lily-dale? She had an X etched on her, too, but nobody talks about her.
> -XOXOXOXO

I sat back, heart thudding. I hadn't heard about the Saint Cloud murder. Why would it come up in a chat now? I searched everywhere for more information, including using Corn's service. It all came back with nothing.

Whoever had posted on the IRC could have been lying. That seemed likely. But if it wasn't a lie, then it was *proof.* Proof that Arsen was alive. I wouldn't need to bear this misery alone anymore, feeling like a girl crying wolf. All I had to do was get to Saint Cloud, track down information on that murder victim. I could interview Liz, Arsen's sister, at the same time.

"I'm hungry."

I slammed the off button on the computer monitor and whipped around in my chair. "Sure, baby. Let me make something for you."

Julia stared at me with wide blue eyes that saw too much of the world. Same eyes as Mom's. "You okay?" she asked.

"I'm fine," I said brightly. "Just tired."

She didn't believe me, but she nodded and padded back to the TV. I walked to the kitchen, my thoughts spiraling. Detective Smith. The Crying Killer. Trixie. It all tangled together, a knot I couldn't untie.

Tomorrow, I told myself. Tomorrow I'd get answers.

He couldn't follow Her as much as he'd like to. He had a regular life to keep up if he wanted to avoid people getting nosy. About this part of him, anyhow, the part that'd been sleeping.

Still, damn, he was glad luck had put him outside the Indian place when that fancy-pants detective, the one who'd shown up outside the Gopher Hole the other night, went up to Her place of employment. It could mean only one thing: The cop was onto Her, tying Her with all of this, tightening the noose.

Had She already confessed to the cop She thought the Crying Killer was back from the dead?

I was never dead.

He couldn't swallow the chuckle. He knew her well enough to know She was crumpling like a terrified tinfoil ball, as afraid of the killer being back as she was of him not being back, which would mean she was going nuts like Pia.

What a sweet mess She was in. He hoped She stepped on at least one or two of the other mines he'd left out there.

Meanwhile, he had a couple more flourishes in mind to put the final shine on Her humiliation.

To put Her in Her place.

Then he'd end it once and for all, and take Julia for his.

But not now. Not yet, he thought, watching Her turn off Her computer.

CHAPTER 32

That night, after Julia fell asleep, I climbed the creaky stairs up to the attic, shivering as the winter air seeped through the ancient windowpanes, warning me away.

The lock was even quicker to pick the second time.

I flicked on the single, naked bulb, ignoring the photos of serial killers and their victims staring at me. I tugged on my boxing gloves and threw the first punch hard, my fist connecting with a dull *thwack*. Then another. And another. The rhythmic impact was hypnotic, but my mind refused to quiet.

Instead, it went to Arsen.

He'd barely reacted to the news break about a possible serial killer as we watched *Jaws 3-D*, just seemed mildly intrigued. Yet he'd hated it when he heard the murderer was being called the Crying Killer. Was it just that he hadn't liked the name, or had something else changed?

My fist connected with the bag again, harder this time. It swung wildly, the chain above squealing in protest. My breath came in sharp bursts, but I didn't stop. Not yet. Not with the wooden box sitting there against the far wall, taunting me. It was unassuming, but I knew what was inside. And I knew better than to open it.

So I kicked and punched and punched some more, until my muscles ached.

When I finally stopped pounding the bag, it swung lazily, no worse for having absorbed my fear. My hands trembled as I removed the gloves. I closed the door to the room but left the attic light on as I went back downstairs.

Somehow, darkness felt too heavy tonight.

If that IRC poster had been right, Arsen had lain low for three weeks after murdering my sister, then killed one more woman in Saint Cloud before disappearing for the next eight years. I had no idea where he'd gone, but I knew why he was back. He'd spotted that article about me in the PI magazine, and he was trying to drive me mad before killing me and taking Julia for his own.

I figured there was no way I'd fall asleep, but muscle exhaustion worked its magic. After showering, slipping into my pajamas, and snuggling under my quilt, I was out in minutes.

It didn't last long.

At first, it was subtle. A tingling in my fingers pulling me to wakefulness, fighting the weight of sleep. Then the sensation tightened, spreading through my chest, until I couldn't breathe, couldn't move, only scream. And scream I did, a soundless, voiceless cry that filled my mind but nowhere else.

A panic attack had trapped me in a coffin with no lid.

I don't know how long I'd have been there if Nic hadn't sensed what was happening. Out of nowhere she was by my side, holding me. "You're okay," she whispered, her voice grounding me. "It's just a nightmare. You're okay."

I wasn't okay. My pulse was erratic, my skin clammy, but I nodded anyway.

"He's back," I said. I hadn't wanted to admit it to anyone, but I couldn't bear this alone.

Nic brushed a strand of hair from my face. "Who?"

I'd reclaimed enough of my body that I could pull away from her. She wore flannel pajamas, her hair in a bonnet.

"Arsen," I said.

She stiffened. "He's dead. You know that."

"I *don't* know it," I said harshly. Then I sighed. "There were two assaults in Saint Paul in the past week. The first one, the victim's body was posed like an X with the same carved in her back. The second one, the woman escaped, but she also had the X cut into her. You *know* the news never covered that detail of the Crying Killer's murders. The only people who know he did it to all his victims are him and the police." I clutched Nic's hand. "He's not dead, and he's going to get Julia."

Nic sat up. When she wore a full face of makeup, she resembled a long-haired Joan Jett, but right now, she just looked like the kid who'd been afraid of the rope climb in gym and favored green gummy bears. "*Both* victims had the X in their back?"

I chewed my lip. Detective Smith hadn't exactly confirmed the first victim, the one in front of the Gopher Hole, had the mark, but I knew it was true. I could feel it in my gut. "Yeah, I'm pretty sure they did. I saw the first body with my own eyes."

She scowled, but didn't speak. I could tell she smelled a lie, so I kept talking.

"The second victim, I visited her in the hospital," I said. "She showed me the X. And that's not all." I climbed onto my knees. "I was in a chat room earlier and read about another woman who was murdered right after Trixie. That woman also had an X on her back!"

I didn't like the hopefulness with which I said it, nor did I appreciate the sudden lightness in Nic's posture.

"What?" I asked suspiciously.

She shook her head, smiling sadly. "Honey, if you saw the X talked about in a chat room, that means *everyone* knows about it. Don't you see? All this time you've thought only the police knew, but someone must have leaked it." She patted my arm. "Someone's copying him," she said firmly. "It's horrible and sad, but it's not him. Arsen is gone."

I wanted to believe her. God, I really, really did. But my silence betrayed me, and Nic seemed to sense it.

"Remember what it was like growing up in Lilydale?" she asked, gently shifting my focus. "You mentioning you might go back there has me thinking about it. There was so much darkness. But there was good in town, too, wasn't there?"

"Lilydale *good*? After how they treated you?" I shook my head. "Let's not even get started with all those terrible crimes. The town's cursed."

"Mrs. Peterson," Nic said, smiling softly. "Remember how she used to leave those paper bags of day-old doughnuts in front of my door at the motel? Never said a word, just dropped them off every Sunday morning. Or Mrs. Garrison. Didn't she bring you a casserole once when your mom couldn't get out of bed?"

"And Mr. Carlson," I found myself grudgingly adding. "He fixed your bike that time, wouldn't take any money."

"Ms. Ruby at the library." Nic's voice went wistful. "She always knew which books to save for us. Never judged what we were reading, even when your tastes ran to true crime and mine to fashion magazines."

The memories came faster then, small kindnesses that'd somehow survived the horror. The lunch lady who slipped us extra butter sandwiches. The neighbor who taught us to ice-skate one winter when Mom was hospitalized. The school nurse who never asked questions when we needed Band-Aids or just a quiet place to rest.

"There were plenty of people who were kind to us," Nic said, reading my mind. "Even when they didn't have to be."

I wanted to set my shoulders against her words, but they'd found a crack.

"You need to see the doctor," Nic murmured after a few beats of silence.

"I know." My voice was small in the shadows. "I called to make an appointment."

Her face lit up and then fell. "Promise you'll keep it?"

"Promise."

She nodded, then was surprised by a yawn. She stretched out beside me, just like the good old days, and I curled into her familiar warmth, letting her be the big spoon. As I drifted off, I thought about patterns—spirals, snowflakes, branching trees repeating endlessly in smaller forms, X marks the spot.

I fell asleep listening to Nic's breathing, steady and sure, and for the first time since I'd seen my photo on that PI magazine, the darkness didn't feel quite so heavy.

CHAPTER 33

By morning, I almost felt like myself again.

Nic always had a way of untangling the knots in my chest. I slipped out of bed with her still sleeping and got Julia and me ready for the day. She seemed unusually excited for school. When I told her it was time to head out, she was already bundled up in her winter gear before I'd even pulled on my boots. Her white coat was a size too large, the hood slipping down over her eyes. It was a poor kid's trick to buy clothes big enough that you could get three times as much use out of them (too large, just right, too small), but she didn't care.

"I'm a marshmallow." She giggled, stomping her feet in her snow boots.

"The cutest marshmallow I've ever seen." I tugged her hood back so I could see her grin.

At school, she hopped out of the car, her backpack bouncing against her small frame. She turned to wave, a mittened hand high in the air.

My whole world in one fleeting gesture.

I waited until she was safely inside, and then a few minutes longer. When a crossing guard signaled for me to move along, I pulled out, heading toward the University of St. Thomas and Hachette's apartment. She hadn't called, which wasn't unusual for a client, but it made the job harder.

The old quadplex she lived in looked worse than it had the first time. The snow out front seemed dirtier, the porch saggier. I climbed the steps and rang the doorbell to apartment 2. No answer. I rang it again, leaning in this time. Still nothing.

I didn't blame Hachette. If I were being stalked, I wouldn't be eager to answer the door, either. Still, I needed to talk to her. I retreated to my car, cranking up the heat against the Minnesota chill. The vinyl seats squeaked when I leaned back to grab her file. I opened it to Hachette's photograph paper-clipped to the corner and settled in to wait.

An hour and seventeen minutes later, her front door opened. The late-twentysomething woman who emerged matched Hachette's photo as far as I could tell from this distance and with her bundled up against the cold, but her movements were wrong—jerky, like she was wearing someone else's skin. She kept glancing up and down the block.

I got out of the car and approached slowly, hands visible. "Ms. Hachette? My name's Tuesday. I work with Corn Stamoran, who you hired to help you. I left my card in your mailbox."

She startled, her hand flying to her throat. Her brown eyes were heavily mascaraed, her lips slathered in nude lipstick lined with brown. "Oh. Right. The police detective."

"Private investigator," I corrected. "Do you have a minute?"

I was asking her the same thing Smith had asked me. Had I looked as scared? Hachette's eyes darted past me, scanning the street.

"Sure," she said. "But my roommate's still sleeping, so we'll have to talk out here."

"All right," I said. "Can you tell me about your stalker?"

She hesitated, glancing over her shoulder, back at the house, before speaking. Her worry was contagious. "I keep seeing this guy around. He's always there. Watching. And someone keeps calling and hanging up. I do star 69, but it just rings and rings."

"What'd the police say?"

Her mouth twisted into a bitter smile. "They said they couldn't intervene until a crime was committed."

I nodded. That part, I believed. But something about her story wasn't sitting right. Movies would have you believe a hardened cop or court-weary DA could spot a liar a mile away. That's 24-karat bull. The easy ones, the ones who looked at their feet or whose voices shook, sure, but most of the time, unless you had a handle on your own crap, how you responded to someone's story was a Rorschach of your own experiences, not some sweet skill. That's why so many cops got it wrong. This woman, though, her eyes were shifting like sand. A kindergartner would've known she was lying about something. But why'd she get Corn involved if she didn't want our help?

Turned out I didn't particularly care. It was her money.

"Can you describe the guy?" I pressed. "Caucasian? His height? What he wears?"

Her mouth twitched. "That's just it. I never get a clear look. From what I can see, he's an average-sized white guy. Brown hair. Always wearing a leather jacket. An unusual one." She scrunched up her face. "What were those jackets that were big in the '80s? The sorta military-style ones?"

My eyes snapped to her pale, doe-eyed face, my blood buzzing. "Members Only?"

She appeared relieved. "That's it."

Like Arsen wore. I battered her with questions just to keep talking. "Lined?"

"What?"

"It's winter. His coat must be lined. Yeah? Cap? Mittens?"

She shook her head, flustered. "I don't know. Maybe."

I asked her about when he showed up (there was no pattern), if she or her roommate was dating anyone (they'd both been single since the fall), if there were any coworkers acting unusual (not that she'd noticed). When I couldn't think of anything more to ask her, I gave her a rundown of basic safety tips and told her we'd be in touch.

The familiar smells of curry and coffee back at Corn's office couldn't settle my nerves. Even the stacks of paper on every surface—the filing cabinet, his desk and mine, the table where we had our meals—didn't give me the cozy nesting vibes they usually did. The further away from Nic's soothing presence I got, the worse I felt.

"What'd Smith want yesterday?" I asked, tugging off my coat.

"Hello to you, too." His blazer was folded so I couldn't read his T-shirt. "She wanted to know how you found out what room Wheaton was in. I told her I got it myself, that it was connected to a stalker case."

Not only was that a lie, but it was also one that could get him in deep trouble. When I made an annoyed noise, he held up a hand. "Yeah, I took the bullet. I assume you squeezed it from Shawn?" His expression went from inquisitive to hangdog. "Look, Smith's just trying to close any leaks in the department, Tuesday. Wanna tell me why you acted like she was here to march you to death row instead?"

Smith had dropped by because she wanted to close some leaks? It was plausible. Plausible but unlikely. "Jumpy these days, that's all." It was true, but it wasn't the whole truth.

He watched me for a moment, stroking his bushy mustache. His skin seemed heavier, droopier than it had yesterday. He looked like he was going to hold his tongue until he thought better of it. "Here's what I know: Wheaton was assaulted within a mile of the Gopher Hole, the bar where *you* saw a fresh murder victim. That victim was posed in an X shape like some hellish snow angel, and she also had an X sliced on her back, which you didn't hear from me."

There it was, finally confirmed. I fell into the nearest chair with an *oomph*.

Corn kept going, his voice scraping like he was carrying the weight of the world. "I don't need my genius card punched to guess the SPPD suspects we have a Crying Killer copycat out there hunting the winter streets. I'd even wager a guess that they're worried the copycat is going to come for *you*, given that you're the surviving sister of his most famous victim." He cleared emotion from his throat. "I'm not going to make you talk to me about this, Tuesday, but I sure as hell wish you would."

An unexpected knot rose in my windpipe. I couldn't speak.

After a few beats, he made a frustrated noise and slid a business card across his desk. "It's Smith's. She seems like a good cop, for what it's worth. Said to call."

I nodded, pocketing the card.

When Corn sat up straight again, I was finally able to read his T-shirt: It's not revenge he's after. It's a reckoning.

CHAPTER 34

The overhead lights of Johnson's Market were dusty, making it feel like we were all swimming in aquarium water. I pushed my cart past displays of marked-down candy canes and chocolate reindeer, marveling that the store sound system was still playing "All I Want for Christmas Is You" over two weeks past the holiday. Mariah's voice bounced off the shelves, making me think of Coretta's fierce hatred of pop music.

"Germans only listen to Wagner and weep," she'd declared, then cackled at her own joke.

My favorite benefit of living on the top floor of her house, besides the cheap rent and free childcare, was the food. Coretta cooked German fare like her life depended on it, piling up mountains of sausages and sauerkraut, dense cakes dripping with cream, dumplings that sat like lard balls in your stomach. And always without warning, just a "you'll come down for dinner tonight, you and Julia." Her troublesome son rarely visited, and so we became her "sad little family."

"You're broken people, you and Julia," she'd announced over one of her German feasts, that one schnitzel and vinegar cabbage. "But broken things, if you glue them right, they hold water just fine. Like my good china."

The last time she'd invited us over, a couple weeks earlier, we'd eaten on that good china, surrounded by her religious art and antique furniture that always felt hard and dusty, and we'd listened to her stories about Saint Paul in the 1940s as we gorged ourselves. Nic had been glad to miss it, but I'd loved it. Julia had too, even the sauerkraut.

I was so lost in the memory that I didn't see him until my cart nearly clipped his ankle.

"Jesus, Tuesday," Shawn said, stepping back. "You trying to maim me?"

"Hey." My heart had jumped into my throat, and it made my voice froggy. "Didn't expect to see you here."

"Yeah, I live just around the corner. Can't believe you don't remember." His expression was hard to read, and not just because of the face fur he was sporting. He glanced at my cart. "Shopping for the week?"

I looked down at my Cheerios, bananas, milk, butter, and noodles. "Something like that."

He shifted his weight, his smile fading. "Lotta stuff happening at the department lately."

"Always is." It occurred to me that I could make the best of this unexpected encounter. Was there any chance I could convince him to tell me the name of the first victim? I tried to keep the eagerness off my face.

Shawn nodded impatiently. "Listen. About what I told you about Wheaton. I didn't tell you. Get me? It's hot right now at the PD with this copycat thing." His eyes locked onto mine.

"Who would I tell?" I asked, the picture of innocence.

"Good," he said, but he didn't relax. Instead, he studied me, *this* expression much easier to read. It's what'd brought us together the first time a few years back, one night at bar close. "We didn't talk much when you dropped by the other day. What're you up to these days? Still doing PI work?"

"Yeah." My nerves were singing. "Still digging that dirt for Corn."

"Huh." His eyes walked over my body. "I've got some time. Wanna come by?"

A familiar jolt hit me low in my stomach. I hesitated for a moment, but the heat coming off him convinced me. "Sure. Why not?"

◈

The steps yelled as we climbed to his second-floor apartment, the stairwell's scuffed white walls badly in need of a touch-up. His apartment was exactly as I remembered: sparse furniture, a weight bench in one corner next to an aquarium hosting a single out-of-place blue fish the size of a dinner plate. There was a massive tub of protein powder on the kitchen counter and a stack of sci-fi paperbacks by the couch. At least he read, I'd thought the first time I came over. That was how low my bar was, how low it'd always been for me and Trixie and probably every other girl who'd grown up with a father who taught them to make a feast out of crumbs.

I hadn't necessarily cured that blind spot so much as limited its ability to harm by only *sleeping* with men, never falling in love. I had only one hard-and-fast rule, which was that I didn't screw married guys. No temporary relief was worth permanently hurting someone else.

"Drink?" he asked, already moving to the kitchen.

"Just water," I said.

He returned with a glass, our fingers brushing. The contact sent electricity up my arm. When he leaned in, I could smell his aftershave, something foresty that took me right back to our first night of me ripping off his clothes. His mouth found mine, tentative at first, then deeper when I didn't pull away. His close-shaven beard and mustache didn't tickle, like I thought they would; instead, they sent an extra thrill through me. For a moment I let myself forget everything. The murder and assault, all the cases I had to work, the weight of my lies.

Shawn's hand slid toward my hair and I tensed, but he read my reaction instantly, redirecting to caress my cheek instead. The thoughtfulness of the gesture undid me. I set down the water and led him to his bedroom, leaving a trail of clothes behind.

His, not mine.

He knew that not only did I not like hands in my hair—thank my mom, who liked to pull it when she was angry—but also, I hated to be naked. I didn't mind a hand up my shirt, but I kept it on, and I only dropped my pants because there was no other way to do the deed. We fell onto his bed, his body pressed on top of me, his breath hot on my neck, and the world outside faded. There was only Shawn, only this moment, and the tangled history between us.

Bliss.

Later, wrapped in his sheets, I watched him sleep. He'd always dropped off right after, no matter the time of day. I didn't mind. In fact, I appreciated it. Let me slip out easier. But his face looked so soft in this moment, kinder. Part of me wanted to stay, to pretend I could have this kind of normal. But Julia would be home from school soon, and Nic would worry, and somewhere out there a killer was watching, waiting.

I slipped out of bed and tugged on my underwear and jeans, moving as quietly as I could.

CHAPTER 35

The punching bag swung in hot little arcs under the bare bulb. Sweat trickled down my spine despite the attic's chill, my hands slick and hot inside the gloves. It was getting easier, coming up here, and I didn't like that.

The good news was that I had an appointment with Dr. Simpson tomorrow morning. When I'd come back from Shawn's, Julia in tow, I discovered his nurse had left a message confirming it, her voice cheerful and efficient.

Nic would be happy, and I always liked making Nic happy.

My punches grew harder, the sound of my gloves connecting with the bag echoing through the attic, under the watchful gaze of Arsen's photo. I'd always wondered how it was that the shooter had missed me with his bullets that night. He was at close range. Had hearing Julia's cry unsettled him?

I threw another punch, even harder this time, and the bag swung wildly on its chain, squeaking like a dying mouse. My thoughts stumbled over to the Hachette case. Tomorrow, I'd need to stalk her to see if anyone was stalking her. The irony. But I'd do my best to crack her case. That creeping feeling of being watched was one I knew too well, like a chill you couldn't warm away.

My stomach tightened as a memory surfaced. Trixie and I'd been sharing a bed in one of our smaller rentals, middle schoolers trying to survive after our father skipped. One spring night, Trixie had woken me up, her voice trembling.

"There's someone outside," she'd whispered.

Half asleep, I'd wrapped my arms tight around her, like I used to back when Dad's whistling froze her. "I won't let anything happen to you."

But then I saw it, too. A shadow outside our window. It passed back and forth, back and forth. We watched it until our eyes grew too heavy to keep open. Whoever it was never tried the windows, never rattled the doors. Just paced. When we told Mom the next day, she said we'd imagined it. But the footprints were there in the morning, a perfect circle in the crusty snow around the house.

Another time, when we were even younger and our parents were screaming at each other in the next room, I became convinced the spirits were going to take Trixie away. I'd covered her in powder from the bathroom cabinet, dusting her pale until she looked ghostly herself. "Now they'll think you're one of them," I'd told her solemnly.

When Mom saw the mess, she'd been furious, yelling about wasted powder and the price of everything. But for one night, Trixie had been protected.

That had always been my job. *Keep Trixie safe.*

I stepped back from the punching bag, my breath coming in gasps. My arms were sore, my knuckles burning inside the gloves. I pulled them off, flexing my fingers. The attic was silent now, the bag swaying gently. *Swing creak. Swing creak.* I grabbed my water bottle and headed for the stairs, flicking off the light as I went.

I made it all of five steps before I screamed.

A figure stood at the bottom of the stairs.

CHAPTER 36

My heart nearly cracked my rib cage before I recognized Coretta, silver hair loose around her shoulders, her face pale and slack in the dim moonlight. Her eyes were open but vacant.

"Coretta?" I whispered, stepping closer.

She didn't respond, her eyes wide but unseeing. *Sleepwalking.* We'd done this dance before. I exhaled shakily and touched her arm. "Come on, let's get you back to bed."

Gently, I took her elbow and guided her downstairs to her apartment. It was no small feat navigating the narrow attic stairs, our shared landing, and another set of stairs down to her level. Her front door to the shared foyer was wide open, her security system disarmed. She must have turned it off without waking up.

I led her to her bedroom. It smelled like lavender and old books, everything precisely arranged except for a photograph on her nightstand that'd been knocked over. I flipped it up to reveal Coretta's son, a young man in an army uniform, flashing the cocky grin of a boy who'd yet to see combat. He had a habit of appearing in her life, causing a couple weeks of havoc, and then disappearing as quickly as he'd arrived.

Coretta let me tuck her into bed like a child, her breathing already evening out. I pulled her bedroom door shut behind me, locked her front door, and padded back upstairs, reengaging both our security systems from my central box.

Then I speed-walked straight to Julia's room.

She was splayed across her bed, clutching her stuffed bunny. One of her feet hung off the edge. I eased it back under the covers, her night-light casting magical star patterns on the ceiling.

My girl. My miracle. My reason for everything. My chest kicked with a fierce, protective love. Whatever nightmares the world held, they wouldn't reach her. Not while I was still standing.

I stayed longer than I needed to, just watching her.

Tomorrow I'd go to the doctor and I'd do my job and I'd take care of my family and I'd figure out how to get to Saint Cloud to talk to Arsen's sister and see what I could discover about that other killing, the one that supposedly happened after the shoot-out at our trailer.

But tonight, in this moment, I would simply be grateful that Julia was alive, and she was mine.

Outside, snow began falling, covering everything in a soft white blanket.

After several minutes, I went to my own bed to wait for sleep or sunrise, whichever came first. I would not think about how off-balance I'd been since seeing that body outside the Gopher Hole, push away how similar it felt to my state of mind leading up to the fracture.

The thing that had marked my last day on the police force.

The real reason I'd had to leave and start working for Corn.

CHAPTER 37

The Fracture

It wasn't clear what made that anniversary different. I'd survived others before, patching myself up with work and routine, clawing my way through the forest of painful memories.

Maybe the problem was that that year, the week began with a terrible mistake: kneecapping that innocent bystander I'd been certain was Arsen.

That event barely registered for anyone else at work, but after that, my skin began to itch whenever I put on my uniform, itch so bad that I rubbed myself raw sometimes without even noticing. Still, I might have made it through the anniversary of my sister's murder, just like I had the other ones, if not for what followed.

It started with me and Mike—the officer filling in for a sick Shawn—responding to a 10-16 domestic on a night so hot the asphalt still shimmered with heat. We rolled up to a modest rambler with a well-kept lawn perched on Saint Paul's north side. The man who opened the door wore a Vikings sweatshirt, but the color was off. It took me a second to realize the purple fabric was soaked dark with blood. The reek of brandy poured off the guy.

And then there was his smile, hollow as a jack-o'-lantern.

"Everything's fine, Officers," he said, swaying slightly, that grin stretching impossibly wider, flecks of blood on his cheeks. "Just fine."

Mike moved fast, cuffing the man while I stepped inside to clear the house, my weapon drawn, heartbeat thudding. The living room was a mess: shattered lamp, overturned coffee table, a phone ripped from the wall. Clothes scattered like confetti.

A baby bottle lay on the floor, formula pooling in a pale stain. Something cold settled beneath my ribs. That's when the silence hit me. Houses with babies were never quiet.

Maybe the gore on the guy who answered the door is all his, I thought, my lungs struggling for air that felt suddenly too thin. *Maybe the baby and mother are visiting relatives.* I kept moving toward the back of the house, gun raised, and with each step the metallic tang of blood grew stronger.

I found them in the nursery, beneath a mobile of yellow ducks that turned lazy circles in the air. The mother was curled around her baby like a question mark, like she'd tried to become a shield with her own body. Like my sister had done for Julia.

Neither of them was moving.

Something broke in me then. Or maybe it re-broke, a fracture that'd never healed, some essential load-bearing wall finally crumbling. I holstered my weapon and reached for them. The mother's leg was already going cold as I gripped it. I cradled the motionless baby with my other arm. *You're coming with me. I'm getting you help.* The hospital would know what to do. They had to. I began dragging the dead woman from the room, down the hall, her head bouncing against the hardwood with soft, terrible thuds, the tiny baby clutched against my chest.

I was going to save them. I was going to get them to the hospital, to anywhere but that blood-splattered nursery where yellow ducks spun endlessly overhead. I'd carry them for the rest of my life if I had to.

"What *the hell* are you doing?" Mike asked when I emerged from the house, his face going white as paper. He was on the front lawn monitoring the handcuffed man in the Vikings jersey who was still wearing a horrible smile, but it was the sight of *me* hauling two dead bodies that'd scared him.

I didn't have time to answer. The ambulance was already screaming toward us.

I made it to the curb just as it arrived, its lights painting everything in strobing red. The corpse I'd dragged had left a trail of blood behind me. The EMTs tried to wrest the baby from my arms, but I held on. I wouldn't let go. Couldn't.

"Officer Kenn." The voice sliced through the chaos, an EMT I'd worked with before, someone whose name I should've known but couldn't remember. "*Tuesday.* They're both dead."

Dead.

That's when—impossibly, miraculously—the baby jerked and began wailing.

The sound pierced the night. For one blazing moment, I felt triumph surge hot through my chest. But as the EMTs rushed the infant toward the ambulance, my mind began to splinter. I thought of Julia sleeping safe in her bed only through luck and grace. I thought of my sister, who would never sleep anywhere again. I was becoming two people in the same skin, the woman who had helped a baby and the sister who had failed to save her family when it mattered most.

I collapsed like a marionette with severed strings.

The rest blurred into fragments: Sitting in the back of a squad car, someone's jacket draped around my shoulders. The station the next morning, everything too bright, too sharp. Everyone's faces looking wrong, like they'd been replaced with rubber masks. I'd screamed at my sergeant that they were all duplicates, that the real police department had been taken over by impostors.

They'd placed me on leave and ordered me to see a doctor.

My life split into *before* the fracture and *after*.

Thank god that Nic finally showed up. I wouldn't have been able to make it if she hadn't. Six years of silence between us dissolved as she held me, told me that everything was going to be okay. She'd gone with me to that first appointment with Dr. Simpson, held my hand as I sat in that sterile office wearing a blue gown that tied in the back and explained about the night I'd tried to drag the dead back to life.

CHAPTER 38

After

Dr. Simpson's office hadn't changed since my first visit. Same pale-blue walls, same framed prints of sailing ships, same glossy leather couch.

I think seeing them both dead—at least, so I believed—and feeling so helpless just did a number on me, I'd told Simpson that first meeting, my eyes pleading. I wanted help, for sure, but I needed to play it just right. Somebody would take Julia away from me if I didn't.

Fill this, he'd said, handing me a prescription. *And see a therapist regularly.*

I'd taken the first and lied about the second. I'd also decided I was done with the SPPD and gone to work for Corn. I kept up my visits with Dr. Simpson, though, more or less. The Haldol dulled the edges of my mind, softening the jagged places where my thoughts snagged. It felt like a gift. I'd managed to get Simpson to refill my prescription a couple times after without visiting, but then he'd instituted the mandatory "every three months" checkup.

I didn't love it, but what choice did I have? I needed the medication.

The waiting room reeked of cheap, powdery perfume that reminded me of scented toilet paper. Was it the receptionist's? I thought about pretending to read a magazine. The nearest one, a water-stained copy of *Time* from July, read The Strange New World of the Internet. Instead I picked at my cuticles and listened to the receptionist's acrylic nails click-clack against her keyboard. Behind her, a dusty corn plant drooped in its brass planter.

One of my fingers was bleeding when I was finally led to an exam room. Doc Simpson was waiting inside for me, even his sweater vest seeming the same as what he'd worn last time I was here—maroon with beige diamonds, like somebody's grandfather who'd gotten lost on his way to a golf game.

"It's been a while, Ms. Kenn," he said as he shuffled through my clipboarded file, several pages thick. "I'm glad you're back. How's the medication treating you?"

"Good," I said quickly, nodding for emphasis. I dropped into an orange plastic chair across from him. "It . . . helps."

He nodded, scribbling something onto the clipboard. "The new formulations are quite remarkable." He cleared his throat. "Did you know that Haldol's become popular on the streets?"

I blinked. "No. I didn't."

"Well, it is." He seemed momentarily embarrassed. "But you couldn't possibly be selling it because it looks here like you ran out a few weeks ago. Are you halving your pills again?"

I nodded, my throat tightening. If he thought I was selling it, he'd be even stricter with my prescription. "I'd prefer not to take it at all. My compromise is half a tablet."

He flipped another page in my file and tapped his pen against the clipboard. "Any unusual thoughts? Visual or auditory disturbances?"

One of Mom's litanies that I collected on our visits came easily to my lips. "Sometimes I think I hear whispering, but I know it's not real. The shadows moved once, but I realized it was the paranoia. The medicine makes a difference." I was twisting the skin of my thigh so tight that my eyes watered.

"Excellent insight." He looked pleased, like a teacher whose slowest student finally grasped long division. "You know, trauma like you experienced, it can quite literally split the psyche. The mind protects itself by fragmenting. I see it all the time. Your psychologist is helping you?"

I nodded. I'd done the one mandatory visit with her. I hadn't gone back. Too much to hide. Would Simpson realize I was lying? It would only take one call to my supposed therapist. Out in the waiting room, the receptionist's phone rang. As muffled as the sound was, it was everything I could do not to jump. This all seemed to be taking longer than it should. He wouldn't withhold my medicine, would he?

"Well, everything seems stable," he said, scribbling a final note in my chart. "I'll write you another three-month prescription, but I want to see you again before I renew it, like usual. Things have definitely improved since The Fracture."

He always said it like that, so you could hear the capital letters. I didn't care, as long as he gave me my meds. I nodded, weak with relief, and took the scrip he offered.

His hand was liver-spotted, nails perfectly trimmed. Grandpa hands. Safe hands. I wondered if he really believed my act or if he just didn't want to dig too deep, afraid of what he might find.

"Thanks again, Doc," I said.

He nodded. "You can find your own way to the lobby?"

"Yep."

I waited until he was gone under the pretense of digging for something in my purse. Once the door closed behind him, I did a quick run through the exam room. He'd taken the scrip pad with him. The only things not locked down were the swabs. I pulled on my coat and made my way out through the lobby, eyes on the ground until I reached the lot. I was planning the shortest route to the drugstore, but when I looked up, I saw a man standing near the far edge of the parking lot, his figure hazy.

He wore a military-style jacket, and for a moment, I was sure he was watching me.

My spine turned to glass.

But then I blinked, and the figure was gone. Just an empty lot, cars dusted with snow. A plastic bag tumbled across the asphalt like urban tumbleweed.

I wanted to scream.

Instead, I made my way to my car, sat in it, watched my breath cloud the windows. The prescription felt heavy in my pocket. Mom's words echoed in my head: *Sometimes I think I hear whispering, but I know it's not real.* Except I'd never heard whispers. Never seen moving shadows. Those were *her* demons, not mine. I just borrowed them sometimes, when I needed to keep my real ghosts hidden.

I reapplied a brick-red lipstick, hands shaking, then started the engine but didn't put it in drive. Across the lot, that plastic bag still danced. For a moment, it reminded me of a ballerina taken to the air.

Then the bag snagged on a light pole and shredded itself to pieces in the winter wind.

I checked all my mirrors before pulling out. No military jackets. No one tailing me. Just me and my borrowed crazy and a prescription for three months' worth of pills.

She stepped out of the clinic, hugging Her coat tighter, the winter wind whipping that ugly short hair. He hated the way She moved. That was the thing about girls like Her. They didn't stay down. Well, soon, She wouldn't have a choice.

He'd gotten good at this. Tailing people. It'd taken practice—years of it—but now it was second nature, the quiet art of knowing exactly when to follow and when to fade. Watching Her had required more than he was used to giving, though. She checked reflections, changed routes, doubled back. She knew the game.

But he played it better.

Just now, he'd let Her catch the smallest flicker of movement. Just enough. A half second of him appearing next to a car before dropping down, vanishing like he'd never been there at all. He imagined the way Her pulse would kick, the way Her brain would start grinding. Had She really seen something? Or was it just Her nerves?

He chuckled.

That was his favorite part. Messing with Her, making Her question Herself. He pictured Her driving home, checking the rearview mirror every few seconds, securing doors and windows tonight with trembling hands.

Soon, he'd be done screwing around. The fun part was almost over, and it was almost time for things to get serious.

Soon, there would be no hiding, not for Her and sure as hell not for Julia.

CHAPTER 39

Sometimes, the best thing you could do for your mental health was clean your kitchen. A deep scouring, the kind that left your hands wrinkled and your mind empty.

I started with the bright-blue counters, wiping down every inch with a soapy rag, scrubbing at the sticky spots where Julia's juice cups had left their mark. A pot of soup burbled on the stove, a ham bone provided by Coretta forming the base, with navy beans, carrots, and celery adding earthy sweetness, a bay leaf and full cloves of garlic providing depth. The kitchen was slowly filling with the kind of homey smell that made even January feel warm.

I'd bring Coretta a mason jar of the soup once it'd cooked and cooled, and I'd put aside another serving for Corn. I stirred the pot, tasted the broth, added salt and white pepper. It was the kind of meal that felt old-fashioned, and something about it calmed me.

Knowing I had access to three months' worth of Haldol didn't hurt.

Soup perfectly seasoned, I moved on to Ajaxing the sink, watching the blue water swirl down the drain. My mind wandered to the appointment with Simpson. I knew my breakdown had started with a single domino falling: thinking I'd seen Arsen right around the anniversary of my sister's murder. Everything went downhill after that.

I'd been feeling on the verge of a similar breakdown this past week. It'd been the picture of me on the PI magazine that'd started it, convinced me Arsen had found us. This time, however, I would stop a full collapse before it happened. It might be helpful to talk to myself like I knew Nic or Corn would. The Arsen sightings I thought I'd had? They could be a simple by-product of stress. And there was a much more rational way to explain the killing outside the Gopher Hole and the attack on Hannah Wheaton, and Detective Smith, Shawn, Nic, and Corn had all said it: There was a copycat killer out there.

What would it look like if I believed that?

Well, for starters, the odds of the copycat tracking down Julia and me were minuscule, especially since I'd changed our last name and no one but Arsen, Nic, my sister, and me had even known Julia was Arsen's daughter. A copycat killer definitely wouldn't. That meant my girl was safe, and I'd keep her that way until the cops caught the predator.

"I'm fine," I murmured, the words massaging the knot in my chest. "Julia's fine."

My hands moved in automatic circles over the stovetop, working away baked-on spills while MTV played quietly in the background. The familiar chords of "All Apologies" drifted through the room as I attacked a particularly stubborn spot. I rinsed off my hands before reaching for the remote. I intended to head into the living room and flip through channels until I found something better—the song had always made me sad—but the bang of the front door opening startled me. Nic burst into the kitchen, her face flushed and hair windswept. She glanced wildly at the remote in my hand. "Look at the TV."

I opened my mouth to ask her what she was talking about but paused when I saw her expression. The remote had stopped on CBS. Sure enough, regularly scheduled programming was being interrupted for a news bulletin.

"Listen," Nic said, her voice tight. "There's been another murder."

The news anchor's professional calm couldn't quite mask her horror: "We're about to play audio from a 911 call received early this morning. We warn viewers that some may find this disturbing."

At first there was only static, then a sound that made my blood freeze. Deep, racking sobs that I knew. Knew like my own heartbeat.

"I had to do it," the high, pleading voice said between gasps. "She reminded me of—" A pause, wet with tears. Then laughter, low and building until it drowned out everything else. Horrible, familiar laughter that planted me right back in that night in the trailer, frozen while bullets rained.

I moaned. It really was Arsen.

The news anchor's voice faded back in, but I couldn't hear her over the roaring in my ears. I grabbed the counter to steady myself. "That's him."

Nic turned to me, her eyes wide with disbelief. "But how can it be? He's dead."

"You just heard the same thing I did," I said, my pulse racing. "That's the original Crying Killer's voice. *Arsen's* voice. We both know it. Would know it anywhere."

Nic was trembling. "It's just a copycat," she said shakily, as if saying it aloud would make it true. "It has to be. All guys sound the same when they're whiny like that."

I couldn't respond. The sound of his laughter echoed in my ears.

"Tuesday?" Nic touched my arm. "Hey, look at me."

But I couldn't rip my gaze from the TV, where the details were scrolling across the bottom. This latest murder victim was a woman, mid-thirties, found in her home. Reports said her body was posed and that a mark was deliberately made on her.

Police are urging anyone with information to come forward. The public is advised to remain vigilant.

The broth on the stove bubbled over, hissing as it hit the burner, but still I couldn't bring myself to move. The smell of scorched beans filled the house.

I had no choice. It was time to confront a piece of my past.

CHAPTER 40

The roads between Saint Paul and Saint Cloud were treacherous, patches of black ice lurking beneath fresh snow. I white-knuckled the steering wheel, squinting through the crystalline flurries. The scenery shifted from urban sprawl to farmland, barren fields stretching white and endless under a pewter sky before turning back to suburban chaos as I neared Saint Cloud. The radio kept cutting in and out, static drowning the voices that all seemed to be discussing the "Crying Killer's return."

CK 2.0, they called him. As if this were a software upgrade rather than the monster who'd murdered my sister.

Either way, I was going to catch him, and I was going to kill him.

Elizabeth Bauer's house was modest, a squat little box near Munsinger Gardens on the east bank of the Mississippi. I parked at the curb and sat for a moment, staring at her home. *Why did your brother become a serial killer? Have you heard of the woman he murdered in Saint Cloud after he was supposedly dead? Do you know that he's still alive? Who was he working with that night he came to my trailer? How do I send him back to hell?*

Liz Bauer and I'd graduated Lilydale High the same year. I hadn't interacted with her much back then. She was one of those quiet types, the kind who blended into the background unless you were looking for her. And I wasn't. Back then, I was too wrapped up in my own life, my own struggles, to notice much of anyone else.

But I knew—everyone knew—Liz was a cop's daughter, which meant she had two paths available to her in life. Like a preacher's kid, she was going to either rebel spectacularly or toe the line so tightly it might snap. As far as I knew, Liz chose the latter. She didn't drink or party, didn't date any of the boys who circled like vultures. She wasn't a cheerleader or class president or anything that put her in the spotlight. She just *existed*, moving through the halls with her books clutched to her chest and her head down.

One interaction stood out, though. It'd been late spring, the air thick with the promise of freedom. The school windows were open, letting in a grass-scented breeze. I was in the library because I was skipping gym and needed somewhere to hide. Liz sat at one of the tables, her notebook open in front of her, her pen scratching steadily across the page. She didn't seem to notice me. I don't know what came over me, but suddenly, I slid into the chair across from her, startling her.

"Hey," I said. She'd just nodded, her eyes darting back to her notebook. "What're you writing?" I asked more out of boredom than genuine curiosity.

She paused, her pen hovering above the page. "Nothing important."

I leaned forward, trying to catch a glimpse. "Come on. Let me see."

Her cheeks flushed, a deep red that spread to her neck. "It's personal."

"You're not writing about me, are you?" I teased, but she didn't laugh. Her eyes flashed up to mine, sharp and serious.

"No," she said quietly. "Not everything's about you."

The words stung more than they should have. I was acting stupid, trotting out my lame social skills in an effort to connect, and she'd made it serious. Simple as that. She went right back to writing, her pen flying now, and I sat there, silent, until the bell rang and she gathered her things and left without a word. I watched her go, feeling something I couldn't quite name. Jealousy, maybe, or embarrassment.

Not everything's about you.

With the gift of hindsight, I was sure she'd survived things I couldn't begin to imagine, things I was only now starting to piece together. A cop father jailed for selling drugs (and worse, if my mother's gossip was to be believed), a brother who'd become a serial killer. Her home-life might even have been as bad as mine. And as much as I hated to admit it back then, she was right. Not everything was about me. But this—Arsen, the bodies piling up—this was about both of us, and I needed her help, though I hadn't the faintest what that would look like.

Might as well figure it out.

I made my way to her front stoop and was raising my hand to knock when her door opened. Liz stood there, not so much older as blurrier around the edges, her pinned jeans and popped collar having given way to a soft-looking sweatshirt and pine-green cords. She wore no jewelry. Her gray eyes were sharp as she took me in. Something about her was familiar. Not in the way of an old classmate. It was something else, something slippery.

"I've been waiting for you to show up," she said, moving to the side so I could enter. "I mean, before you called today."

The house smelled of some flowery air freshener, almost aggressively normal. I stepped past her. The interior was as modest as the outside. The furniture was old but clean, the walls decorated with faded prints of flowers and landscapes with lakes.

"Thank you for seeing me." I stamped my boots on the mat. I wasn't sure whether to remove my coat, and she didn't offer to take it.

"I've got cookies in the kitchen," she said, leading the way. She'd grown into herself since high school, her movements deliberate, controlled.

A survivor's walk.

I removed my boots and followed, taking the seat she indicated at the kitchen table, still unsure where to begin.

"I like your hair short like that," she said, grabbing a plate of chocolate chip cookies off the counter. They appeared to be homemade. "Makes you look different. Grown-up. I suppose we both are."

"I suppose," I said. "I'm here because—"

"I know why you're here," she said flatly. "Arsen's not back. He's dead."

The skin at the back of my neck grew cold. Of course she knew about the most recent killing, how it bore her brother's signature. "There was another murder right after my sister was killed," I said, swallowing hard. "Here in Saint Cloud. The same mark carved in her back. Do you know anything about it?"

Liz shook her head. "I don't. Why do you ask? Aren't you a *cop*?" She said it like it was a dirty word. Couldn't blame her.

"I . . . I was," I said.

"Well, can't you ask someone you used to work with about that other woman?" She tipped her head when I didn't respond. "You don't know for sure there *was* another woman. You're here to fish."

I figured I might as well try honesty. "I read about it in a chat room and was hoping you could confirm, because you're right, I don't know for sure." I wished I'd taken off my coat. I was suddenly too hot. "What I *do* know is that two women in Saint Paul have recently been murdered following Arsen's MO, and a third was attacked, the signature X sliced into her skin."

She set the cookies down in front of me, hard. "But whoever did that—whoever is attacking those poor women now—it's not my brother. The police shot him dead."

Her words were firm, but I realized with a jolt that the shadow in her eyes said otherwise. I took the opening.

"The police shot someone wearing his *jacket*," I countered. "His face was destroyed. They never ran any tests on the body." I leaned forward, rapping the table with my knuckles. "Arsen was too mean to die easy, Liz. You know that."

Her posture went ramrod straight. Without warning, she turned and lifted her sweater. A raised scar curved across her lower back.

"He did this when I was sixteen," she said. "The X turned into a keloid. My body overreacting to the trauma, the doctor said. Fitting, right?" Her laugh held no humor.

Something between horror and pity cracked open beneath my ribs. I studied her face in profile—the sharp cheekbones, the wide-set eyes. She could have been any of his victims. That's when I realized who she reminded me of.

Trixie.

My throat closed up. Liz must have been Arsen's patient zero. My heart shattered for her, but I didn't have the luxury of laying off. Arsen was back, and she might not want to believe it, but I could tell she had her doubts. If I could get her on my side, I stood a chance.

"What about the phone call confession the news played today?" I asked. "If you've heard it, you know it's him."

Liz dropped her shirt and turned, her hands tightening on the back of the kitchen chair, her words slicing out. "Here's what I know about, Tuesday. I know about *shame.* How it eats you from inside, how everyone tells you to swallow it down, hold it tight, don't talk about it." Her eyes were blazing. "But the shame. Isn't. Ours. It never was. It's his. You need to hand it all back to him. To the *memory* of him. Once you let that pain go, you can let him go." She waved a hand in the air. "He's gone. This new monster has nothing to do with us. Let the police deal with it."

Something tickled my brain. She'd said "gone." "Gone" didn't mean "dead."

"Why'd he do it?" I hadn't expected to ask the question, and she clearly hadn't expected to hear it, but suddenly, I was starving for the answer. "What happened to him to make him kill?"

A slice of sound, almost laughter but not quite, cut her mouth. "You watch horror movies? You hoping for some backstory of a cannibalistic clown dragging Arsen into the woods and turning him evil? Well, sorry to disappoint, but he was just another guy who felt entitled to more than he got. He wanted someone to blame, and he chose women." She took a deep, ragged breath.

I was still trying to balance it all out. "Your dad hit him?" Arsen had said as much, back when we all hung out, but I wanted to hear it from her.

Liz's chin jerked in an imitation of a nod. "Sure. It got so bad that he'd hide in the cupboards. He was always good at disappearing into small spaces. Dad hit me, too, and Mom. She could have gotten Arsen and me out of there, but instead, she acted like it wasn't happening, walked out in the community like the queen of the world with her head held high." Her eyes glittered. "Kind of like your mom."

The last of the armor I'd been wearing sloughed off. We were just two girls who'd been born into a raw deal. "But we didn't turn into killers."

Her mouth twisted. "We sure didn't."

There was no recovering from this conversation, no gliding gracefully into small talk, so I asked her any question I could think of, more to find my way back to myself than because I expected revelations: who else Arsen hung with back in the day (an alternating cast of losers, plus my sister, Nick, and me), if she'd seen anything unusual recently (no), if her mom or dad had (she didn't talk to her dad, and her mom hadn't mentioned a thing), if she knew the two women who'd recently been murdered and the one who'd been assaulted (she didn't think so, but their names had yet to be announced; when I shared Wheaton's name, she said she'd never heard of her).

In short, she had nothing. No insight, no leads, just a fervent hope-bordering-on-belief that her brother was dead. Her skin seemed almost translucent when I left, her under eyes bruised. She looked like I felt. I had to sit in my car for several minutes to collect myself.

That's when I realized I was closer to Lilydale than Saint Paul.

I could feel that dark little town pulling at me like an addiction. I ignored it and headed home. By the time I reached the Victorian, the streetlights were already on, trying to hold back the gloom of early afternoon. I had about an hour before I could pick up Julia. Maybe Coretta was home. I'd grab her mail and mine and drop by.

The mailbox was cold under my fingers, the metal biting into my skin as I wrenched it open. I pulled out a stack of letters, leaning over to make sure I got everything. There was a shape in back. I reached for it. Drew it out.

A worn paperback copy of *Helter Skelter*.

I felt like I'd been drop-kicked in the ribs.

My hands shook as I turned it over and then paged through it. There were no markings. I stumbled into the house and up to my apartment, grabbing Smith's card off the bulletin board in the kitchen, the card Corn had given me.

Screw this Lone Ranger act.

I had to report the book, no matter what it cost me. Julia must be protected.

CHAPTER 41

I kept glancing over at Julia as we drove home from school, her face half hidden behind a Baby-Sitters Club book, dog-eared from countless rereadings. "Hey, sweetie," I finally said, my voice an octave higher than usual. "A police officer might stop by tonight. To talk about a case."

Julia lowered her book, her brow furrowing in that way that made her look far older than eight. "What kind of case?"

"Nothing for you to worry about." I forced a smile. "Just routine stuff."

"Okaaaay," she said, drawing out the word. She turned her gaze to her window, watching the city blur past. When she looked back at me, she seemed like she wanted to say something, but she stopped herself. She looked so much like Pia. She held her silence until we got home. I parked in the driveway and ushered her upstairs, my stomach full of knives. Inside our apartment, she kicked off her boots, leaving them haphazardly near the door, and ran to her room with a shouted "I'm hungry!"

I glanced at my wristwatch. I had time. I hustled to the kitchen to cut up some celery, which I arranged on a plate around a scoop of chunky peanut butter. Normally, I required Julia to keep food at the table, but I didn't want her to overhear what Smith and I would be talking about.

"You can chow down in your room," I said, bringing the plate to her.

"No way!" she said, wrapping her arms around my waist. She grabbed the food and brought it to her window, where she'd been curled up with her book.

I barely had time to close her door behind me when the knock came. It was firm, deliberate. I opened my front door to find Detective Smith standing there, her coat immaculate, her hair pinned back in a sleek twist. Her eyes were hawkish as she took in the hallway behind me, eyes pausing on the security panel that I'd disarmed in anticipation of her arrival.

"Detective," I said, stepping aside. "Come in."

She tipped her chin and crossed the threshold, her heels clicking softly on the wood floor. She stood in the entryway for a moment, her gaze sweeping over the modest decor. The mismatched furniture, the stack of Julia's books on the coffee table, the lingering stink of burned bean soup from this morning. I could almost hear her brain whir as she cataloged it, filing it away.

"Let's talk in the kitchen," I said.

She followed, removing her coat to reveal a crisp and polished taupe pantsuit that probably cost more than my rent. She kept up her survey in the kitchen, her gaze glancing off the dishes drying in the rack, Julia's broccoli-tree artwork magneted to the fridge, the African violet struggling for life on the blue-and-white windowsill, the worn copy of *Helter Skelter* in a Ziploc bag on the kitchen table.

"Nice place," she said, sitting down elegantly, her eyes settling on the book. "Very homey."

"Coffee or tea?" I asked.

She pointed at the Suisse Mocha canister. "I'd love a cup of that, if it's not too much trouble."

I filled two mugs with water, then popped them in the microwave. While they heated, I grabbed spoons and the tin of coffee, setting them on the table. When I'd called the cop shop, I'd been patched straight through to Smith. I'd told her about finding *Helter Skelter* in my mailbox, about Arsen Bauer's obsession with Charles Manson. I said whoever this killer was—because I'd realized it was safest to go along with the story that it was a copycat instead of Arsen—he knew private details about the original case, and he was targeting me. I said I'd bagged the book, and that it'd be lousy with my fingerprints.

She'd asked to come right over.

I told her I had to pick up Julia but that we could meet when I returned home.

The microwave beeped, and I jumped. I grabbed the two bubbling mugs, handing her one. She set down the notebook and pen she'd been holding to flip the lid on the Suisse Mocha tin and scoop two heaping mounds of brown powder into her mug before stirring. I wrapped my hands around my own cup, letting the warmth ground me. I wanted tea but suddenly couldn't summon the wherewithal to grab a bag.

"What do you need from me to catch him?" I asked.

"Everything you can tell me about the recent murders." Her dark eyes were steady, assessing. "Especially any connection you see to Arsen Bauer."

"It seems like his work," I admitted, dancing around any reference to certainty. "The placement of the bodies, the X engraved onto their backs . . ."

"It *sounds* like Arsen Bauer," she finished, her gaze piercing. "But it can't be. He's dead."

Was she asking or telling? "Right," I stammered. "He's dead."

She studied me for another long moment, her pen poised above the notebook. I could feel her curiosity pressing against me, like she was trying to pry me open without asking too many questions.

A gust of wind rattled the loose kitchen window in its frame. Before I could get to it, Nic glided silently into the kitchen, an annoyed look on her face. My pulse stumbled. I'd thought she was at work, but nope, here she was at home. She stared at Smith then at me, her eyebrow speaking more eloquently than her mouth. *Cop?* it asked. I shrugged. Nic glowered and stomped straight to the window, which had always driven her crazy with its rattling. We'd finally been able to fix it by wedging a piece of cardboard into the gap.

Detective Smith glanced up, her jaw tightening almost imperceptibly. While I'd assumed she would have more natural curiosity, I wasn't surprised by her reaction. Nic had that effect on people, especially authority figures. They saw she was different, and they either ignored her or attacked her. I suppose I was grateful Smith had chosen the former. I didn't have the energy for anything else.

I stood quickly to help Nic. The glass was cold under my fingers as we worked the cardboard into place. The frame was old, the wood warped, and it took more effort than I expected. We finally wedged the cardboard deep enough to keep the window still.

"You get much company?" Detective Smith asked.

She was referring to Nic, of course. It was a Minnesota Nice version of asking to be introduced to someone who should have already introduced themselves. I didn't need Smith to know how close she was to the Nicholas Gajdusek she'd been searching for. Since she wasn't here investigating us, she had no right to push. Still, I had to think fast.

"I prefer to keep my homelife private." I threaded my tone with what I hoped was the right amount of annoyance. "If you don't mind, let's just you and me talk."

Before Smith could press further, I gave the window and then Nic a pointed look. "It's all good," I told her, hoping she didn't make the mistake of opening her mouth. I wasn't sure why she'd even come out. Curiosity? A passive-aggressive impulse to make my life more difficult? Thankfully she took the hint, leaving as quickly as she'd come.

"Fine by me," Smith said curtly, though I suspected we'd return to a conversation about this person living with me very soon. She flipped back a couple pages in her notebook. "You probably heard that both murder victims were found in similar positions to Arsen's previous targets," she said, clearing her throat. "But the violence is escalating. The most recent woman was stabbed over sixty-one times, compared to seventeen for the woman in front of the Gopher Hole."

"Like I said at the hospital, I read about the Gopher Hole murder." I retook my seat. Still no need to mention that I'd been outside the bar in its aftermath, seen the police lights painting the snow red and blue. "But Arsen's dead. The police shot him that night in the trailer."

Smith was scratching something into her notepad. "You sound very certain."

Thank god. I was worried I wasn't pulling it off. "I saw his body." The half lie tasted as bitter as bark on my tongue, but it was easier than the truth—that I wasn't certain of anything anymore.

"Let's say for the sake of argument that Arsen is alive," she said delicately. My chest grew cold, and I suddenly understood why she'd given Nic so little attention. She had a much, much bigger fish on her line. She continued. "And I'm certainly not saying he is, but if he is, why do you think he's surfaced now?" She spread out her arms, indicating, presumably, all of Saint Paul. "Why here?"

The answer stuck in my throat. I didn't think she believed Arsen was still alive. In fact, I was certain she was trapping me somehow, but how could I keep the words down if saying them might protect Julia? So I uttered the truth I'd intended to carry to my grave. "Because he's coming for his daughter."

Smith stiffened, but she was looking toward the hallway, where Julia was peeking around the corner, her wide eyes fixed on me. I sucked in my breath.

"Jules," I said gently, stepping toward her. "Do you need some more snacks?"

She didn't answer, just looked up at me with a mix of curiosity and horror. Smith's voice broke the tension.

"Is this your daughter?" she asked, her tone deceptively playful.

"Yeah," I said. "Julia, this is Detective Smith. She's just here to ask some questions, like I mentioned."

Julia nodded slowly, her fingers twisting the hem of her sweater. "Hi," she said shyly.

Smith offered her a small smile. "Hi, Julia. Don't worry, I won't be here long."

I ushered Julia back toward her room, my heart pounding. How much had she heard? When I returned, Smith was standing, her notebook tucked away, the bagged book in her hand.

"Walk me to my car?" she asked.

She waited until we were on the front porch to ask, and I was grateful for her discretion. "Julia is Arsen Bauer's daughter?"

I meant to nod but instead could only jerk my chin. "His and Trixie's. He didn't know until the night he murdered her." I blamed my sudden burst of honesty on my desperation to distract from Nic. "I've raised Julia as my own child, and as far as the world knows, she is."

Smith's mouth pursed, and she stared angrily off into the distance. "You should have led with that."

"It's no one's business," I said.

Her eyes locked onto mine. "Thank you for your time," she said, her tone gone formal again. "If you think of anything else, please let me know."

I watched her drive away, the iron weight of the conversation settling heavily on my neck. She'd seen Nic. No way was she not going to follow up on that. What had I done, inviting her into my home?

CHAPTER 42

Before

The leaves were dying in spectacular fashion, painting the banks of the Crow River in shades of amber and rust. The Three Musketeers had claimed their favorite spot under the spaghetti arms of a huge willow, the leaves forming a tent around them.

Trixie sprawled on her back, arms flung wide, a Marlboro balanced between her fingers. She exhaled into the sky. Her Walkman headphones were loose on her ears, tinny echoes of Tears for Fears leaking out. Tuesday sat cross-legged beside her, algebra book open but mostly ignored. Nicholas was leaning against the tree trunk.

"I've been thinking," Nick said, dramatic as though he were onstage. "Maybe one day I just disappear. *Pfft.* Gone." He snapped his fingers, the jelly bracelets on his wrist flashing. "No one would even know what happened to me. I'd show up somewhere new, maybe O'Gara's or maybe even Hollywood, and I'd start over. Be whoever I want."

"Don't be stupid," Tuesday muttered, eyes on the equations she wasn't really solving.

"It's not stupid." Nick leaned forward. "It's survival. Imagine it. A place where no one expects me to be the weird one, or the funny one, or the not-man-enough one. A place where the cops aren't always busting me, trying to pin everyone else's shit on me just because I'm different. A place where I just . . . am."

Trixie stubbed out her cigarette. "You'd last, what, two days before you missed us?"

"Maybe." Nick grinned, but then his gaze flicked sideways. "I was talking about it with Arsen. He gets it. He says maybe we'll go together."

Tuesday's head snapped up, the book sliding off her lap. "You talked to *him* about it?"

Nick shrugged. "Why not?"

"Because he's poison," she shot back. Trixie glared at her, but she ignored it. "He's not your way out, Nick. He's a dead end."

Nick bristled. "You don't know him like I do."

Tuesday was gearing up for an argument when a gray ball of fur fell from the branches.

Trixie shrieked and scrambled backward, Tuesday grabbing her arm, while Nick yelped and nearly fell over. A squirrel shot away from them, tail bushed high. The three of them erupted into laughter, breathless as the fight dissolved.

"You screamed like a girl," Trixie gasped, wiping mascara streaks from her eyes.

Nick tossed his hair, trying to recover his dignity. "Correction. I screamed like *you*, girl." He mimicked her shriek so perfectly she punched his arm.

Tuesday shook her head, still smiling. "You're impossible."

"Maybe." Nick's grin cracked wide. "But admit it. You'd miss me if I disappeared."

They all knew it was true.

CHAPTER 43

After

After Detective Smith drove away, cold settled into my marrow.

I lingered in the foyer, trying to will my heart rate back to normal. Would she discover Nic lived with me? Track down who she used to be and start harassing her like everyone else did? And worst of all, had Julia guessed I was talking about her?

I shuddered. She couldn't have. She'd scampered back to her room, oblivious to the storm brewing. For now, she was protected. For now, she didn't need to know the cracks spiderwebbing through my world.

But the guilt at hiding who her father was surged like acid up my throat. She'd go through periods when she'd ask what his name was, what kind of work he did. I always told her I hadn't known him very well but that I had two parents' worth of love for her. The truth. Just not the whole truth.

I hoofed it up the stairs and reset the security system before walking to her closed door. I raised my hand. Dropped it. Raised it again. Knocked. "Jules?"

"Yeah?" Her voice sounded tiny.

"Can I come in?"

A pause. "Sure."

She was lying on her bed, her hands at her sides. She seemed so small, so vulnerable. I dropped next to her, pushing hair out of her eyes.

"How about a Lazy Day tomorrow?" I asked, forcing brightness into my voice. "It's been so long since we've had one."

Her face lit up, and she popped onto her knees. "Really? Like, 'sleep late and watch cartoons' lazy?"

I searched for any sign that she'd had her worldview upended. I saw none. "I was thinking more we'd go to Belcamino's and the Minnesota Zoo."

She squealed and wrapped her arms around my neck, nearly knocking me off the bed. I inhaled her scent as deeply as I could. "I have my meeting tonight, though," I said. "You okay going to Corn's? I'll leave you both money to order pizza."

She couldn't have been happier. I thought about checking in with Nic before we left, telling her to do a better job lying low, but I didn't want to slow Julia's happy momentum. I bundled her into her coat and drove to Corn's home above his office, his daily life contained to a building whose stairwell smelled of cumin and turmeric.

The scents followed us up the narrow stairs, making my empty stomach growl. The first time I'd brought Julia here, she'd curled her nose and said it smelled weird. I'd tousled her hair. "That's what good food smells like, baby," I told her.

Thanks to Corn, she'd had plenty of opportunity to try it since. Matar paneer was her favorite—she said the chewy cheese and mushy peas were a "mouth-splosion"—but she never passed up a samosa. Maybe she and Corn would order from downstairs rather than get pizza.

Passing the second level, Julia behind me, I was surprised to see the light on in Corn's office. I'd expected him to be up in his apartment. I probably should have called, but he knew it was an AA night. I opened his office door.

He was hunched over his desk, reading glasses perched on his nose. His office looked like a library had exploded, even more so than usual. Papers everywhere, Styrofoam coffee cups breeding in corners. He glanced up as we entered, his face brightening at the sight of Julia.

"Hey, kiddo," he said. "Your mom here to hit me up for something?"

Julia grinned. "It's her meeting night. She said we can order pizza!"

"That's right!" He pushed back from the desk, shaking his head at his own forgetfulness. "Well, that's good news for me, because I'm starving."

"Can I grab the camera for the Hachette case while I'm here?" I asked. Then I swallowed before saying the last bit, the part I'd been rehearsing ever since I'd discovered *Helter Skelter* in my mailbox. "Plus, I need Hannah Wheaton's home address."

His bushy eyebrows drew together. "The woman from the hospital? Why?"

I glanced at Julia, who was examining the collection of snow globes on Corn's windowsill. I leaned in close. "I think she's in danger." It was true. If her memory came back, she could potentially identify the killer. He'd want to finish what he started, which meant that if I tailed Wheaton, I might catch him. It was also true that as much as I believed Smith was good at her job, I wasn't putting all my eggs in one basket. I'd follow up on every possible lead I could.

"If the woman's in danger, it's the cops' job to protect her," he said gruffly.

"The guy who attacked her, it wasn't random." I heard the desperation in my voice.

He studied me for a long moment, his dark eyes worried. "Tuesday . . ."

"I'll be careful," I promised. "Scout's honor."

"You were never a Scout." But he was already on the horn. Minutes later, he wrote down the address, which he offered to me. I read his T-shirt: WE ALL GOT IT COMIN', KID.

"Don't make me regret this," he said.

I tried to pull the scrap of paper out of his hand, but he wouldn't release it. His lips were pressed into a thin line, his brow heavy with worry. "You're not bulletproof, Tuesday. Don't act like you are."

"Thanks, *Dad*," I said dryly. When he finally released the paper, I tucked it into my pocket. Then I went over to kiss Julia goodbye.

"Can we get Indian instead?" she was begging Corn as I closed the door behind me.

CHAPTER 44

The folding chairs were arranged in their eternal circle. I poured a paper cup of coffee and took a swallow, the bitter heat grounding me as I slipped into an empty seat. The room buzzed with the low hum of shared vulnerability. I needed to be here, needed the routine of it, but I felt like I was splintering into a hundred different pieces.

That's when I caught him staring at me.

The same guy who'd asked me out last time I was here, the teacher with a drinking problem, *J*-something. He still had the black-rimmed glasses, the neat hair, and that unsettling intensity in his gaze. As soon as our eyes locked, he sidled over and slipped into the empty seat next to me.

"I couldn't help but notice—" he started, leaning too close.

"Back off," I snarled. Heads turned. Conversations died.

He raised his hands, palms out. "Hey, just being friendly."

"I don't need friends." My voice carried even farther in the sudden quiet. Everyone was staring now, coffee cups frozen halfway to mouths. "So don't look at me, don't talk to me, don't even think thoughts about me. You're here for your reasons, I'm here for mine. Stay the hell out of my way."

Not in a million years was I going to be the woman who gave up her seat when she hadn't done anything wrong, so I stared at him until he slunk away. Coretta took his place, her face creased with concern.

The rest of the group started talking again, wallpapering over the awkwardness I'd caused.

"When can I watch Julia again?" Coretta asked brightly. "I miss our time together."

The uncharacteristic gentleness in her voice made me want to scream. "Don't," I warned. "Don't treat me like I'm crazy."

She put a hand on my arm. "Nobody thinks you're crazy, honey."

But her eyes said different.

So did everyone else's. They might be talking to each other, but they were watching *me*, and I couldn't stand the way they were doing it—with pity, with worry, like I was a problem that needed solving.

Like I was making this all up in my head.

"I need to leave," I muttered, grabbing my coat and heading for the stairs. I heard Coretta sigh. It sounded like surrender.

At least that guy hadn't tailed me out.

Still, I waited in the parking lot another half an hour to be sure.

He followed Her and Julia to Cornell's building, keeping his car far enough back so She wouldn't notice. That was the trick. Not too close, not too distant. She thought She was so careful, so aware, but She never saw him coming. Never had, never would, not unless he wanted Her to.

He drove up to the church ahead of Her, parked where he could see the door. When She finally went inside, She looked beat down. Smaller. That straight back She always had was starting to slump, and damn if it wasn't nice to see. Her shoulders rolled in now. Her hands looked shaky.

All his work, all his waiting, finally paying off.

When She came storming out soon after, face all twisted up, moving like a woman losing it, he knew She was nearly cooked.

He even got to watch Her pace back and forth by Her car in the parking lot. Back and forth, back and forth, like some zoo raccoon. She kept pulling at Her hair. Real nice little meltdown.

The trap was almost fully set.

He thought about little Julia, staying with some stranger right now. Sweet kid. She was gonna be so happy when she finally got to meet her real family.

CHAPTER 45

The next day dawned bone-white and bitter. After a lazy morning playing cards and coloring, Julia and I bundled up and headed to Belcamino's on West 7th, her favorite restaurant in all the land. The place had the feel of an old-school Italian market. The walls were lined with ginormous, neatly stacked cans of San Marzano tomatoes, the glass cases filled with wheels of cheese and loaves of focaccia. Exposed brick walls were hung with old photos of Saint Paul's Italian immigrants, and that smell—*oh, that smell*—of garlic and basil and red sauce that'd been simmering since dawn.

It was enough to melt the coldest heart.

Julia's face lit up as she ran to press her nose against the glass, pointing at a massive slice of pepperoni pizza sprinkled with sausage crumbles. "That one! That's mine!"

We ordered, me opting for the rigatoni al forno, baked in molten glory with ricotta bubbling up from the center. Julia insisted on adding a cannoli "for later," which I knew meant the absolute second she was done chowing down her pizza.

The dining area was cramped, every table occupied by families and students on lunch break. A group of high schoolers laughed loudly in the corner, their varsity jackets slung over their chairs. I found us a spot near the front, where the frost traced delicate patterns along the window. Julia dug into her pizza with gusto, her face a canvas of sauce and happiness. I sat back with my pasta, soaking in the moment. These days didn't happen often enough, and I had a terrifying sense they wouldn't last.

"Can we go to the zoo next?" Julia asked ten minutes later, licking ricotta from her fingers. Her eyes were bright, almost feverish.

"Of course." I glanced around the restaurant, scanning faces, looking for one in particular. But there was just the usual lunch crowd trickling in and out: elderly couples sharing plates of pasta, businessmen in salt-stained shoes, young mothers with toddlers who attacked the paper place mats with chunky crayons.

We bundled up and headed to the Minnesota Zoo, which in January was a ghost of its summer self. Most of the outdoor exhibits were closed, but that's how Julia liked it. She'd always preferred the indoor stuff, especially the tropics trail with its humid air and secret corners. We wandered past the gibbons, their coal-black eyes following us, their long arms wrapped around thick branches.

"Mr. A says monkeys are our closest relatives," Julia said, pointing upward, her tone certain. "He knows *everything* about animals."

I was only half listening, my attention caught by a man in a leather jacket disappearing around a corner. *Not Arsen. Just another dad out with his kids.*

"He's the best teacher I've ever had," Julia continued. "When Tommy kept interrupting me during reading time, Mr. A made him stay in at recess. He said it's important to protect the quiet ones." She smiled, pointing her thumb at herself.

A group of schoolkids thundered past, their excited shrieks echoing off the glass enclosures. I knew Julia deserved my full attention, but I was too busy studying the crowd, searching for a particular set of shoulders, a certain way of walking.

"I'm glad you like your teacher," I said absentmindedly. "Hey, I want to get out of here. You ready for the playground?"

She hopped up and down, which I took as a yes, so we forwent our usual trip to the zoo's gift store and instead drove to Cherokee Park. The playground equipment was dusted with snow, the swings creaking in the wind. It was surprisingly full of families with little kids playing on metal equipment slick with frost. I shouldn't have been surprised by how many people were out. If you were a Minnesotan who stayed inside when it was uncomfortably cold, you'd be trapped in your home at least half the year.

Julia hesitated at the edge of the playground, her breath coming in visible puffs as she surveyed the swings. "I'm too big for this, right?" she asked tentatively.

I shook my head, jogging forward to brush snow off the seat of the only open swing. "Never too big to play."

She climbed on, pumping her legs shyly at first, then with more confidence. I gave her an underdog to help her along. The chains screeched, and soon she was soaring, her giggles riding the wind. I leaned against the monkey bars, watching her silhouette against the steel sky.

After a few minutes she slowed, dragging her boots in the snow. Then she hopped off and ran toward me, her cheeks pink from the cold. "Mom," she said, her voice conspiratorial, "I *really* like my new teacher."

"Oh yeah?" I crouched down, brushing ice from her mittens. The only man at the playground had left, so I could relax. "Tell me his name again."

"Mr. A. He's old, like maybe even thirty." Her eyes widened for emphasis. "But he's really nice. And patient. He helped me with my spelling test last week."

"That's great, baby," I said, smiling. But her words stirred something in me. I couldn't put my finger on it, an uneasy hum. She'd been trying to tell me about her new teacher for a couple weeks now, and I needed to listen.

"Yeah, he's the first boy teacher I've had," she continued, tugging at my sleeve. "He said I'm really smart. Smarter than most kids." Julia grinned and made straight for a tornado slide, one of several. I perched on a bench where I could see all the approaches to the playground, my breath making clouds in the frigid air.

She slid down again and again, her laughter pealing across the park. Each time she climbed the ladder, I counted the rungs with her, thirteen up to the platform. Each time she disappeared over the top, my heart stopped until she emerged at the bottom, cheeks flushed, eyes sparkling.

"Watch this trick Sarah's dad showed me!" she called out, and proceeded to go down the slide backward, arms crossed over her chest like a mummy.

My attention snagged on movement at the edge of the park—just a dog walker, bundled against the cold. I forced myself to relax. We were safe here in the weak winter sunlight. Arsen wouldn't dare. Not in public.

"Do you know that Sarah's dad plays guitar?" Julia said, plopping down beside me on the bench, snow dust shimmering in her hair. "He says he could teach me, too, that everyone should know how to play an instrument. Sarah's mom said that's a good idea, and I'd probably learn right away because I'm really something special." She leaned against me, her small body vibrating with playground energy. "Is that why you're always watching for bad guys? Because I'm special?"

I wrapped my arm around her shoulders, pulling her close. "Something like that, bug."

She hummed against my side, some garbled tune I didn't recognize, while I scanned the tree line.

CHAPTER 46

That night, as I tucked Julia into bed, she looped her arms around my neck and held on tight, her breath warm against my cheek. Her small hands, still soft with childhood, cradled me. "You're the best mom in the whole wide world," she said solemnly.

It hit me like a sucker punch. Julia couldn't know that every ounce of my devotion to her was poisoned with guilt. I kissed her forehead, brushing back the hair that always fell in her eyes, and whispered back, "I love you more than anything."

That, at least, was true.

She smiled sleepily, letting her head sink into the pillow, her lashes already fluttering shut. Her breath evened out, but I stayed for a while longer, watching her, burning this image into my memory. Then I slipped out, closing the door softly behind me.

The attic was waiting.

I checked and double-checked the alarm system and then made my way upstairs, tugged on my gloves, and worked myself until my muscles screamed, until sweat plastered my T-shirt to my back.

The box sat in the corner, patient as a cat.

I'd been avoiding it for nearly two weeks. Tonight felt like the night to face my fears. I might find something helpful, right? I hurried to it before I could change my mind, dragging it below the bare bulb, my breath hitching as I knelt. The lid resisted at first, like it knew what I was up to, but finally, it gave way.

Inside was the detritus of a life I'd tried to bury.

The paperback-size lockbox sat on top. Fat. Heavy. It'd been here since The Fracture, to quote Doc Simpson. I shoved it to the side. I wasn't ready for that. Not yet. Beneath lay a drinking glass in a Ziploc, smudged with prints I'd been saving for—what? Evidence? Insurance? I set that aside as well.

The past rose up below in fragments: ticket stubs from the Lilydale Community Theater's production of *Our Town*, a dried corsage from sophomore homecoming. The cork from the first bottle of wine we'd ever tried, stolen from Nick's mom. One of Trixie's report cards. Straight A's, except for gym. "You can't measure my worth with a dodgeball," she'd said when Mom asked about it, her tone so defiant it'd made me laugh. A photo of her and me at the county fair, fingers sticky with cotton candy.

Another picture slipped free: our father, looking like a recruitment poster for the American Dream in his shiny, dark-brown Sunday suit over a mustard-colored shirt and a red tie. But I remembered how those hands that waved at the camera would turn to fists by Monday, how his voice would swing from honey to hornets. Some days he took us for ice cream. Others he took off his belt, and it was never clear what to do to win one and avoid the other.

No wonder the Hendrickson girls were inclined to fall for abusive men. Dad had laid the blueprint: Love meant learning to duck.

"Visiting memory lane?"

I startled. Nic stood in the doorway, still wearing her bartender blacks, her hair damp from melted snowflakes.

"They cut me early," she said, crossing the floor to sit beside me. "Dead night."

I nodded, noting how tense she looked, the pinched skin around her mouth and eyes. "Hey, what the hell was that," I asked, "coming into the kitchen to fix the window yesterday?"

She tossed it back in my lap. "What was a *cop* doing in our kitchen?"

Fair enough. "She's helping me with a case." I didn't know why I suddenly felt evasive. "Side note, you'll want to stay out of her way."

Nic nodded. She looked like she wanted to say more before her eyes caught on the stack of photos still inside the box. She reached for the top one. "Oh my god, look at this."

It was us at the homecoming game: me, my sister, and Nic when she was Nick. My sister was mid-laugh, her head thrown back. I was trying to look cool and failing. Nick was watching us both with that gaze he always wore, like he knew something the rest of us hadn't figured out yet.

"Remember what happened that day?" Nic asked, her voice soft. "Under the bleachers?"

I did. We'd smuggled some wine coolers in our jackets, huddled in that steel cave while the crowd roared overhead. It was a good time until a pack of senior boys found us, started calling Nick names. We ran, giggling but also terrified, until we lost them. We ended up spread-eagle in a wheat field, watching stars punch holes in the Minnesota dark.

"We made all those promises," I said, the memory unreeling like old film. "You were planning to move to the Cities and start working at O'Gara's so you could go to all the magic shows. I was going to teach English and save the world one comma splice at a time."

"And Trixie was gonna throw me the biggest 'Finally Me' party ever when I was ready." Nic's laugh caught. "God, remember how many gummy bears we ate that night?"

"You always took the green ones," I said.

"And you hoarded the lemon." Nic huffed, sounding like she was swallowing a bubble of sadness. "Trixie loved orange."

We both went quiet, remembering who'd claimed the red ones, who'd said they tasted like sweet blood. Nic flipped to the next photo: three kids in summer dresses, balanced on the railroad tracks. Looking at it now, I could see we were all posing, me trying to hide, my sister showing off her curves, Nick posing like he thought a girl would. But we were smiling, real smiles that reached our eyes. We were content in that moment, wrapped in the certainty that we'd always have each other's backs.

"She was supposed to make it," I whispered.

Nic reached for my hand, squeezed once.

Outside, the wind picked up, rattling the windows like someone trying to break in.

CHAPTER 47

The next morning, after dropping Julia off at school, I steered my car toward Saint Paul's West Side, where Hannah Wheaton lived. The sky was thick with clouds that threatened snow, but what else was new? Winter would have its way with us until we reached our breaking point, and then it'd last for another couple weeks.

Hannah's neighborhood was modest but well-kept, rows of postwar bungalows with stoops sunken into hardened snowbanks. Her house was at the end of a quiet street, its paint a fading white, its chain-link fence rusted where the winter salt had chewed on the metal. I parked along the curb and killed the engine, watching her home for a beat, just like I'd done to Liz Bauer's. Had I expected to see Arsen lurking just outside, hiding behind a tree like a cartoon villain?

The house was small, with white curtains drawn tight across the front window. A welcome mat lay crooked on the icy stoop.

She probably didn't feel very welcome anywhere right now.

I left my car, strode up the sidewalk, and knocked, my knuckles stinging by the time the door finally opened. Hannah stood on the threshold, glaring defiantly, clutching the edge of the door with one hand. She seemed smaller than she had in the hospital, her face pale against the backdrop of her living room. The bruise on her jaw had changed color, mottled now in sickly greens and yellows. She cradled her arm in its cast close to her chest.

"The police detective." Her voice was hoarse. "What do you want?"

"PI," I corrected again. "I wanted to check in. Make sure you're okay." I'd layered warmth into my voice, though I doubted she'd buy it.

Her eyes bounced past me to the street, scanning for something—or someone—before she stepped aside reluctantly. "I guess you can come in."

Her living room was cramped but clean. A plaid couch sagged against one wall, a crocheted blanket draped across its back. The coffee table held a neatly stacked pile of *TV Guides*, and the air smelled faintly of microwaved popcorn.

She perched on the edge of the couch, her injured arm resting against her body. "Why are you here?" she asked, her voice tight. "Because like I said at the hospital, I already told the cops everything I know, which was nothing. It was dark. He came from behind. I was unconscious for the rest of it."

A radio on a nearby shelf played Cities 97 at low volume, Melissa Etheridge singing about coming to my window. I hadn't moved from the rug just inside the door. "Sometimes our minds protect us by hiding details. But they're still in there."

She shook her head, her walls visibly shooting up. "You sound like my therapist."

I took a breath, felt the familiar tightness in my chest. She wasn't going to be vulnerable with me if I wasn't vulnerable with her. I unclenched my fists. I wanted to make eye contact with her, but my body refused. "I know it's hard to talk about," I said through gritted teeth. "But the man who did this—he's done it before. To someone I loved. My sister."

I was able to pull up my gaze just in time to see Hannah's lips parting. "Your sister?"

"He murdered her in June of 1986." The words drew blood as they dragged up my throat. "She had an X cut into her back. Just like you."

Her free hand clutched a throw pillow, and she glanced away. "I'm sorry," she said, her voice barely audible. "But I don't know anything else. I've told you everything."

"Hannah," I said firmly, "if you want to stay safe, you need to talk to me. Anything you can remember might help."

Her gaze snapped back to mine, and for the first time, I saw something like anger behind the fear. "Stay safe?" she said, her voice rising. "What the hell do you know about staying safe?"

"I know more than you think." My jaw was so tight that it was difficult to speak. "That's why I'm here."

She shook her head, a bitter laugh escaping her lips. "I know who you are," she said. "I suspected the second you showed up at the hospital. You're the sister of the Crying Killer's old girlfriend, aren't you?"

My vision narrowed to the thin slice of light falling between us. "I am."

Hannah stared down at her lap, her fingers plucking at a loose thread in the pillow. The tension in her shoulders drained, leaving her slumped and exhausted. "Well, he's dead and you should go," she said. "I want to be alone."

The room pressed in on me. "Before I leave," I said, "there's something you should think about. I train at an MMA gym downtown. It's nothing fancy, but it's a good place to learn how to protect yourself. If you're interested, I'll write down the address."

I saw a flash of the carefree person she must have been as she snorted. "Me? Doing MMA? You're serious?"

I nodded, my gaze steady. "Dead serious. You don't have to feel helpless."

She studied me for a long moment, a handful of expressions flitting across her face—disbelief, anger, fear. Then she sighed. "Maybe. I'll think about it."

I scribbled down the name and address and then showed myself out. Back in my car, I let out a shaky breath, scanned the neighborhood—no one was out—then checked my watch.

Time to shadow Melissa Hachette.

She'd filed the stalking report three weeks ago, and so far, we had nothing to give her. I hadn't yet visited her at work, a vintage shop on Grand Avenue, so I figured I'd start there today. Its bay window was a riot of mismatched mannequins and 1970s velvet, and on the other side, Hachette was talking to a customer. She kept it up for the next three hours: helping people shop, checking them out, arranging displays. Nothing suspicious happened inside or outside the store.

When Hachette left for her lunch break, I saw she was pure '90s in her Doc Martens and baggy flannel beneath a peacoat, her long brown hair twisted up with a pencil. She ran errands, stopping by the bank and then the corner store before ending up at the coffee shop two doors down from the vintage store. She sat by the window, her fingers curled around a steaming mug while she wolfed down a muffin the size of her head.

After about ten minutes, she glanced at her watch and then left the coffee shop, heading back to work. She didn't seem anxious or jumpy, but there was a slight stiffness in the way she moved, like she was bracing for something.

I was beginning to think this was another dead end when I spotted him.

A man lingering on the opposite sidewalk, his face partially obscured by a hood. He wasn't close enough to be immediately threatening, but there was something suspicious about him. I grabbed my camera from the seat next to me and snapped a few photos, my pulse quickening. The way he stood, the tilt of his head as he watched Hachette, set my nerves jangling.

She was his absolute laser focus, his world.

Was this her stalker?

When she disappeared inside, he stuck around for another beat before turning and walking away, his movements smooth and deliberate. I leaped out of my car, planning to follow him at a distance, but he disappeared into the maze of side streets before I could get a better look.

CHAPTER 48

Corn's office door was ajar, faint strains of public radio bleeding into the mangy-rugged hallway. I knocked as a courtesy before pushing the door open, greeted by the familiar sight of him at his desk, a pencil tucked behind his ear and his reading glasses perched on the end of his nose. He glanced up when I walked in, his sharp blue eyes narrowing as he took in the camera in my hand.

"You get anything good on Hachette?" he asked, gesturing toward it. Today's T-shirt read THERE'S ALWAYS A FASTER GUN.

I handed over the camera. "Some guy for sure tailing her. He was too far away for a clear picture, but there might be something useful in there."

Corn grunted, running through the rest of the film in the camera with a couple clicks before snapping open the back. He handed me the 35 mm roll. "Next time you leave, drop this off at the drugstore. Tell 'em it's a rush." He offered me the Nikon back along with a fresh roll of film. "Keep this, too. I don't need it for a while."

I stuffed the camera and film into my purse. "You cool if I work off the database while I'm here?"

Corn gave me a look that said he wanted to ask what I intended to look up, but he didn't push. "Sure," he said. "Just don't lock me out. I've got my own searches to run."

I pulled a chair up to the corner desk, brushing aside a stack of outdated phone books to get a clear view of the monitor. The computer was ancient by today's standards, its tan casing yellowed with age. I booted it up, the hard drive groaning and whirring like someone had trapped a dozen fat hamsters in there and told them to earn their keep. I could feel Corn watching me with the faux disinterest of someone who knew better than to ask too many questions. "You haven't told me about the copy of *Helter Skelter* in your mailbox," he said finally, his voice too casual.

Of course word had gotten back to him. "Because I don't want to talk about it." I kept my eyes on the monitor as the system finally loaded.

"You were the one who called Smith to tell her?"

My eyes slid to the window. No snow, just gray. "Yeah," I said softly. "I had her over."

A squeaking sound told me Corn was leaning away from his desk. "You tell her you were at the Gopher Hole the other night, too?"

"I wasn't *there*," I snapped, turning to glare at him. "I didn't see the murder. I showed up after the fact."

"Okay," Corn said reasonably. "So, you tell her that?"

"There's nothing to tell," I said through tight lips.

He didn't respond. I turned back to the computer, my fingers hovering over the keyboard as I stared at the search bar. This was a database I couldn't access at home. I angled the monitor away so Corn couldn't see it and typed in *Arsen Bauer*.

The results filled the screen in seconds, a list of articles and records I'd pored over a hundred times before. The mugshot from a teenage arrest. The grainy high school yearbook photo where his eyes seemed to follow you. The police reports that barely scratched the surface of who he really was.

Nothing new.

So I dug deeper, scrolling through every document, every fragment of information I could find. My chest tightened as the frustration built. Arsen was still as slippery as mercury, his truth slipping through my fingers no matter how hard I tried to grab on.

I switched gears, pulling up the archived articles about Trixie's murder. Within seconds, her face appeared on the screen, frozen in time, her smile bright and full of life. I reached out instinctively, my fingers brushing against the monitor's cold surface.

I scanned the article, one I'd read at least a dozen times.

Tragedy Strikes Sunrise Estates Mobile Home Park: Killer Dead in Police Shoot-Out Following Murder of Local Girl

Lilydale, Minn.—A domestic dispute turned deadly at Sunrise Estates Mobile Home Park last night when Arsen Bauer, 22, shot and killed his former girlfriend Trixie Hendrickson, 16, before dying in a shoot-out with police.

According to Chief Bill Everson, officers who were already at the trailer park for an unrelated dispute heard the gunshots around 11:45 p.m. Upon arrival, they witnessed Bauer exiting the residence. When ordered to surrender, Bauer turned his weapon on officers, resulting in return fire that proved fatal to Bauer.

"It's a tragedy that hits close to home," Everson said, referring to Bauer's connection to former police chief Aramis Bauer, who is currently serving time at Stillwater State Prison for drug trafficking.

Sources close to the investigation say Arsen Bauer is being considered as a suspect in the so-called "Crying Killer" murders that have terrorized the area since 1985. The killer, known for making

> tearful phone calls to police after each slaying, is believed responsible for four unsolved homicides.
>
> "We're exploring all possibilities," said Minnesota State Trooper William Kent, who has headed the Crying Killer investigation out of St. Cloud.
>
> Following standard procedure, officers involved in the shooting have been placed on administrative leave pending the investigation. Chief Everson emphasizes there is no ongoing threat to the community. Anyone with information about this incident or the Crying Killer murders is urged to contact the Lilydale Police Department.

The tears came before I could stop them, hot and unwelcome. I wiped them away angrily, but the damage was done.

Corn broke the silence. "You okay?"

"What do you think?" I asked, but there was no heat in it.

He stood, offering me a pastel-colored box of tissues. "I think you're carrying too much."

I shook my head at the Kleenex. "This sort of get-in-my-business is why I left the police force."

His voice was low and steady. "Tuesday, I *know* why you left the force. And it wasn't office politics."

I froze, my hands curling into fists. He'd never brought this up before. "You don't know shit."

"I know about the domestic call," he said. "The one with the murdered woman and the baby. I know what it did to you."

"Shut up," I hissed.

"And I know what you survived in Lilydale," he continued, his words unyielding. He'd been waiting to have this talk with me for years,

I could tell it in the way his mouth stayed tight below his mustache. "What you went through with Arsen, with your sister. I know."

"Stop," I said, the word barely a whisper.

He didn't. "I don't give a damn about the past, Tuesday. I don't care what broke you. I care about what you're doing to put yourself back together."

The phone's scream made us both jump.

Corn answered it. "Stamoran Investigations," he said, his gravelly voice sharp with irritation.

I couldn't hear the other end, but I saw the way his jaw tensed, the lines around his eyes deepening. He glanced at me once, then scrubbed a hand down his face.

"Yeah, she's here," he said finally. "Uh-huh. I see." He shot me another glance, his eyes narrowed. "Right. Thanks for the courtesy call."

He hung up with a heavy click and remained still for a moment, his hands resting on the desk. When he finally turned, there was a pinched quality to his expression I didn't like. It was worry, sure, but something else. Something harder.

"Well?" I asked, breaking the silence.

"That was Smith." His voice was low enough that I had to lean forward. "She thinks they've got the guy who left *Helter Skelter* in your mailbox."

I blinked, the words taking a moment to sink in. "What? Who?"

Corn hesitated. "Someone from your AA group. Guy named Jackson. Ring any bells?"

The image flashed in my mind instantly: the teacher with the black-rimmed glasses and the too-intense gaze. The one who'd followed me after his first meeting, asking me for coffee like he wasn't breaking every rule in the book.

"You're kidding," I said.

Corn shook his head. "He admitted to it. Said he was pissed when you rejected him, wanted to . . . what'd she say he called it? 'Do some light harassing.'"

"Light harassing?" I repeated, my voice rising. "He left *Helter Skelter* in my mailbox. That's not 'light harassing,' that's—" I stopped, pressing my lips together, my breath coming too fast.

"The cops are holding him. They don't think it's just about the book."

"They think he's the one behind the Gopher Hole murder," I said flatly. "And the attack on Wheaton, and the murder after that."

Corn nodded slowly. "They do. He's denying it, but you know how that goes. They're holding him for now."

I shook my head. "It's not him. It can't be."

"How do you know?"

"Because this distraction is exactly the kind of thing Arsen would do. It's a setup."

Corn pulled himself to his full five feet, ten inches. "Tuesday, listen to yourself. You're saying Arsen Bauer, who's been dead for nearly nine years, set this guy up? You hear how that sounds, right?"

"I'm not saying Arsen's alive," I snapped, though the words rang hollow even as I said them. I'd gotten caught up in fear and shown too much of my hand. "I'm saying . . . I don't know what I'm saying. But Jackson didn't kill anyone. And he didn't attack Hannah Wheaton. This was designed to make us look the other way."

Corn studied me for a long moment, his gaze unflinching. "Okay," he said finally. "Let's say you're right. Let's say it *is* a setup. Who'd allow themselves to be framed for murder? Who in their right mind would risk life in prison for someone else?"

"Maybe Jackson didn't know," I said quickly. "Maybe he thought he was just confessing to the book. To the harassment. Maybe someone put him up to it."

Corn's eyes shuttered. "You think Jackson, what? Just happens to be the unlucky idiot who got manipulated into taking the fall for murder?"

"Yes," I said stubbornly. "That's exactly what I think. How else would he even know to leave a copy of that particular book?"

"By finding out your real name and what you'd been through in high school, just like I did about a minute after we met?" Corn exhaled, dropping back into his chair. "Jesus, Tuesday. You're twisting yourself into knots."

"Because it doesn't make sense!" I wailed. "Jackson's too *normal* for serial murder. He's too . . . small."

"And what? Arsen's larger than life?" Corn slapped his desk. "A mastermind pulling strings from beyond the grave?"

I didn't answer. My throat felt tight, my thoughts spinning too fast to catch.

Corn sighed. He looked so tired all of a sudden, the lines around his eyes deepening in real time. "Tuesday," he said softly, "whatever you think is happening, you can't keep doing this to yourself."

"I'm not doing anything to myself," I said. "I'm just trying to figure out what's real."

"And you think *this* is real?" He flapped both hands in the air, indicating the swirling mess of words I'd just thrown at him.

"I don't know," I said. "But I know it's not over. And I know Jackson didn't kill anyone."

Corn squinted at me. "Tuesday," he said. "I know you think you're holding it together, but you're not. And if you don't let someone help you—"

"I don't need help," I said, cutting him off. "What I need is answers. And unless you're offering that, just stay out of my way."

For a brief, flickering moment, I felt a pang of guilt for pushing Corn away. But then it was gone, swallowed by the familiar weight of anger and fear. I stood and grabbed my coat, heading toward the door.

"I'll go drop off the photos. Call me when they're ready," I said, my words clipped.

Corn didn't stop me. He didn't say another word as I walked out, the scent of cumin and turmeric clinging to my skin like smoke.

CHAPTER 49

A couple of days passed in a haze of monotony. I interviewed all of Hachette's neighbors and coworkers, transcribed notes until my fingers were stiff, and hunted through the emerging labyrinth of the internet, learning the cryptic language of the new search engines. The green glow of the computer monitor had become a strange comfort. The film roll containing photos of Hachette's stalker got misplaced by the developer, though they swore they knew just where it was and would drop off the images as soon as they were ready.

I barely spoke to Nic, who worked her usual night shift at the bar. I struggled to listen to Julia, who buzzed around me, chattering about her new teacher and friends and homework and socks. I nodded when I had to, grunted when I couldn't muster more. Her world was as bright as mine was dull.

It felt like breathing underwater. Arsen was out there, but where?

All I could do was be vigilant and wait.

The days pressed down, heavy and shapeless, until Wednesday evening, when the phone rang. I was standing at the stove stirring Campbell's tomato soup, adding a dash of milk the way my mom taught us. Julia sat at the kitchen table, multiplication worksheets spread before her, pencil tapping against her teeth.

"Mom," she said, her voice rising slightly, "are you gonna get that?"

I startled. I'd been hypnotizing myself with the stirring, watching the marbling of the milk fold into the velvet soup.

The number on the caller ID was unfamiliar. Still, I answered, clutching the receiver tighter than I needed to. "Hello?"

"Tuesday?" The voice on the other end was cautious, female.

"Speaking," I said. "Who's this?"

"It's Margot Andrews."

I froze, the wooden spoon clattering onto the counter. I hadn't heard that name in almost a decade, not since high school. Margot had been short and intense, with bristly blond hair and a perpetually sunburned nose. The whole Andrews family had that tight yellow hair, like the kind on an antique porcelain doll. I knew because we rented a farmhouse on their land for a few months. They all talked too loud, too, their words sharp and desperate. They had six daughters and then, finally, exhausted, a boy.

Margot was their fourth daughter.

"Margot?" I stretched out the phone cord so I could turn down the heat under the soup, which'd started to bubble aggressively. "Wow. It's been—"

"Forever, can you believe it?" Her laugh hadn't changed, still that same pop of sound that back in the day seemed to startle even her.

I was brought back to junior high. The Three Musketeers always sat at the same table, the one with the wobbly leg that someone had tried to fix with wadded-up notebook paper. One day, Margot approached us, clutching her brown bag like a shield.

"Can I sit with you guys?" she'd asked.

I remembered being impressed. She was attempting the Queen's Gambit of junior high: joining a new clique. I'd looked at my sister, who looked at Nick, and we all three shared that silent communication that came from years of having no one else to count on. We didn't need a fourth. We were complete, self-contained, bound together by empty refrigerators and fathers who disappeared.

"Sorry," my sister had said, not sounding sorry at all. "Table's full."

It wasn't, of course. But Margot, with her clean clothes and balanced lunches, couldn't have understood that the less you had, the stronger the grubby, greedy impulse to hoard it. She walked away, head down, to sit by herself at another table.

I remember feeling so bad that I hunted her down later, when my sister wasn't around. Margot and I started hanging. It lasted all of two weeks. One Saturday night, she and I met up in the city park and passed strawberry Boone's Farm back and forth until our lips were stained sweet and tart. I never knew which of us started it, only that one second we were laughing and the next our lips were locked together, our hands everywhere, scrabbling at buttons, chasing something that felt urgent and forbidden.

It was clumsy, frantic. And then it was over.

It was awkward to see each other the next day, and by the end of the week it was as if we'd never been friends.

"Listen, this is kind of weird," she said, pulling me back into the present moment, "but I saw your picture in a magazine someone left on one of my flights. I'm a stewardess now, based out of Atlanta."

My stomach dropped. "A magazine?"

A beat of silence. "Yeah, some private investigator thing. Rising star or some crap. Your last name was different, but I recognized you right away. You still have that famous Hendrickson smile."

"Dammit," I muttered, then immediately glanced at Julia. She was absorbed in her homework. "How'd you get my number?"

Margot made a smacking noise. "My brother knows someone who . . . look, does it matter? I had to find you. It's about Trixie."

A bolt of cold spiked through my spine. I turned away from Julia, lowering my voice. "What about her?"

"Not over the phone." Margot's voice dropped to match mine. "I have a layover at MSP tomorrow. I'll be staying at the Embassy Suites near the airport. Could you meet me at the bar?"

The smart answer was no. My instincts were waving their hands, telling me that this wasn't a coincidence, her showing up at the same time as Arsen. But walking straight toward the trouble was better than having it sneak up on me.

"What time?" I asked, already mentally cataloging Corn's availability.

"Six work?"

"I'll be there." I hesitated. "Margot? How exactly did a PI magazine end up on your flight?"

"Oh, you know how it is. Passengers leave all sorts of things behind. Magazines, umbrellas, their dignity." That pop of laughter again. "See you tomorrow."

The line went dead. I stared at the receiver for a long moment before hanging up.

"Who was that, Mom?" Julia asked, glancing up from her math.

"Just an old friend." I poured soup into bowls, added floating islands of oyster crackers the way she liked. I was surprised at how steady my hand was. "Hey, what's eight times seven?"

"Fifty-six," she answered automatically. "Can we have hot chocolate later?"

"If you finish your homework," I said, setting her bowl in front of her. "Careful, it's hot."

CHAPTER 50

The sky the next morning was a pale, bruised gray. Corn called just as I was halfway through my first cup of coffee, steam curling into my face.

"I know you're already up to your eyeballs, but I have a new one for you," he said. I detected a welcome note of amusement in his voice. "Man says his neighbor's been stealing his newspaper every morning for the last two weeks. Wants us to catch him in the act."

"Corn, please tell me you said no."

"Oh, I said yes." Now I could practically hear the grin in his voice. "But only because I know you need something light for a distraction. Come on, it'll be fun."

I groaned but agreed, packing a thermos of coffee and a pair of binoculars before I dropped Julia off at school. The guy lived on the south side of Minneapolis, right on its border with Richfield, and the stakeout was as dull as expected. I sat in my car, engine running every so often for warmth, watching as the elderly suspect shuffled out onto his porch, his slippers dragging against the icy steps. He didn't steal his neighbor's paper that day, though he did pause to stare directly at my car for an unnervingly long time before shuffling back inside.

When the man who'd hired Corn grabbed his own paper, I snapped a photo of him before driving crosstown to follow up on another case Corn had handed me about a month ago. A cheating husband, classic and straightforward except I'd struggled to find proof of him doing what he'd been accused of. I'd tailed the guy on and off, and his movements had been predictable: gym, work, liquor store.

This morning, though, as I followed him, he took a sudden detour into the Como Park Zoo. I parked and followed at a distance, surprised to find him sitting on a bench near the polar bear exhibit, holding hands with a woman I'd never seen before. *Bingo.* The two of them were laughing, their breath fogging in the cold air. I was snapping pictures when a man in a full Santa suit wandered into view, shouting something incomprehensible about "Christmas justice."

I went rigid, half convinced I was hallucinating until the cheating husband glanced up, startled, and hurriedly pulled his companion away. Out-of-season Santa began humming, managing to stumble across my path. The smell of cheap liquor wafting off him was strong enough to give me a buzz.

"You're not gonna believe this," I said when I called Corn later.

"Try me," he replied. When I told him, he whistled. "Sounds about right for the zoo. Did you get the photos?"

"Yeah," I said. "But I'm starting to think this job is bad for my sanity."

"You know you can take a break if you—"

"I'm good," I said, cutting him off. "I was joking."

The only positive news I got that day was Corn agreeing to watch Julia while I met up with Margot. He acted like he was doing it grudgingly, saying he was only willing to watch her an extra night because I'd worked so hard this week, "filing and tailing like a beaver," but I knew hanging out with Julia was the highlight of his life.

Even better? She knew it, too

CHAPTER 51

The Embassy Suites loomed against the January night sky like a concrete wedding cake, its interior blazing yellow against the purple dusk. The whole front wall of the hotel bar was a window, the people inside more on display than the zoo creatures I'd seen today. I parked, shut off the engine, and watched the steady stream of folks flowing in and out of the bar, the bank of windows not twenty feet away and unobstructed.

The winter air crept through my car's weather stripping, but I didn't dare run the engine. If Arsen was watching this lot, I didn't want to call attention to myself. Instead, I pulled my wool coat tighter and kept my eyes fixed on the hotel. The bar was pure Midwest corporate: brass railings, hunter-green carpet, fake rubber trees, a wall of Naugahyde booths. The kind of place where middle managers sipped cheap scotch and waited for their mistakes to resolve themselves. A cluster of men leaned on the bar, and I could almost hear the false bravado in their voices, how they talked too loud, slapping each other on the back like it meant something. I'd staked out a dozen places just like it.

A woman wearing an oversize red blazer was seated at the end of the bar nearest me. She threw her head back and laughed at something her companion said. Not Margot. Another woman sat on the opposite end of the bar, shorter, with a sleek black bob. She checked her watch and glanced down at her roller bag. Not Margot either.

I had no intention of going inside, of course. I just needed visual confirmation it was really her, then I'd wait for her to call again so I could get whatever information she claimed to have over the phone. Safer that way. Smarter.

My windows were starting to lace with frost, so I gave in and ran the car for a couple minutes. The gassy smell of exhaust turned my stomach. Across the parking lot, a man in a camel-hair coat trudged through the slush toward the Embassy Suites entrance, his breath clouding above his head like a thought bubble in a comic strip. Behind him, the airport shuttle pulled up, disgorging a fresh batch of travelers into the lobby.

Still no Margot.

The first prickle started at the base of my neck, like spider legs crawling up my spine. *Someone was watching me.* I knew it with the same bone-deep certainty that used to tell me when Mom was about to slip into one of her spells. My hands tightened on the steering wheel, and I wished desperately for a gun. I hadn't held one since The Fracture, didn't trust myself enough.

The feeling intensified: pins and needles spreading across my shoulders, tiny electrical charges dancing along my scalp. I checked my mirrors. Nothing but shadows and snow. But the sensation persisted, grew stronger. Like hands hovering just inches from my skin.

That's when the need for a drink hit me like a physical blow. Just one. Just enough to quiet the whisper in my nerves that'd begun with that dead body in front of the Gopher Hole and grown steadily since until it was nearly a scream. I kept a bottle of bourbon in the Cabinet of Lost Hope, just behind the vases. I joked with Nic that it was there in case of emergency. The truth? I needed to know I could resist. I wouldn't drink unless I was out of choices.

And right now, I felt dangerously close.

O'Gara's was only ten minutes away. Nic would be working. She'd talk me down like she had a hundred times before in the two years since I'd gotten sober. But she would also ask questions I couldn't answer. Not yet. Not until I knew what Margot's game was, why she was really here.

If she was here at all.

I gave it another fifteen minutes, as long as I could stand it, and then fumbled with my keys, fingers clumsy with cold and fear. The sensation of eyes on me had become unbearable, ants crawling under my skin. As I pulled out of the parking lot, my headlights swept across the hotel's facade one last time.

Still no Margot.

I pressed hard on the gas, not caring about the slick roads, checking behind me for a tail. I needed to be somewhere warm and bright, somewhere with voices and movement and life.

Somewhere that wasn't this haunted land between past and present.

He watched outside the Embassy Suites. He waited. Two moves left before the trap snapped shut.

CHAPTER 52

Shawn opened the door, the surprise on his face lasting exactly two seconds. Then understanding blazed like a match strike, followed by a wolfish grin. He stepped aside to let me enter.

No words. No need. He knew what this was.

The door hadn't even clicked shut before he threw me on the couch. The floor lamp crashed to the carpet with a dull thud, the bulb flickering once before going out. It was exactly what I wanted. Raw, feral, meaningless, no time wasted on kissing or foreplay. My fingers tangled in the hem of his sweater, yanking it over his head, but when he reached for my shirt, I shoved his hands away.

"You know better," I growled.

He studied me like he was trying to decode some foreign language, but then he shrugged, almost amused. "Whatever you say." He gripped my thighs and lifted me.

My body registered the ache of his grasp, the bruises that would bloom by morning, but my mind was a blank slate, every corner wiped clean of thought.

That was the point.

Afterward, we lay on his area rug, tugging on pants, not looking at each other. I'd left scratches down his neck that would be hard to explain tomorrow.

"So, that's what we're doing now?" he asked.

I zipped up my jeans. "Don't read into it," I said. I couldn't afford to give him even a glimmer of softness.

"Oh, believe me," he said. "I'm not."

I grabbed my coat off the floor and slipped it on. The room smelled like sweat. "Thanks," I said. I meant it.

He might've laughed, but I didn't stick around to know for sure.

The drive to Corn's lasted just long enough for guilt to set in, my skin bristling with the phantom touch of other hands, other nights. A streetlight caught my reflection in the rearview—mulberry lipstick smeared, short hair wild. I fixed what I could at a stop sign.

Corn opened his door before I could knock, took one look at me, and his face did that disappointed-father thing that made me want to simultaneously apologize and tell him to go to hell.

"She's asleep in the back room," he said, voice carefully neutral.

You're not perfect, I wanted to say.

I found Julia curled up in the spare bedroom, her little face buried in the crook of her arm, one hand gripping her favorite blanket. Her hair was a mess of curls sticking up in every direction. My heart squeezed painfully. I scooped her up, breathing in her apple shampoo smell, trying not to think about what kind of mother goes from rough sex to picking up her sleeping child.

She stirred, her eyes fluttering open. She looked at me with a bleary, confused gaze before nuzzling against my shoulder.

"Thanks for watching her," I whispered, turning back to Corn.

I was startled to find him standing immediately behind me, an immeasurable sadness in his eyes. "You know I love you. You and Julia both."

I took a step back. "Yeah, I know." He'd never said it before, but I felt it. His sudden intensity made me uncomfortable. "I gotta get her home."

He brushed his hand over his face. Tonight's T-shirt? WHEN YOU HAVE TO SHOOT, SHOOT. "Yeah. Of course. Do you want me to carry her to the car?"

"I got it." I shifted Julia in my arms as I brushed past him. "Good night, Corn."

"Tuesday," he said as I headed for the door. I paused but didn't turn. "Take care of yourself."

I could hear the weight of everything he wasn't saying in those five words.

I left without answering.

CHAPTER 53

Before

A door inside the house slammed like a gunshot, sending the sparrows that had been pecking at crumbs near the front step scattering into the muggy air. Tuesday and Trixie looked up from where they'd been sunbathing on faded beach towels, their eyes wide.

Daryl Hendrickson's voice spilled out of the rental, low and dangerous. He was leaving again, *this time for good*, he'd announced over breakfast, banging his coffee mug down so hard that Trixie had jumped, spilling orange juice down the front of her Holly Hobbie T-shirt. He'd spent the hour since packing his clothes and tools.

"Don't go, Daryl," their mother was pleading from somewhere near the kitchen, her voice thin and desperate. "The girls need their daddy. *I* need you."

Tuesday's and Trixie's eyes met, reflecting the same thought: *Need him?* They might love him, but it was a plain fact that life was easier when he wasn't around.

The front door crashed open and there he was, filling the doorframe like a thundercloud. He was a tall man, all shoulders and fists and eyes the color of dirty ice. His dark hair was greased back with Brylcreem. He wore his good shirt.

"Girls," he called out, his voice switching to that false-sweet tone he used when he wanted something. "Come say goodbye to your old man."

Neither of them moved. Tuesday's hand found Trixie's automatically, their fingers lacing together.

Behind him, Pia appeared in the doorway, her face red and puffy, hair half unpinned and sticking to her neck. She was wearing her yellow sundress, the one with the tiny flowers. "Daryl, please," she tried again, reaching for his arm. "We can work this out. The girls—"

The sound of his hand meeting her cheek cracked across the lawn. Pia stumbled backward, one hand flying to her face, and Tuesday felt something cold settle in her gut. Trixie's eyes filled with tears. They'd seen him hit their mother plenty, but it never stopped feeling like the world was tilting sideways.

"Don't," he said, his voice deadly quiet. "*Don't* tell me what's best for my girls."

He turned back to where they sat frozen on their towels, his expression shifting into something that might have looked like fatherly affection to someone who didn't know him.

"Trixie," he said, holding out his hand. "How about you come with Daddy? We'll have an adventure, just you and me. Get you some gummy bears. A whole bag just for you. Start a new life. Whaddya say?"

There was something in the way their father was looking at Trixie, something hungry and possessive that made Tuesday's skin crawl. And how had he known gummy bears were her favorite candy these days?

"Come on, baby girl," he coaxed, his voice syrup-sweet. "Daddy's going to take real good care of you."

Trixie was fifteen, far from a baby girl, but she started to rise, drawn by the promise of attention, by the fantasy that maybe this time things would be different. But Tuesday moved faster, scrambling to her feet and stepping between her father and her sister.

"No," she said, her voice stronger than she felt. "She's not going anywhere with you."

Trixie hugged herself, like she was trying to make herself as small as possible. Pia watched, glaze-eyed, her hand on her swelling cheek. Tuesday stood alone.

Her father's face darkened, the mask of false kindness sliding away. "You little *shit*. You think you run this family?"

"I'll call the police," Tuesday said, lifting her chin even though her heart was exploding with fear. She wished she weren't wearing a bikini. She put her fists on her hips, desperate to make herself bigger. "I'll tell them you hit Mom. I'll tell them everything."

They stared at each other. Tuesday was about ready to grab Trixie and run when her father's lips twisted into something that wasn't quite a smile.

"Go ahead," he said, backing toward his rusted Camaro, full to the brim with everything he thought was his. He'd have had to throw something out to make room for Trixie. "Call whoever you want. You'll never see me again, you understand? I'm gone forever, and it's your fault, Tuesday. You didn't learn the most important lesson, which is that nothing on this earth matters more than family." He turned his hateful gaze on Trixie, all the earlier coyness stripped from it. "And don't think I'll forget you let me down, *Trick*sy. Pretended to care for your old man, and then refused to give him what he needed. You're no better than your mother. Hell, you're no better than *my* mother."

He whipped the car door shut and gunned the engine, tires squealing against asphalt as he tore out of the driveway. In the silence that followed, Tuesday could hear Pia crying softly in the doorway and the distant sound of a Fleetwood Mac song drifting from someone's radio. She looked down at Trixie, who was still sitting on the towel, clutching her knees.

"Was he telling the truth?" Trixie whispered. "Is he really gone this time?"

Tuesday didn't answer. Only sixteen, she already understood that when you were raised by a man like that, he'd follow you around for the rest of your life, one way or another.

CHAPTER 54

After

The drive home from Corn's was silent except for Julia's soft breathing and the swish of wipers clearing snow. By the time I carried her up to her bedroom, my arms were trembling. Not from her weight—she was still bird-boned, all elbows and knees—but from the heaviness of life. The watching eyes at the Embassy Suites. Shawn's hands. Corn's judgment and, even heavier, to someone as messed up as me? His love.

I tucked Julia into her bed, turning on her yellow-star night-light on the way out. She didn't stir. Back in the kitchen, I puttered aimlessly. Made tea I didn't drink. Logged onto CompuServe but couldn't focus on the screen. Wished Nic were home instead of slinging drinks at O'Gara's. She'd pour me a club soda and tell me I was being too hard on myself, the way she always did. Finally, exhaustion won. I shuffled to my bedroom, already thinking about a hot shower and my flannel jammies.

I flicked on the light.

Three gummy bears lay in the center of my secondhand quilt, arranged in a neat row: yellow, green, orange. A silver pin pierced them all, fixing them to a Polaroid.

The air turned to gravel as I stumbled closer.

The Polaroid was grainy but clear enough. Me, leaving Shawn's apartment building. My coat unbuttoned. My hair a mess, lipstick smeared. Time stamp in the corner: 8:47 p.m.

I dropped it and ran to Julia's room.

It was ten steps away. Nine. Eight. Each footfall seemed to take hours. My pulse was a hammer at my throat.

I hit her doorframe at full speed, bounced off, caught myself. Whipped open her door.

My hand flew to my mouth.

Her bed was empty.

CHAPTER 55

My heart stopped, then lurched into overdrive. The night-light cast monstrous shadows on her walls, her stuffed animals watching with dead button eyes as I scanned the room. Suddenly, I caught the soft whistle of her breathing. I rushed forward, peering between the bed and wall.

There she was, curled up tight, wedged into the narrow space like a hiding mouse.

Asleep. Alive. *Right?*

I pressed trembling fingers to her neck, felt her steady pulse. Checked her breathing. Normal. Deep. Untroubled. I moaned with relief. Then I eased back to clear her room, checking everywhere for an intruder. Closet. Drawers. Behind the curtains. Under the bed. When I was sure there was no one waiting to snatch her, I pulled her door shut, dragged a side table in front of it, and moved into the kitchen to grab a butcher knife.

Whoever had left the gummy bears and the photo knew my security code. That much was clear. But it was the missing red gummy that chilled me to the core. *Red.* Arsen's favorite. He always picked them out first, leaving the others behind.

It had to be him.

Arsen had been here.

I was halfway through clearing the apartment—Nic's room, the living room, the hall closet, the bathroom—when a pounding at the door shattered the tense silence. Had I not reset the security in the foyer? Panic clamped down. I kept the knife clutched tight in my hand and edged toward the peephole.

Detective Tayari Smith.

She appeared immaculate as always, her coat buttoned up tight against the January cold, her scarf perfectly knotted. Her dark hair was pulled back into a sleek ponytail, not a strand out of place.

I ripped open the door. "You know about the gummy bears, don't you."

Her brow furrowed, eyes flicking to the knife I held. "What? No. What're you talking about?"

I stopped short. "Why are you here, then?"

She sighed, pulling off her gloves and tucking them into her coat pocket. "Jackson's clean." She stepped past me into the apartment. Her heels clicked against the hardwood. "The guy from AA who left the Manson book in your mailbox? He definitely did that. The fingerprints match. But he has a solid alibi for the recent attack and two murders. Plus . . ." She trailed off, turning to look at me with unnervingly focused eyes.

"Plus what?" I wanted to continue my sweep. Smith's perfume, something expensive and French, tickled my nose. Beneath it was the smell of cigarettes.

"There's been another murder," she said carefully.

"Who?" I walked over to double-check the security system. Someone had disconnected the foyer from my apartment. My skin felt too tight all over my body.

Smith didn't answer right away. Instead, she waited until I turned to her, her face carved from stone. "Where's Nicholas?"

"I don't know," I said automatically.

She took a step closer. "He's been missing since the night Trixie was murdered. His parents kicked him out the week before, they said. They don't care where he is, but they thought you might know."

"I don't," I said again, louder this time. I glanced toward Nic's room.

Smith's gaze followed mine, lingering on the closed door. "I'm not asking you to turn him in," she said, her voice tight as wire. "I just need to know if you've seen him. If you know anything."

I didn't answer. Instead, I stepped out of my apartment to check the lock on the attic door. It was still secured from the outside.

"I haven't seen him," I said. *Tell the truth, never the whole truth.* Automatic to me as breathing.

Smith's eyes tracked my movements as I returned to the apartment to check the window locks. She crossed her arms. "Fine. But I need you to know something."

Her tone stopped me in my tracks. "What?"

Her expression shifted, a jarring mix of hesitation and resolve. "Cornell Stamoran's dead," she said flatly. "Murdered in his home about an hour ago. We got an anonymous tip."

CHAPTER 56

The knife slipped from my fingers, clattered against the floor. The sound seemed to come from very far away. "That's impossible," I heard myself say. "I saw him tonight. I just picked up Julia from—" My voice cracked. "He was fine. He was alive."

"When exactly did you leave his place?"

I checked my watch, had to focus to make the numbers make sense. "Nine thirty? Maybe nine forty-five?"

"Time of death is estimated between ten thirty and eleven." She pulled out her notebook. "How was he behaving?"

I opened my mouth to answer, but no words came. Images of Corn flooded my brain. His voice, warm and certain, cutting through the chaos of my life. His laugh, a deep chuckle that started in his belly. That bushy mustache and his ridiculous Western quote T-shirts. And tonight. Tonight, when he'd said . . .

"Tuesday," Smith said again, pulling me back. "Did he say anything unusual?"

The words clawed their way out of my throat. "He told me he loved me and Julia."

Smith's brows lifted, just a fraction, but she didn't speak. She let the silence stretch, let me fill it.

"You know what I said in response?" A cry was building in my gut, and if it came out, it was going to rip my head off. "*I know.* That's it. That's what I said."

That's not what Smith was after. "Did he seem afraid? Distracted?"

I shook my head. "Just disappointed. In me. Like always." The weight of it hit me all at once, a locomotive to the chest. I covered my face with my hands, trying to hold myself together, but the grief was tearing through me. I needed to move. "I have to show you something," I said, too loud. I wiped my face with the back of my hand and led her to my bedroom. The door creaked as I pushed it open. The photo was still lying on the quilt, the gummy bears pinned neatly in a row.

Yellow, green, orange. No red.

Smith stepped closer, her eyes scanning the scene with a practiced detachment. "Explain this to me."

"It's us," I said. "Me, Trixie, Nicholas, Arsen. We used to eat them all the time, back in high school. Arsen always took the red ones."

Her gaze flicked to me. "And the photograph?"

I hesitated, but what was the point? "It's me leaving Shawn Fenton's. He's an officer with the SPPD. Sometimes we hook up. Tonight was one of those nights. Corn had Julia," I said defensively. "Arsen—" I caught myself, stopped. "Whoever did this was watching me. Photographed me leaving Shawn's. Brought the gummy bears and photo here while I picked up Julia, then killed Corn after we got home."

Smith didn't react, not visibly. She just nodded, like she'd been expecting it. "Who else knows about the gummy bears?"

The words burned my tongue. "Just the four of us."

"So, Nicholas?"

"Yeah," I said.

She watched me for a beat longer, then strode to the kitchen to use my phone. When she returned, she was all business. "The police are on their way," she said. "We'll need prints and to remove the evidence."

I nodded, holding myself as the sound of sirens grew louder outside. Minutes later, uniformed officers overran my apartment, their movements brisk and efficient as they cataloged and bagged everything. The photo. The candy. The pin.

Somehow, Julia slept through it all. Thank god, because I didn't know what I'd tell her if she hadn't. I'd moved the side table so she could get out when she woke up.

"Was there a 911 call after Corn's murder?" I asked Smith, my voice scratching. "Like the others?"

She paused in her notetaking, silver pen hovering above the page. Through my bedroom doorway, I could see the crime scene techs still working, dusting for prints, their cameras flashing as they documented the gummy bears, the photo, every detail of this home invasion.

"Yes," she said finally. "Same voice. Same pattern."

"I need to see him."

Smith tipped her head. "Who?"

"Corn. I need to make sure it's him."

Her eyes flashed. "One of the officers on the scene knew him. He's been positively ID'd."

"I need to see him. Tonight."

She paused for a moment, then nodded.

CHAPTER 57

In all my years on the force, I'd never visited the morgue, so I was surprised to see that the sheet covering Corn was blue, not white like on TV. Something about that detail broke me all over again. When the coroner pulled the sheet down, Corn's face was peaceful, his eyes closed, almost like he could've been asleep if not for the butchery across his chest.

Corn, who'd been more of a father to me than my own. Dead because of me.

Smith had told me on the drive over that he'd been stabbed multiple times in the torso and posed like the others but that he hadn't had an X carved on his body.

"If this is a copycat," she said, "we're very worried he's now preying on male victims."

My brain sought refuge in facts. Statistically, most serial killers started with caution. They began by intentionally testing the waters, perfecting their methods under the radar. But, if they weren't caught, a switch inside them often flipped. The crimes came faster, the scenes grew bloodier, the risks became bolder. Their compulsion outweighed their need for caution, the satisfaction fading faster and the cravings hitting harder. Once a serial killer escalated, their timeline collapsed. They could go from months between murders to mere days. They got sloppy, frantic, and that made them even more dangerous.

That was the common path. But sometimes, serial killers could lie in wait for years before striking again, every move of theirs calculated. Like Arsen.

"Take me home. Please."

◈

Saint Paul was steeped in an eerie predawn calm. A man with a dog, both of them wearing bright-orange vests, shuffled down a side street. We passed someone leaning over a windshield, the squeak of their ice scraper rhythmic.

I recorded it all from a great distance.

"An all-night locksmith has been called to your place." Smith's voice was careful, and she didn't look over at me as she spoke. Her hands stayed fixed at ten and two. "They won't be able to touch that fancy security system that didn't work for jackshit tonight, but they will change your locks."

"Thanks," I said. Or at least I think I did.

"You okay?"

I nodded, because "okay" was easier than the truth.

She pulled into my driveway, the crunch of tires on packed snow needling me. I wanted to tell her to leave me there, to slip into the house with no further conversation. But Smith wasn't having it. She killed the engine, turned to me, and waited. The techs' cars were still lined up out front. They'd been ordered to stay until we got back, and Coretta had been called up to watch Julia.

I sighed. "Fine," I said to her unasked question. "You can come up. Tea?"

"Tea sounds good."

Inside, I checked on Julia first. Her room was dark and warm, the moonlight catching on the tangle of her blond hair. Coretta was curled up in the old armchair beside her bed, a quilt pulled to her chin. She snored softly, the sound oddly comforting. I tried to let her presence anchor me, tried to tell myself Julia was safe, but my hands shook as I tucked her blanket tighter around her small shoulders.

"Safe" wasn't a word that belonged to us anymore.

CHAPTER 58

Smith had the tea ready when I came into the kitchen. The cheap kettle I'd thrifted years ago squatted on the stove, steam curling lazily from its spout. She must have preferred it to the microwave. Two mismatched mugs sat waiting on the table, the scent of chamomile and mint filling the air. She'd shed her blazer, and her cream turtleneck made her look softer somehow, less the hard-edged detective who'd been riding me for days.

I sat down across from her, staring into the tea as if I could find answers in its swirl.

"Have I mentioned I like your kitchen?" she asked, as if she hadn't cataloged every inch of it already. "Very lived-in."

I snorted. "You can say 'cluttered.' I won't be offended."

She didn't laugh, just cradled her mug between her palms, watching me. Waiting. She was good at her job. Most cops filled silences with noise. Questions, accusations, heavy breaths. Smith let the quiet stretch until it pulled something loose.

"Look, I get it," I finally said. "You want to talk about what I think is going on."

"That matters," she said evenly, "but that's not what I'm most concerned about right now."

"What are you concerned about, then?"

She set the mug down, leaned forward slightly. "You."

I blinked. "I'm fine."

She held herself still. “You know I read your file. Your *real* file.”

I stiffened. “You’re digging into my history?”

“Professional curiosity. Sorry.” She didn’t sound the least bit apologetic. “You know what it says? Says you were a smart cop, if a little reckless. Intuitive. Says you noticed things other people didn’t. And it says you had . . . a difficult time at the end.”

I swallowed hard, my throat suddenly dry. “Is that what we’re calling total breakdowns these days?”

She was quiet for a few beats, and then: “Tell me about Corn.” Her voice was gentle in that way cops use when they’re trying to crack you open. “How long did you work for him?”

“Two years.” I blew across the tea’s surface, watching ripples form.

“And how did that arrangement come about?”

I knew what she was doing. Starting with the easy questions, lulling me into a false sense of security before she went for the jugular. I’d done it myself, back when I wore a badge.

“He knew me from before. Thought women who grew up with trauma made the best investigators.” I shrugged. “Said we could smell predators coming.”

She nodded like I’d confirmed something. “Your father—did you know he served time in the late ’80s? Assault charge.”

The room tilted slightly. “I don’t know anything about the man after ’84.”

“You didn’t wonder?”

“Why would I? He’s the one who ditched us. He’s been dead to me ever since.”

She tilted her head, her gaze like a scalpel. “Like Nicholas is dead to you?”

I kept my face carefully blank, the way I’d learned to do when my high school boyfriend would show up in my bedroom after midnight. “I lost touch with everyone.”

“Everyone except Nicholas. Right?” Smith’s whiskey-colored eyes fixed on mine. “The one no one’s seen since that night in the trailer.”

The room felt suddenly airless. A car drove past, its headlights sweeping across the ceiling.

"I need to tell you something," I said, the words tumbling out before I could stop them. I wouldn't give up Nic, but there was something else I could come clean about. "I don't think Arsen died that night. I think he switched places with someone—put his leather jacket and ID on them, shot them in the face. He's alive, and he's come back for Julia."

For the first time, I saw something slip in Smith's professional facade. She picked up her mug with exaggerated care. "That's quite a theory."

"You think I'm crazy." I laughed, but it came out more like a sob. "That's fine. Everyone does."

"I think you're traumatized," she said carefully. "I've read your psych eval from when you left the force. That scene with the mother and baby—"

"Don't." The word cracked out.

She held up her hands in surrender. After a moment, she reached into her briefcase and pulled out a thick manila folder. "Here. Everything we have on the original Crying Killer case and the new murders. Maybe a fresh set of eyes will help."

I stared at the file like it might bite me. What trap was this? But curiosity quickly got the best of me, and I flipped through the pages—crime scene photos, witness statements, forensics reports. Some I recognized, some I didn't. My hands shook when I came across the photos from that night at the trailer.

"I should go," Smith said finally, standing. "But call me if you need anything. Day or night. In the meanwhile, I'm stationing two officers outside your house."

I walked her to the downstairs front door. When the techs finished up, I walked them out, too. By then, a cop car was sitting across the street, two shadowed officers inside.

Smith was efficient, and a woman of her word.

When I got back to the apartment, Nic was standing in the doorway to the kitchen, hand on cocked hip. She must have come in while Smith and I were at the morgue and taken my advice to stay out of Smith's way.

"Good lying," she said. "You almost sounded like you believe it yourself."

I didn't have the energy to deal with her, to tell her about Corn, about the gummy bears and the photo. "Stay out of it, Nic."

She raised an eyebrow. "Where am I supposed to go?"

"Where *do* you go?" I asked, slow fury building in my gut. I'd never have made it through if she hadn't shown up when she did two years ago. I'd needed her, and so I hadn't asked many questions. What had that mistake cost me? "Where do you go when you're not at work?"

She knew what I was asking because she knew me better than anyone else. A broken half smile cracked her face. "I've always taken winding roads to get anywhere. You know that." Her expression hardened. "And I've never killed anyone." She walked off to her bedroom, her shoulders set in anger.

I leaned against the wall, my bones made of lead. Once I could move again, I grabbed Smith's file off the kitchen table and took it to the couch. I wouldn't lie in my bed tonight.

I was sure of only two things.

Arsen Bauer didn't die that night, and I was running out of time.

CHAPTER 59

I spent the weekend cocooned with Julia, loving on her in a frantic way. I told Nic about Corn's death, but I couldn't bear to tell Julia, not yet. We watched *The Secret Garden* twice, buried in blankets on the couch, the sunlight low and gold through the frosted windows. I braided her hair, cooked chocolate chip pancakes shaped like Mickey Mouse, followed her from room to room. By Sunday night, she wrinkled her nose and told me to "go relax or something," so Nic pulled me to the kitchen for a hand of cards.

My guilt was a constant companion, raw and bloody.

Coretta and I had new locks—she was surprisingly quiet about the hassle—and I'd reprogrammed the security system. Someone had gotten the code, somehow. Coretta and Nic both swore they hadn't shared it with anyone, so one of us must have been watched plugging it into the front door.

When Monday came, I didn't want to let Julia go to school, but Nic convinced me we had to keep her life as normal as we could. Still, I walked her almost all the way to her classroom even though it embarrassed her. She glanced over her shoulder twice, pink-cheeked and glaring, before—just shy of her homeroom—she rolled her eyes. "You can go, Mom."

I told her I wanted to meet her new teacher, but she insisted I'd have to wait until conferences, so I walked out to my car and pointed it toward the last place on earth I wanted to go: Lilydale. I didn't know what answers I'd find, but I had nowhere else to look. Might as well return to the source of all ills, see what I could see.

I passed Saint Cloud with no problem, but when I exited the freeway, my skin began to crawl.

Sometime in the past eight years, the road had changed, a new four-lane rerouting the traffic directly from Saint Cloud to Lilydale, skipping all the small towns. Rockville. Cold Spring. Richmond. I cracked the window as I drove, sucking in mouthfuls of frigid air like a brutal balm. The closer I got, the quieter the world seemed to grow.

My hands tightened on the wheel as I passed the LILYDALE—COME HOME FOREVER sign, its paint peeling at the edges. The dark ring of trees that circled the town proper loomed ahead, their bare branches making a stark lacework against the winter sky. You had to drive through them to reach downtown, like passing through a portal. *Pop.* Then suddenly you were inside, trapped in a pocket with the other poor souls.

I started at the Sunrise Estates trailer park, where Arsen had destroyed everything. The metal homes huddled together against the cold, their windows dark and watchful. Our trailer was still there, wedged between the woods and a gravel lot. I expected a wave of great sadness seeing it again, but I felt only numb. It looked exactly the same. Stained blue siding, the front steps sagging with rot, like time hadn't moved at all.

I could almost see the three of us the night we'd brought Julia home. My sister glowing like she'd swallowed the sun, Nick making faces at the baby. Me, promising—*swearing*—we'd all make it out of there. That we'd be better than this place.

The memory made my gut churn, so I pulled out and drove to the Dairy Queen where the three of us used to hang. It was boarded up now, its red roof faded to the color of old blood. We'd sit on the concrete picnic tables out front, letting the ice cream drip down our fingers while we talked about escape plans—California, New York, anywhere but Lilydale. Nick decided that after he got discovered at O'Gara's, he'd move out to San Francisco, where he could finally be herself. My sister and I agreed we could make that work.

I cruised past Saint Patrick's Church, where Mom took us every Sunday she was well enough, its spire stabbing the sky. Past the elementary school, where Mrs. Hamline had caught Nicholas passing me notes in fourth grade and made us read them out loud: "Do you think Bobby Larson is cute? Circle one: YES, NO, MAYBE." Past the park where me and my sister played red rover until the summer when games started feeling too childish, when boys' stares started following us home.

Somehow, everything looked smaller than I remembered, compressed by time and memory. I kept going until I reached the Andrews home, situated at the edge of Lilydale, where farmland bled into town. Their house was as I remembered, a weathered two-story with a wraparound porch and dormant flower boxes. I killed the engine but left the keys in the ignition, wondering why Margot and I hadn't built on our friendship after we got over our embarrassment at making out.

But I knew the answer. The Three Musketeers didn't let anyone in, not for long.

A sharp rap on my window yanked me back to the present. I jumped, my heart slamming against my ribs, before I recognized Bob Andrews's weathered face. His eyes narrowed as he bent down to peer into my car.

"Can I help you?" His breath fogged the glass between us.

I rolled down the window, mustering a smile. "Mr. Andrews? I was friends with your daughter Margot in high school. I'm in town and was hoping to catch up with her. Is she around?"

He shook his head. "She's stationed in Germany. Army life suits her." He smiled. "She just made sergeant."

The blood in my veins turned to ice water. There was suspecting, and then there was hearing it. Margot wasn't a stewardess, wasn't even in Minnesota. Which meant the phone call, the hotel meeting . . .

"You all right?" Mr. Andrews asked. "You've gone nearly as white as the snow."

"Fine," I managed. "Just surprised. I could have sworn someone said they'd seen her recently."

He grinned, proud papa. "Nope. Joined the army straight out of high school, been in Europe six months now. What did you say your name was?"

I could barely hear him over the roaring in my ears. Arsen had set me up. He was watching me, playing with me, seeing how close he could get.

And I'd walked right into it.

I mumbled something to Mr. Andrews about needing to go, cranked up my window, and threw the car into reverse. As I peeled away from the curb, I caught a glimpse of him in my rearview mirror, still standing in the road with his hand raised in confused farewell.

The trees closed around me as I fled, their shadows reaching across the road like grasping fingers. I didn't breathe properly until I crossed the town limits.

CHAPTER 60

Before

The August heat pressed down on Lilydale like a damp towel, making the town feel smaller than it already was. Trixie adjusted the straps of her nearly new Esprit tank top, bright pink with white piping. The fabric clung to her fourteen-year-old frame in a way that made her feel like she was somebody worth looking at.

Tuesday rolled her eyes from across their shared bedroom. "You're gonna get a sunburn wearing that."

"Better than looking like I shopped at Kmart," Trixie shot back. She grabbed her shoplifted Watermelon Slice lip gloss and slicked it on.

Nick appeared in the doorway wearing cutoff jeans and a Duran Duran T-shirt that hung loose on his skinny frame. His curly hair was feathered and held in place with enough Aqua Net to survive a tornado. "You two ready? The DQ's gonna run out of ice cream if we wait much longer."

They walked through the heavy air. Lilydale appeared peaceful enough in the summer light. Tree-lined streets, tidy lawns. But if you looked close, you could see how it was a trap, the way the dark ring of woods circled it, the way everyone knew everyone else's business but pretended not to see the bruises.

The Dairy Queen sat on the edge of downtown, a handful of cars parked in the lot, mostly pickups. The three of them claimed an open picnic table out front.

"I'm getting a Peanut Buster Parfait," Nick announced, digging quarters from his pocket. "Live a little."

Tuesday's eyes narrowed. "Where'd you get the money?"

"None of your beeswax."

Trixie was starting to ask Nick if he had enough for onion rings, too, when the rumble of a motorcycle drowned her out. A black Kawasaki pulled into the parking lot, chrome gleaming beneath a layer of road dust. The rider killed the engine and pulled off his helmet, shaking out dark hair.

"MTV video much?" Tuesday muttered under her breath.

The guy was older—maybe twenty-two or twenty-three—with the kind of lean build that looked good in tight Levi's and a black T-shirt. But it was the leather jacket he wore that caught Nick's and Trixie's attention. Military-style, worn soft with age, molded to his body like armor.

A second bike pulled up behind the first, ridden by a guy with sandy hair and nervous eyes, no helmet. The two of them headed toward the DQ window, but the dark-haired one caught sight of their table and changed course.

"Well, well," he said, his voice low and amused. "Look what we have here."

He had pale-green eyes and a smile that made Trixie's stomach flip. She'd seen plenty of boys try to look dangerous, but it seemed to come naturally to this dude.

Tuesday caught the desperation written across her sister's face and wanted to tell her to cool it.

"You guys from around here?" he asked, though his eyes stayed fixed on Trixie.

She tilted her chin, meeting his gaze. "Depends who's asking."

His smile widened. "Arsen Bauer. And you are?"

"Not interested," Trixie said, but the way she was playing with the strap of her tank top said otherwise.

Tuesday shifted uncomfortably on the bench. Nick stayed quiet.

"Cute," Arsen said. "I like a girl with backbone." He glanced at Tuesday and then back to Trixie, ignoring Nick. "You two wouldn't happen to be Daryl Hendrickson's kids, would you?"

Tuesday sat up straight. "How do you know that?"

"My dad." Arsen squinted toward the sun. Tuesday thought he was doing it intentionally, knowing how good he looked. "Aramis, he's the police chief. He and Donny McDowell used to hang out with your old man before he skipped town." Arsen's expression shifted, something calculating flickering behind his eyes. "Thought I saw Daryl around last week, actually. But I must've been mistaken."

Trixie's throat went tight. "He's been gone awhile. Hasn't been back once."

"That true?" Arsen seemed genuinely surprised. "Huh. My mistake."

The sandy-haired guy had finished ordering and was walking back toward them, carrying a cone that was already dripping in the heat. "Come on, man," he called to Arsen. "I wanna hit the road."

Arsen ignored him. "You hear about those boys who were abducted for a minute?" he asked, his voice casual but his eyes still sharp. "Lilydale boys?"

By that time everybody had, just like everyone knew Arsen's dad, Police Chief Rammy Bauer, was in charge of the case. "Yeah," Nick said carefully. "We heard."

Arsen studied Nick for a minute before speaking. "Strange thing," he said. "Makes you wonder what kind of monsters are hiding in a place like this."

The way he said it made Tuesday's skin crawl, but she kept her expression neutral. "Every place has monsters."

"True," he said, and his smile returned, aimed directly at Trixie. "Anyway, maybe I'll see you around, Hendrickson."

"Maybe you will," Trixie replied, her own smile widening.

He was walking back toward his motorcycle when Tuesday stiffened. "I have to go," she said quickly. "I just remembered—I'm supposed to be somewhere."

"Where?" Trixie asked suspiciously.

Tuesday was already standing, color rising in her cheeks. "Just . . . somewhere. I'll catch up with you guys later."

"You going to see that creep again?" Nick asked.

Trixie made a gagging noise. "Not the teacher. Mr. Anderson?"

Tuesday told herself she didn't owe either of them an explanation. She was the oldest. She could date who she wanted to date. Without another word, she turned and walked away, her shoulders rigid.

Trixie went back to making googly eyes at Arsen, who was mounting his bike like a cowboy.

Nick, though, watched Tuesday until she was out of sight.

CHAPTER 61

After

I roared away from Lilydale, gripping the wheel so tightly that the leather cording left imprints on my palms. Me and my sister, so lost, so desperate for some guy to love us. Where had it gotten us? One of us dead, the other to blame. I pushed the gas pedal harder. Cars lurched out of my way. Maybe they could smell the desperation rolling off me, or maybe I just looked frenzied enough to be dangerous. The thought almost made me laugh. *Frenzied.* Was this what my mom felt like during a spell?

The radio crackled with a Spin Doctors song, and I stabbed it off. I needed to think. I'd always assumed Arsen was the only one left besides me and Nic who knew all the details. The X's carved into backs, his obsession with *Helter Skelter*, the way we'd sort gummy bears by color. But had we told anyone else? We were outcasts, sure, huddled together in our dark little corner of the lunchroom, but my memories of Margot reminded me that none of us had been joined at the hip. My brain traveled in and out of the rabbit warrens of memory.

Suddenly, I was in Saint Paul.

It seemed like I'd just left Lilydale.

Highland Park Elementary rose ahead, its brick walls solid and institutional against the winter sky. Its flag hung limp in the dead January air. I pulled into a visitor spot, my tires crunching rock salt.

The clock on my dash read 12:47. Still over two hours until dismissal, but I was going to die if I didn't make sure Julia was safe right now.

The secretary's eyes showed their whites when I burst through the office door. "Ms. Kenn? Is everything all right?"

"Fine." I was too jittery, too obvious. My pulse pounded in my throat. "I'm here for a family thing. A quick check-in. Julia's expecting me."

She studied me for a long moment, and I fought the urge to check my reflection. Could she see Arsen's evil hovering over my shoulder?

"I'll have someone grab her," she said, reaching for the phone.

I paced the narrow office while I waited, avoiding the concerned glances from the staff. The walls were covered with student artwork, tempera-paint snowmen with crooked carrot noses, cutout snowflakes, Popsicle-stick houses. A job chart with glittering metallic blue, red, and green stars bore children's names. Everything so innocent, so safe.

Soon Julia appeared in the doorway, her face pinched with worry. "Mom? What's wrong?"

"Nothing, sweetie." I wrapped my arm around her shoulders, guiding her away from the front desk. I ran my hand down her stubby braid, the gesture meant to soothe both of us, and knelt in front of her. "I just wanted to see you."

Julia squinted at me, her mouth squeezed into a frown. "You're being weird."

"Yeah." I laughed. It sounded dull. "Maybe I'm just tired. I'll pick you up after school like usual. We'll grab some rainbow sherbet on the way home. Okay?"

She nodded, but the crease in her forehead didn't smooth. "Okay."

I kissed that worry line, lingering for half a second longer than I needed to. "Love you, sweets. Now go back to class."

She glanced back at me once as she walked away. I stood in place until she was out of sight, and then I forced my feet to move, retracing my path down the hallway. By the time I hit the parking lot, my chest ached.

Where to go, with Corn gone?

There was only one place.

The familiar smell of sweat and leather hit me. The guy at the front desk barely glanced up from his newspaper, just waved me toward the changing room. I swapped my clothes for the sports bra and shorts I kept in a duffel in my car, not bothering to wrap my hands before attacking a heavy bag.

Left jab. Right cross. Left hook. The rhythm was automatic, my muscles remembering what my brain was too fried to think about. Each impact sent shock waves up my arms, and I reveled in the pain. It was cleaner than the fear.

Whack. Thud.

Who else had Arsen told? Nic had been right that the X's weren't an airtight secret—the IRC chat had confirmed as much—so what other lowlifes might have known about *Helter Skelter*, about the candy? Did they also know about Arsen sneaking into Trixie's room at night, whistling that awful song, the one that trapped her in her body? The bag swung wildly as I unleashed a flurry of strikes, my breath hitching. My knuckles split, leaving crimson smears on the vinyl.

"Jesus, lady." The desk worker's voice cut through my haze. "Take it easy."

I stumbled back, suddenly aware of my burning lungs, my trembling arms. How long had I been here? The sun slanting through the high windows had shifted, painting orange stripes across the floor.

"Sorry," I gasped, swiping sweat from my eyes. My hands throbbed in time with my heartbeat.

He tossed me a towel. "Whatever demon you're fighting, I hope you beat it."

I caught my reflection in the wall mirror—flushed face, wild eyes, blood trickling down my knuckles. I looked exactly like what I was: a woman falling off the edge.

"Me too," I said.

CHAPTER 62

That night, I curled up near Julia on the worn couch, a faded quilt tucked around us. The erratic glow of the television bathed the living room in pale blue, flicking shadows across the cracked ceiling. We had a metal bowl of popcorn on the table, buttery kernels barely touched. The movie—*Home Alone 2* from the VHS shelf—played on, Kevin screaming about being lost in New York, but my ears were trained elsewhere. Every sigh of the old Victorian, every gust of wind rattling the windows, every murmur from the pipes sharpened my brain.

Julia didn't seem to notice. She laughed at the funny parts, her small shoulders shaking. She leaned into me when the scenes turned too loud, her slight weight a comfort I didn't deserve.

"Mom, you're not watching," she said, and I realized I'd been staring at the window.

I blinked, trying to smooth the edges of my thoughts. "Of course I'm watching. The part where he drops the bricks on the guys? Classic."

Julia gave me a side-eye, a skill she'd perfected early, one of the many ways she reminded me of my sister. "Liar liar. You weren't paying attention."

I smiled faintly and tugged the quilt higher around her shoulders. "You're too smart for me, you know that?"

She rolled her eyes with exaggerated flair and reached forward for a handful of popcorn. "Mr. A says that, too."

"Your teacher?" I asked, distracted by the sound of a branch scraping against the window. I still hadn't told her about Corn because I couldn't bear to watch her heart break. She hadn't seemed to notice the cop car parked out front.

"He also said I'm a good helper," Julia announced, munching. "He let me tutor Jenny with spelling today."

I reached for my own handful of popcorn. "That's nice."

"He said my handwriting is really neat, too. Like cursive, even though we haven't learned that yet." She beamed, butter shining on her chin. "He gave me a gold star sticker and said I should be proud."

A car door slammed somewhere down the street. I jerked, spilling popcorn across my lap.

"Mom? Are you listening?"

"Of course, sweetie. Gold star. That's great."

"I want to join band next year," she said. "Do you think I could play the flute?"

"Mr. A sounds nice," I said, my ears tunneling another sound—a distant thud, maybe something in the alley. Probably a trash bin knocked over. I tried to write it off, but my body was taut, my muscles coiled.

Julia watched me, her expression sharpening. She was too young to carry that look, like she could see right through me. "You're *not* listening."

"Sorry, baby. I'm just tired. What did you say?"

Her voice dropped, becoming almost uncertain. "Coretta told me the other night that her son's back in town. Did you know that?"

I turned to her slowly, my throat tight. "What?"

"Coretta said it. Yesterday. She was mad about something he did. She said, 'Damn fool's back in Saint Paul, makin' a mess of things again.'" Julia imitated Coretta's raspy voice almost too well. "Have you seen him?"

No, I wanted to say. *I haven't seen him. I haven't seen anything.*

But the truth was I couldn't *stop* seeing things—shadows in windows, shapes across the street. Arsen's evil had become a constant presence, always just out of reach.

"I'll have to ask Coretta about that," I said finally.

Julia studied me, unblinking. When I didn't offer more, she switched tactics. "When can I see Corn again?" Her tone was light, but her fingers twisted the quilt between us. "I want to tell him about my teacher. He'd think it's cool that I have a boy one. And maybe he has a flute we could borrow. Corn has everything."

Her words gutted me. I tucked a piece of hair behind her ear and managed a weak smile. "We can see him soon," I lied. "Corn sure loves you, Jules. He thinks you're smarter than Einstein."

"Yeah?" She beamed. "When is soon?"

"Soon," I repeated softly.

She didn't ask again. Instead, she leaned against me. I kissed the top of her head, her hair smelling of fake apples and buttered popcorn.

The movie rolled on, its cheerful music discordant against the horror closing in on us. I held Julia tight, staring at the dark window across the room.

When she finally fell asleep, I carried her to her bed.

I wanted to sleep in the same room as her. Wanted to drag my mattress onto her floor, lock her bedroom door, and sit in the dark holding a knife until the sun rose. I thought of all the locks I'd already checked twice, the updated security system glowing steady and green.

But I couldn't sleep with her, I knew that.

Once you gave in to fear, it ruled your life.

CHAPTER 63

Morning crawled in gray and slow. I guided my car through Saint Paul's slush-covered streets, Julia silent beside me. She'd put her pigtails in too tight, like she was trying to pull her thoughts straight. She wouldn't let me loosen them.

"You don't have to walk me in again today," she said as we approached her school, her voice carrying that new edge she'd developed in the past couple days, keen as a paper cut.

"I want to." I needed to see her safely inside, had to know where she was every second now. The weight of Corn's death clotted my throat. I scanned the parking lot and sidewalks as we exited the car and made our way to the school. The parents were bundled in parkas and scarves, kids darting through the powdery snow with shrieks of laughter.

Harmless, I told myself. It was all harmless.

Until I saw him.

The shape of his shoulders, the slump on the left side. Was it from a bullet he'd taken that night? He stood near the playground, half turned away, his back stiff against the wind. He wore a leather, military-style jacket. My heart stopped, my breath hitching painfully in my chest.

Arsen Bauer.

Without thinking, I let go of Julia's hand and broke into a run.

"Mom?" Julia called after me, but the word was faint, lost in the pounding of my boots. The world narrowed to that figure, the curve of his head as he started to move, slowly at first, then faster when he noticed me bearing down. He disappeared around the side of the building. I pushed harder, adrenaline surging through my limbs as I took the corner after him.

For a second I thought I'd lost him. Then I spotted the back of his jacket disappearing into the staff entrance. I lunged forward, slamming against the heavy door just before it closed. My shoulder screamed in protest, but I shoved my way inside. Looked around. The hallway in this part of the school was empty. My breath came in harsh gasps, echoing against the tiled walls.

"Arsen," I yelled, my hands up near my chest, ready to strike. I moved forward slowly, scanning each door, each shadow.

Suddenly, a man stepped out of the nearest classroom. He wasn't poised to run. He wasn't even startled. Instead, he blinked at me, confused, his hands raising as he instinctively mirrored my posture. He was tall, maybe thirty, with a clean-shaven face and brown hair that curled slightly at the ends. He was wearing the leather jacket I'd just seen.

"Can I help you?" he asked, his voice polite but edged with unease.

I stopped cold, the adrenaline crashing into confusion, then humiliation. I was staring at a man who had all of Arsen's notes but none of the tune. He looked so bewildered that I wanted to crawl out of my own skin.

"Mom!" Julia's voice came from down the hall, drenched in embarrassment. She was approaching with the principal, Mrs. Linden. Julia's face had gone scarlet.

"This is Mr. Abrams," Mrs. Linden said, clearly trying to smooth over the scene I'd just caused. "He's Julia's new homeroom teacher."

"I . . ." My voice faltered, my chest still heaving. "I'm sorry."

Mr. Abrams just nodded, stepping aside to let Julia enter, his eyes pinned on me. She wouldn't even look at me. "I'll pick you up later," I said to her back, my voice weak.

She didn't say a word.

CHAPTER 64

I couldn't put it off any longer. It was time to return to Corn's office.

I found it cold and dim, the blinds half drawn against the morning light.

Empty.

It wasn't just the absence of him. The place felt hollow, drained of the energy that usually filled it. His coffee cup still sat on the desk, half full, the cream powder he used forming a rainbow skin across the top.

I couldn't help but imagine him here, alive. Pushing his glasses up his nose, calling me "kid," handing me a file, his blazer opening far enough for me to see whatever silly Western movie quote he was wearing today. It was too much. I closed his office door and climbed the narrow stairs to his apartment. Yellow crime scene tape still clung to the doorframe. Smith had told me they were done here, so I pushed it to the side and entered. His place, usually much neater than his office, looked ransacked, though I imagined the techs had done their best to be careful.

Inside, everything felt wrong. The air stank with the mineral scent of old blood, furniture was slightly out of place from where the evidence team had worked.

I made my way to his bedroom.

They'd taken his mattress. That must have been where it happened.

Smears of fingerprint powder coated the nightstand, the doorknobs, the window frames. The peace lily in the corner drooped, forgotten.

Swallowing the lump in my throat, I went to the kitchen and began to clean. I wiped down the counters, watered his plants, the few that'd survived his haphazard care. As I put his home in order, I thought about his funeral, who was in charge of it. He had a great-aunt who lived in Michigan. Had someone told her? I'd help with the planning, do whatever needed doing.

Anything to keep moving. Because if I was still, I'd have to think about how he'd looked the last time I saw him, worried and caring. So I cleaned like Lady Macbeth on speed. I straightened papers, wiped down surfaces, tried to restore order to the chaos. It took the better part of the morning, but when I was done, his apartment smelled of Lysol and looked like it was ready for a shoot in *Retired Man* magazine.

It didn't matter to anybody but me.

I couldn't put it off any longer. Time to do the same to his office.

Once inside, the mail caught my eye, gathered as it was on the floor inside the door. On top was the envelope from the drugstore where I'd dropped off the photos I'd taken of Hachette's stalker. They must have located the film they'd misplaced.

I opened it, flipping through the images, my gut tightening with each one.

The stalker was familiar, painfully so. It wasn't until I reached the last photo that I could be certain. The slumped shoulder. The shape of his grainy profile. Older, but unmistakable.

"Oh god." *It's Arsen.*

I maintained that train of thought for exactly one second before I realized what was happening, the same thing that had just happened at Julia's school. I thought every man looked like Arsen now. Every stranger with a limp, every shadow in a dark alley. They all wore his face. They all haunted me.

I dropped the photos, my hands shaking. I needed to acknowledge it, the thing I'd been refusing to face: I was unraveling, exactly like I had right before I'd left the force, exactly as I'd seen my own mother do, day by aching day. I sank into Corn's chair, the leather still holding the memory of his shape. The office was a tomb, dust motes dancing in shafts of winter sunlight. Everything I'd lost pressed in around me—my dad and then my mom, my sister, Corn, my grip on reality. I couldn't lose Julia, too. I couldn't survive it.

"I need help," I said to the empty room.

The words hung there, honest and terrifying.

CHAPTER 65

The top photo on the stack I dropped slid down, falling on top of the Hachette file. The pages shivered as I flipped the file open. Corn's cramped handwriting filled the intake form, precise as chicken scratch: "Client specifically requested Tuesday Kenn. Prefers female investigator."

Corn wouldn't have thought twice about that note. He preferred working with women, too. But in light of everything that'd happened since then, the words stared up at me now, threatening.

Client specifically requested Tuesday Kenn.

Maybe, just this once, I wasn't wrong about everything. I flipped through the file, rereading details I already knew. Hachette had said she was being followed by a man, someone she'd noticed lurking near her apartment and her workplace, presumably the same guy who was calling her and hanging up. According to Hachette, he hadn't written her any notes, had never spoken, just left her with the oppressive weight of being watched. But I saw something new in the file, a tiny margin note in Corn's handwriting: "Roommate?"

I closed the file with a snap. I'd been coming loose all morning, but this was something I knew how to do. I grabbed my coat and headed out.

The front security door to Hachette's place was propped open with a phone book, letting in a knife of winter air. I entered a narrow foyer, her door to my right, the door to apartment 1 to my left. Hachette's doorframe still had Christmas tinsel taped to it, gone dull and limp.

A woman in her early twenties answered my knock. She had the sallow, underfed look of a college student who'd recently discovered cigarettes could substitute for meals. Her dark roots showed beneath fading purple hair.

"Yeah?" She examined me through the crack, chain still latched.

"I'm looking for Melissa Hachette." My voice came out steadier than I felt. "I'm from the detective agency she hired."

"Oh, right, the stalker thing." She rolled her eyes and closed the door to undo the chain. When she pulled it open, she stepped aside so I could enter. "She's not here. Took off for Cancún this morning. Some last-minute travel deal she nabbed."

The apartment smelled of Cup Noodles. A futon sprawled against one wall, draped with a tie-dyed tapestry. Kurt Cobain stared out from a poster, already looking like a ghost. MTV played silently on a tiny TV perched on milk crates.

"When will she be back?" I asked, fighting to keep my body language relaxed.

The roommate shrugged, collecting empty Diet Coke cans from the coffee table. "Week, maybe? She was pretty vague about it."

I nodded, going for reflective. "She trying to get away from the man who's been following her?"

The roommate snorted. "That was all bullshit. Some guy hired her to *pretend* she was being stalked. Paid her to call up someone claiming to be an old friend from high school, too. Said he was trying to get back at a girl." She caught my expression. "What?"

I felt like I'd fallen in a washing machine, fear and anger sloshing me around. Anger came out on top. "What kind of woman pretends to be stalked?" My voice rose. "Do you have any idea what that does? How it hurts real victims?"

She took a step back, eyes wide. "Hey, don't shoot the messenger. I just live here."

She was right. This wasn't her fault. I pressed my palm against my forehead, trying to push back the pounding in my skull. "I'm sorry. Do you know the name of the man who hired her?"

"No idea. Some guy she met at a bar, I think." She was edging toward her bedroom. "Look, I've got class."

I knew I was taking up too much space, but I couldn't rein myself in. "Did she leave a number where she could be reached?"

"Nope." Her tone said that even if Hachette had, she'd never give it to me. "Said she wanted to get off the grid."

The roommate was all but backed into a corner. I needed to hit the road before she called the cops on me. I left her a card, told her to get ahold of me if she thought of anything else. She nodded. I wondered if she waited until I reached my car to throw the card away, or if she tossed it as soon as the door closed.

Once outside, I drove to the nearest phone booth and dialed Detective Smith's direct line at the precinct. A receptionist answered.

"Detective Smith isn't available. Can I take a message?"

I gripped the phone tighter. "Yes. Please tell her Tuesday Kenn called. It's urgent she contact me as soon as possible."

A shockingly red cardinal landed on the snowy ground next to the phone booth, cocking its head at me. Its black eyes held no answers.

CHAPTER 66

The sun was painting the snow in dirty shades of bruise when I got home. Detective Smith stood on my front porch, breath clouding. She had her hands jammed in her pockets, shoulders hunched against the cold.

"You sure respond quick to phone messages," I said, fumbling with my keys.

"We're going to exhume Arsen Bauer," she said without preamble. "I wanted you to hear it from me."

Her declaration hit me like a two-by-four. The world narrowed to her face, her amber eyes steady, and for a moment, I couldn't speak. Did I want to hug her or punch her? "Why?"

She studied me with her hawk's gaze. "Mind if we take this inside? It's freezing out here."

She was holding something back. I could see it in the tightness around her mouth. But I nodded, stepping past her to unlock the door. The keypad beeped as I entered the new code. When we reached my apartment, it was chilly. I lowered the heat during the day to save money. I turned it up now, flipping on lights as we moved through the rooms. In the kitchen, I filled the kettle and set it on a burner, mostly so I had something to do with my hands.

Smith settled at the table but didn't remove her coat and hadn't taken off her shoes. "The voice analysis came back on those 911 calls," she said, watching me. "The ones after the two recent murders, plus

Corn's. It's not an exact science, but the techs say there are a lot of similarities to the voice from the Crying Killer's original calls to the radio station."

A terrible pain pierced me on the left side. For a moment, I wondered if I was having a heart attack. I leaned against the stove.

"There's more," Smith continued. "Jackson Lightman, the AA guy who admitted he planted that copy of *Helter Skelter* in your mailbox? He claims a man matching Arsen's description paid him five hundred bucks to do it."

"And you believe him?" The kettle screamed, and I jumped. I'd only put enough water into it for one cup. I poured it into a mug, dunked a tea bag, offered it to Smith. My heart was doing a terrible dance behind my ribs.

"We didn't at first. Sounded like bullshit when we brought him in. But now?" She shrugged. "And then there's the partial print we lifted from Corn's apartment."

My mouth was so dry that my top lip stuck to my teeth. "Arsen's?"

She nodded. "It's possible. We're fast-tracking the DNA testing once we have the exhumed remains from his grave. This case is priority now, given the potential connection to an active murder investigation."

My head spun. I did my best to hide my thoughts, but Smith's gaze dissected me with the precision of a surgeon.

"You never believed," she said, her tone surprised, almost accusatory, "that he was the body they'd buried."

"He's not." The certainty in my voice seemed to surprise us both. "He's alive. He's been alive this whole time."

Smith nodded slowly. "I think you might be right."

Something in my chest cracked open. All these years of feeling paranoid, and finally someone was listening. The liquor of relief was so strong that it made me dizzy. "I think Arsen might've paid a woman to pretend she was being stalked, too. Melissa Hachette. She came to Corn and specifically requested me. I took pics of the guy following her, and they look like Arsen."

Smith sat up straighter. "Can you get me those snaps?"

"Yeah," I said. "But none of them show his face clearly."

She nodded. We were both silent for a couple beats.

"When?" I asked. "When will they dig up the body?"

"Tomorrow, we're hoping." She met my eyes. For a moment, neither of us spoke. The only sound was the faint hum of the radiators, the house settling around us. Then Smith closed her notebook and tucked it back into her coat, her tea untouched. "If he's alive, we'll find him," she said.

My throat tightened, but I nodded. "Yeah. We will."

She glanced around the room, her eyes lingering on Julia's art stuck to the fridge. Then she turned back to me. "I'll keep you updated," she said. "And I'll let you know as soon as we have the DNA results."

I walked her down to the exterior door, the cold air rushing in as she stepped outside. She paused on the porch, looking across the street at the cop car that'd been a steady presence. Then she turned to me. "Take care of yourself, Tuesday."

I watched her walk down the steps, my heart pounding like a war drum. But it wasn't fear anymore. It was something else entirely, something powerful.

I no longer had to fight alone.

CHAPTER 67

Kids streamed out of Highland Park Elementary's double doors wearing bright coats, their backpacks heavy with homework. Julia stood apart from the crowd, hair coming loose from her morning pigtails. Something in her posture—shoulders tight, chin lifted—reminded me so much of my sister that my throat ached.

She saw me and waved, her blueberry-colored mitten a bright spot against the dreary sky.

"Hey, kiddo," I said as she climbed into the car. I forced a smile, but it felt brittle. I knew what I had to do. No putting it off any longer.

"Hi, Momma!" she chirped, her cheeks pink from the cold. She'd already forgotten about the embarrassment of this morning, in that glorious way that only children could pull off. She wriggled out of her backpack and buckled herself in. "Mr. A let us play *Oregon Trail* today. Sarah's wagon fell in the river again, and she got so mad she almost cried."

I pulled out from the curb and over to the nearest lot so I wasn't holding up the pickup lane. I put the car into park and turned to her. I unbuckled her and held her mittened hands. "Sounds like a rough day on the trail."

"Yeah, but I made it all the way to Oregon! No dysentery or anything."

Her voice was bright, bubbling with excitement, and I was about to extinguish that joy like rain on a match. I drew a shaky breath. "Julia," I began, my voice breaking. "There's something we need to talk about."

Her chatter stopped instantly, and she stared at me with wide eyes, her curiosity quickly replaced by fear. "What is it?"

"It's Corn." My voice was reedy. "He . . . Someone hurt him. He's gone."

She looked confused. "When's he coming back?"

I swallowed. "He isn't, baby. He's dead."

A tear leaked down her cheek, and then she scurried over to bundle herself into my lap, barely fitting below the steering wheel before she started wailing. I held her, breathing in the scent of chalk dust and shampoo.

"I'm so sorry," I whispered into her hair. "I'm so sorry for everything you've lost."

Including the things she didn't even know about. Was that the way of parents everywhere? Holding back life's storm clouds so their children could walk in the sunlight? She and I sat there for several minutes weeping together, the car's heater struggling against the chill. Finally, Julia's sobs ebbed.

"Who hurt him?" she asked, sniffling. "Is that why there's a policeman outside our house?"

My cheeks blazed. I'd thought I was saving her from worry, and here I was only keeping secrets. No more. "Yeah, baby, it is. They don't know for sure who hurt Corn, but they think they do, and until they catch him, they want to make sure we're protected."

I could feel her nod in my arms. She stayed like that for a few more minutes before pulling back. "Mr. A asked about you today," she said, wiping at her tear-swollen face.

"What?" The change of subject gave me whiplash.

"After this morning? He was pretty freaked at first, but then he said he thought he recognized you. Asked if we lived in his neighborhood." She sniffled.

I'd given her so much to carry alone. "Julia." I tipped up her chin. It was like looking at a miniature of my sister. "Listen to me. Don't tell grown-ups where we live unless I okay it first, like with Sarah's parents."

"But—"

"No one," I repeated. "Promise me."

She nodded, chin trembling. I buckled us both up and pulled out. We drove in silence for several minutes, heading for Corn's. She deserved some closure.

Behind us, darkness gathered in the corners of the city, waiting its turn.

CHAPTER 68

I could feel the cold working its way through the soles of my boots as we stomped toward Corn's building, Julia chirping at my side about some fight on the playground. It wasn't hard to pretend I was listening—I had plenty of practice—but I refused to keep letting her words slip through me, weightless, snowflakes melting on contact.

"He said it was none of my business, but I wasn't going to let Sarah get pushed around, Mom. You'd understand." She stared up at me with those earnest blue eyes, my mother's eyes. Her Hendrickson nose crinkled slightly, the way Trixie's used to.

"Of course I do, baby," I said, holding the door open and ushering her upstairs. The familiar smell of curry comforted me, and I hoped it was doing the same for her.

The cops on bodyguard duty had followed me to Julia's school, then here. The plan was for Julia to do her homework while I cleaned some more, plus for her to pick out something that reminded her of Corn. I hoped it'd give her some comfort to be here as I finished getting his effects in order. I was probably out of a job now, but that seemed the least of my worries.

"You ready to go in, Jules?" I asked her outside Corn's office door.

She nodded resolutely.

We stepped into the familiar scent of burned coffee, the faint mildew of papers, and Old Spice. *Corn.* For a moment I was shellacked to his door, worried what this would do to Julia. She darted ahead, her sneakers squeaking. She went straight to his snow globe collection and picked up the one he'd brought back from Isla Mujeres.

"This was his favorite," she said. "He thought it was funny because there's no snow in Mexico. He said he'd take me sometime. Do you think you and me could go?"

I blinked back tears. "That'd be nice, baby. Are you okay starting your homework while I go through this pile on Corn's desk?"

"I'm not a *baby*." She huffed and dropped to the floor with her backpack, narrating her every move to drive home her point. *"Now I'm taking out paper. Now I'm reaching for a marker. All without supervision."*

I smiled despite myself and started in on the stacks, paper clips scattered across them like spilled candy. It took an hour to arrange the main paper mountain into three piles: closed cases, open cases, and garbage. I planned to bring the open cases home with me and contact the clients from there, tell them Corn was closed for business.

Once the desktop papers were arranged, I moved on to the drawers. The top one stuck when I tugged it, the way cheap office furniture did in the winter. I had to give it a good yank, and when it finally slid free, a manila folder labeled TUESDAY sat right on top, fat with papers.

"Look at this, Momma!" Julia had been telling me about the Valentine's Day party coming up, segueing to how Tommy Jenkins recently ate twenty cherry Pixy Stix and got sent to the nurse because of a terrible tummy ache. Now she held up a sheet of homework with a red "100%" on it next to a gold star. "Corn would have been proud of this one."

I nodded, my hands trembling as I opened the folder. My vision blurred reading the letterhead: LAST WILL AND TESTAMENT.

"I know he would've been proud, sweetie." The words were pebbles in my mouth.

Julia's voice faded as I scanned the pages.

It was all there, outlined in Corn's no-nonsense tone, even in his writing. The PI agency was mine. The building was Julia's. The rent from the restaurant below would cover the mortgage until she turned twenty-five, when she'd inherit it outright.

I slid off the chair and sank to the ground, the cold linoleum pressing against me. Corn had always treated us like family, but this was more than I could bear. A sob ripped through my chest. All this time, he'd been planning, preparing, making sure we'd be okay.

Small arms wrapped around my neck. Julia's voice, high and earnest: "Don't cry, Momma. It's going to be okay. I miss Corn, too."

I tried to speak but couldn't. Instead, I pulled her into my lap, clutching her like an anchor in the storm of my grief.

"It's okay, Momma," she repeated, patting my back with all the solemn authority of an eight-year-old. "We'll be all right. We still have each other."

Her words split something open in me, and I cried harder, holding her tighter.

Corn was gone, but even in death, he'd managed to wrap us in his love.

CHAPTER 69

Later that same night, I ran Julia a bath at home, dumping in extra Mr. Bubble until the foam rose like meringue. She splashed happily, making up stories about her rubber duck being a secret agent.

"He needs quackup!" She dunked her plastic shark toy beneath the suds. "Quick, Mr. Chompers, save Agent Quackerton! Momma, can you get me another cup? I need to bail out the boat."

"Sure, baby."

I padded down the hall to the kitchen, where Nic leaned against the blue counter, arms crossed, her gaze dancing. She must have come home while I was getting Julia's bath ready. "Are you *literally* trying to keep her in a bubble now?"

I rubbed at my temple. The headache had returned the second we'd walked through the apartment door. "I brought her to Corn's with me. A bath after seemed like a good idea." I didn't mention the will, and I didn't want to examine too closely why not.

I'll tell her later.

"But you're still going to let her go to school?" Nic asked.

When I didn't answer, she continued. "Julia needs routine. Structure. School is important—"

"Yes," I said angrily, interrupting her. "I'm going to keep letting her go to school!"

Julia's splashing stopped. "You okay, Momma?"

"You're scaring her," Nic said softly.

"I'm okay, baby girl!" I called out. Then, to Nic: "I'm *protecting* her."

When Nic stared at me rather than answering, I felt something growing in my stomach, riding on the backs of all the people who'd shown up for me since I'd moved to the Cities with Julia. Coretta, always there when I needed her, even in the middle of the night. Smith getting someone to change our locks, assigning cops to protect us, pursuing the possibility that Arsen was still alive. Corn, taking care of Julia and me from beyond the grave.

For the first time since my sister's death, I considered that I might not be completely worthless. It gave me the strength to ask the questions I should have a long time ago. "Nic, where were you when those two women were murdered and the third attacked, all of them with the X on their back? Or when Corn was killed?" My voice was rising of its own accord. I forcibly reined it in. I didn't want to freak out Julia.

"You think I—" She recoiled as if slapped. "That's not fair," she said quietly.

"You're right." Something bitter curled in my throat. "It's not. But neither is any of this. So tell me. Every time something terrible happens, you conveniently vanish. Where do you go?"

The silence stretched taut.

She stared at me for a long moment, her lips pressing into a thin line. Then, without another word, she turned, grabbed her coat, and stormed out the front door, the echo of her boots fading down the stairs.

CHAPTER 70

Smith now had a task force devoted to the case, and Julia's school knew she was never to be out of their sight. For all her weird moods lately, Nic had been right. Julia needed normal, not a mom who showed up at recess wearing night vision goggles and a bulletproof vest. So, after a breakfast of Marshmallow Mateys for her and instant coffee for me, I dropped her off at school, trying to swallow past a gluey ball of fear the entire time.

On the drive, out of the blue, Julia said, "I think I saw Coretta's son last night."

I yanked the car to the curb, ignoring the angry honk behind us. She'd never met him, something Coretta was vigilant about. She'd told me her son was not to be trusted. To Julia, he was simply someone Coretta referred to, a man who lived inside that one picture frame in her bedroom.

"What time?" I asked Julia. "What did you see exactly?"

"I don't know." Her face crumpled. "It was dark. I couldn't sleep and went out for water. I thought I saw a man walk out our door, then I heard someone on the stairs out in the hall, but maybe I didn't?"

Tears spilled down her cheeks. I'd pushed too hard, let my fear infect her. I gathered her close again, feeling her shoulders shake. "Shh, it's okay. You're safe. I've got you. You're sure it was last night? Because I've been working out up in the attic with my punching bag. You might have just seen me."

"I miss Corn," she whispered against my coat.

"I know, baby. I know. I do, too." I stroked her hair, wishing desperately for my own mother. Not the one who couldn't keep her worlds straight, who required constant care and kid gloves. No, I wanted the one who kissed away hurts and made the monsters disappear.

After a few more minutes of cuddles, I drove Julia the rest of the way to school. She didn't turn to wave like she usually did. I watched her tiny form disappear through the doors, wondering how much longer we could keep going like this. Thanks to Corn, we had options now. We could take a trip far away. Me, Julia, maybe even Nic if she ever spoke to me again. Hell, we could bring Mom if they'd let her out, turn it into a full dysfunctional family adventure. There was enough money to escape to somewhere warm, somewhere safe, not returning to Minnesota until the police had done their job.

I updated the cops keeping an eye on me and headed back to Lilydale.

I hesitated outside Evie's Flower Shop on Main Street, my hand on the door handle. I'd graduated with Evie. Would she recognize me? Ask how I was doing? For a lot of us, growing up in a small town had been a master class in swallowing our screams. But there were those lucky kids who didn't even know they were supposed to be scared all the time, who hadn't even known that survival was on the table. Which category had Evie landed in?

I supposed it didn't matter. She was the only game in town. When I stepped inside, the warmth and the sweetness of fresh flowers wrapped around me. Surprisingly, no one pointed, no one whispered accusations about "that Hendrickson girl." The clerk smiled politely, and that was it. I wasn't the center of anyone's world, for better or worse, exactly as Liz Bauer had informed me all those years ago.

I chose a bouquet of red roses, their petals so velvety they seemed unreal. It was the fanciest flower my sister and I could think of as kids, back when our imaginations were the only thing we owned outright.

◈

The cemetery lay just outside town, its wrought iron gates flanked by bare oaks reaching their skeletal arms to the sky. The snow I walked through was crystalline, a million flakes joining to form tiny, crunchy blocks.

Her headstone was smaller than I remembered. TRIXIE HENDRICKSON, the granite proclaimed. Below that, dates that made me dizzy to look at. I didn't know what to say. What was the proper etiquette for grave-visiting when you were only brave enough to come back because someone else you loved had just been murdered?

"Hey, sis," I murmured finally. "It's been a while."

The silence stretched. I felt foolish, but then I remembered the way she used to laugh-snort, how she'd say my name like it was a code only we understood, the promises we made to each other. I knelt, setting the scarlet roses on the pristine white snow.

"I love you and I'm sorry," I whispered, tears blurring my vision. "For everything."

CHAPTER 71

Before

The night before Julia's birth, Trixie, Tuesday, and Nicholas sprawled in the old trailer's living room, high on anticipation and terror. Trixie, huge with baby, had her feet propped up on a stack of Tuesday's textbooks, which she'd, of course, bought months in advance. Nick was painting Trixie's toenails a shocking purple.

"Like grape gumballs," Trixie declared, wiggling her toes. "My girl's gonna come out loving color."

"You're sure it's a girl?" Nick asked, his voice lilting with curiosity.

Trixie grew serious. "I don't care what it is, as long as it's born healthy." She rubbed her churning belly. "No third arm, no antennae. That's all I'm asking for."

"You'll love the baby either way," Tuesday said firmly. "And if she does have an antenna, we can rent her out to NASA."

Trixie grinned. "Yeah, you'll be paying for all of it, Professor Tuesday. Or is it Dr. Tuesday? Which one makes more money?"

"Neither," Tuesday said. "But it's not about the money. It's about . . ." She trailed off, searching for the right words. "Making the world better. Or at least less stupid."

"Good luck with that," Nick said. "All I want is to live in a place where I can"—he gestured to himself—"be me. *Fully* me. I heard they've got these surgeries in Europe. Like, full-body transformation stuff. Can you imagine?"

Trixie sat up straighter, her curiosity piqued. "Europe? What's wrong with here?"

Nick snorted. "Have you met America? It's not exactly a beacon of tolerance. And Minnesota is like living in a time capsule."

Tuesday rested her elbows on her knees. "You'll get there," she told him confidently. "We'll all get there. I'll teach college, Trixie'll raise the most adorable alien baby, and Nick?" She paused, smiling. "You'll be exactly who you're meant to be."

His last two flourishes were complete. The gummy bears on Her bed, the killing of Her friend, the one who'd played daddy to Her.

No more messing around, no more hiding. Only him and Her.

Ticktock, Ms. Hendrickson. Ticktock.

His lips curled. Time was always running out. For everyone but him, at least. She thought She could forget about him. Thought She could pick a new name, walk away from Lilydale. Thought She could keep that little girl to herself, never letting her meet her real family.

He pressed a hand flat to the floor, felt the pulse of the old Victorian, everyone inside weak and breakable.

It wouldn't be long.

Ticktock.

CHAPTER 72

After

The drive out of Lilydale should have felt like relief. I'd said my apology to my sister in person. I'd attended Trixie's burial eight years earlier, of course, Mom and newborn Julia and me. But I'd been a lightning bolt of grief, not a person. We'd just put her in the ground without a ceremony because who would have arranged it?

But now I'd gone back to her grave and said what needed to be said.

So why did I feel even more unsettled as I drove past the trailer park? I didn't want to keep expecting the worst. I also didn't want to pack up Julia and Nic and my mom and hide somewhere where we didn't know anyone. I wanted to stay in Saint Paul, in my sweet apartment.

Why not imagine that Smith was going to capture Arsen? Why not picture living my life without constantly looking over my shoulder? Maybe I could finally upgrade to that home computer Corn had been after me to buy. Get the database access at the house, really build up the business. He'd left me his legacy; the least I could do was grow it, make a home for Julia and me, one where we were truly, actually, safe.

Didn't I deserve to hope?

Suddenly, I was itchy to be back in Saint Paul, closer to Julia, so of course the drive back stretched out so long it felt like I was caught in a time loop. I fiddled with the radio, but everything was Boyz II Men or that "Kiss from a Rose" song, which always made me think of Nic. She had opinions about Seal.

I finally reached the Cities with an hour left before Julia's school let out. Enough time to rush home and make some cookie dough that she and I could bake later. I was running through a mental ingredients list when I spotted Detective Smith's Crown Vic sitting in my driveway.

My stomach dropped through the floor of my car.

The detective stood on my front steps like she'd been expecting me. Well, I supposed she had, through the cops who were tailing me. She looked as put together as usual—a tailored black winter coat, her sleek hair held in a bun—but something was off, I could feel it from a distance. Her usual cool professionalism had been replaced by an electric energy that made me wary.

"We need to talk," she said as I approached. No hello, no how-are-you. Just that barely contained urgency.

"I have to pick up Julia soon." I clutched my keys, suddenly uncertain whether I was coming or going.

She watched me with those whiskey-colored eyes, sharp as cut glass. "We opened the grave this morning. Arsen Bauer's." She walked off the porch and stood in front of me. "There's a body in there, but it's not his."

The keys slipped from my fingers, hitting the ground with a sound like mouse bones breaking. "What?"

"The body in the coffin was the same one put in there in 1986, but it's not Arsen Bauer. Whoever it is had a full set of wisdom teeth, and Arsen Bauer had his extracted when he was fifteen years old. We're running the DNA, but we already know what it's going to tell us. Arsen wasn't the man shot and killed that night."

I crumpled, my legs no longer interested in holding me up. I'd known, but I hadn't *known*.

Smith crouched next to me, close enough that I could smell her expensive perfume. "We're going to find him, Tuesday. But I need you to tell me everything you remember about that night. Every detail."

I closed my eyes, but all I could see was my sister's body, blood blooming across her back like peonies. And somewhere out there, the man who'd killed her was walking free.

Just as I'd always suspected.

◈

Back in my kitchen, Smith moved with practiced precision, pulling mugs from the cupboard and setting the kettle on to boil. Our tea ritual.

I sat at the kitchen table, my hands flat against its worn surface. I'd known that corpse in the leather jacket wasn't Arsen. Or thought I'd known. But because of my mother's condition, I'd never trusted myself. Smith had confirmed it, though. No take backs.

"So, it wasn't Arsen who was buried," I said numbly. "How does that even happen?"

Smith sat across from me, her blazer creasing as she leaned forward, her expression serious. "DNA testing wasn't routine in 1986," she said. "And the police had every reason to believe it was him. They chased him into the trailer, the body matched his build, and it had his jacket and ID on it. It seemed open and shut."

"Except it wasn't." I gripped the edge of the table like it was a life raft. "So who's in the grave?"

Smith sighed, her eyes scanning my face like she was measuring how much more I could take. "We're not sure. It could have been a transient, someone Arsen paid or coerced to join him that night. Or it could have been a friend."

I shook my head, the idea refusing to settle. "What kind of friend takes a bullet for a guy like Arsen?"

"Nobody willingly." She was calm, measured. "But there's another possibility."

Her tone had shifted just enough to make my stomach twitch. I glanced at her, my voice dropping to a whisper. "What?"

"It could have been Nicholas's body."

The world tilted. For a second, I wasn't in my kitchen anymore. I was back in that trailer park, the air thick with the smell of gun smoke and blood, my heart pounding so hard it felt like it was ripping through my chest.

"No," I said, shaking my head fiercely. "That doesn't make any sense. Nicholas ran."

Smith's gaze was steady, but there was something softer in it now, a trace of sympathy. "You're sure?"

I opened my mouth to answer, but the words caught in my throat. Had Nic told me that? Or had I just decided it was true because the alternative was unbearable?

"I need a minute," I murmured, pushing back from the table. My knees felt weak as I stood. Had I taken my meds today? Or even yesterday?

Smith reached out a hand but stopped short of touching me. "Take your time," she said.

I stumbled over to the sink because I didn't know what else to do. My reflection in the window stared back, pale and shaken, hair sticking up at all angles, lipstick faded. I'd spent years trying to convince myself that the worst was over, that Arsen was dead, that the bodies in that trailer were exactly who the police said they were.

But it'd always been water slipping through my fingers.

When Smith next spoke, her words shattered the last flaxen thread holding me together. "We need to exhume your sister's body, too."

The room went crystal clear, then blurry, then sharp again. Like someone was turning a focus knob in my brain. "What?" I asked.

"We have to consider the possibility that Trixie left with Arsen that night. That they staged the whole thing."

"No." I turned, reality warping and reweaving itself. "No, I saw her. I saw her body."

"Did you?" Those amber eyes were too knowing. "Think carefully. What *exactly* did you see that night?"

Blood. Screaming. Blue and red lights strobing through the trailer windows. But Trixie's face? Had I actually seen her face?

"She wouldn't." My voice cracked. "She wouldn't leave Julia."

Smith's expression tightened. "Sometimes people make choices we don't understand."

The kettle whistled, a shrill, grating sound. I walked over and turned it off with shaking hands.

Smith continued. "I don't think this is easy to hear. And I don't think it's likely to be true. But we need to be certain. For Julia. For you. I'd like to take a swab of your DNA before I go."

For a moment, all I could do was stare at the steam rising out of the kettle. My life, carefully rebuilt piece by piece, was crashing down. A wave of panic grabbed me. "I need to get Julia." I moved so fast I knocked a mug off the counter. "I need to—"

"I've sent officers to her school," Smith said, standing, holding out her hands to calm me. "We're not letting anything happen to either of you."

But they'd let plenty happen already, hadn't they? They'd let Arsen walk away. They'd tried to convince me we were safe for eight years while he was out there somewhere, breathing the same air as my Julia. I rushed to the doorway.

"I threw up on a crime scene my first week as a rookie," Smith said, blocking my exit. "Barfed all over key evidence."

I stopped, blinking at the non sequitur.

She squinted, smiled, continued. "Veteran cops, they see this vacant look come into someone's eyes, they know they're about to lose them. Start talking about anything else, that's the trick. Gets them back in their body."

The world felt like it was hurtling past me on a conveyor belt. "Is that what you're doing? Getting me back in my body?"

"Is it working?"

I glanced down at my hands. They'd stopped shaking. "Maybe."

"Good." She gripped my arm. "Because I need you clearheaded, Tuesday. I need you to remember everything about that night. Every detail you can give us about Arsen, about Nicholas, about your sister. All the things you've been trying to forget."

The weight of eight years of carefully constructed normalcy pressed on my throat. Eight years of building a life that now felt as substantial as tissue paper in the rain. I swallowed hard. "I don't know if I can."

"You can. You have to." Smith's face was granite. "Because if Arsen is alive, if your sister is out there somewhere? This isn't over. And Julia needs you."

Julia. My North Star. My reason for everything. "Okay." I took a deep breath. "Where do you want me to start?"

"The beginning," Smith said. "Tell me everything."

I rubbed my arms. "I can do you one better. I can show you."

I led her to Nic's room.

CHAPTER 73

I was so calm. Preternaturally so. The kind of peace that came after a tornado had stripped you bare, when all that was left was your shattered body and an echoing quiet. My hands were steady on Nic's doorknob, my breath coming in huffs as I revealed the thing I should have told her from the very beginning.

"It's not Nicholas in that grave," I said. I felt like I was free-falling. "And I can prove it."

She cocked her head, the movement suggesting anger, but she let me finish.

I tapped the door, not quite ready to open it. "All through school, Nicholas knew who he was, knew that he hadn't been born in the right body." My words marched out like soldiers, my breath evening out as I felt the truth of it. "It took incredible bravery for *her* to get here. She faced hell, and she survived. Nicholas lives with me now. As Nicolette."

Smith's face screwed up like she'd just caught the scent of something burning. "She's here?" Her voice was dangerously tight.

I nodded. "Yeah. She lives with me and Julia."

Smith's eyes gleamed with something fierce, something nuclear. "Where is she now?"

"I'll show you." Nic's door squawked as I pushed it open, revealing a neatly made bed, the dresser bare, not a single decoration on the wall.

My throat tightened. "She's gone," I whispered, my voice breaking.

Smith walked around Nic's room, her expression unreadable. She opened drawers, looked under the bed, in the closet. There was nothing. The room was empty, dead, smelling of dust and disuse.

My voice rose, shaking with the force of everything I'd been holding back. "Everyone leaves me," I said, tears spilling down my cheeks. "Everyone."

Smith stepped to me, her voice low and steady, like she was trying to soothe a scared animal. "Tuesday, listen to me. You're *not* alone. I'm here. But you need to take your medicine."

I shook my head, backing away. "I can't. Nic hates it when I take a whole one. She disappears."

"Tuesday." Smith drew out each syllable. "Nic isn't here right now. I need you to trust me. Where do you keep it?"

I told her about the Cabinet of Lost Hope. I realized I was weeping. Somehow, she led me to the couch and had me sit down. When she returned, she held out a pill and a glass of water, her gaze steady. "Just this once," she said. "Let me help you."

"Cut it in half," I pleaded.

"Not this time," she said gently. "The whole thing. I'll make sure you're safe, and I'll make sure Julia is taken care of."

Still, I hesitated.

"What would Corn want you to do right now?" she asked.

It was a low blow, but it worked. With jittery hands, I took the pill and swallowed it. The water was cold, searing my throat. I imagined the world beginning to go gloriously smooth, imagined how nice it would be to be taken care of, to feel safe in my body for the first time in years.

I heard Smith make a phone call, her voice muted. "I won't be back in today," she said. "Something came up."

When she returned to me on the couch, she covered me in the pink-and-orange afghan my mother had crocheted. "The officers are pulling up with Julia. I'll be right back with her."

She left. The winter light filtered through the windows, painting shapes on the ceiling. I followed them with heavy eyes. At some point, the front door opened.

Julia's voice, bright as pennies: "Momma?"

"Your mom's resting," Smith said. "How about we get you a snack and you can tell me about school?"

I floated in and out, catching fragments. Julia explaining multiplication. Smith's quiet laugh. The smell of grilled cheese. Had I told her where the bread was? The pans?

"Is my mom sick?" Julia's question carried.

"She's just tired." Smith's voice was warm honey. "Sometimes grown-ups need extra rest. I have two kids of my own. They're in high school now. There were days I needed rest, too."

"Did you make them grilled cheese?"

An easy laugh. "And chicken with stars soup. Want to see if your mom has any?"

Their voices faded into kitchen clatter. I should get up, help them, but the couch held me like quicksand, and my limbs were made of warm, melting gold. Later—minutes? hours?—Smith's face appeared above me. "Julia's in bed. I read her three chapters of *Charlotte's Web*. Hope that's okay."

I tried to nod. "Appreciate it."

She perched on the coffee table, her suit wrinkled now, her face sewn with concern. "Will you let me keep helping you, Tuesday?"

"Yeah." The word came easily, wrapped in pharmaceutical cotton.

She set her mouth in a line. "I want to bring you both in, keep you in a safe house until we've caught Arsen."

I shook my head. The movement felt underwater-slow. "I have a better idea. Tomorrow night."

Her brow furrowed. "What happens tomorrow night?"

"My plan." I closed my eyes. I meant to open them again, but they were too heavy. "Just let Julia have one more regular day. Let me visit my mom. Then tomorrow night, we do it my way."

I explained what I had in mind.

Silence stretched between us. I could feel her weighing it, this gift I was asking for. One more day of normal for my daughter. I dragged my eyes open.

"Okay," she finally said. She didn't like it. I could see it in the set of her jaw, the tension in her shoulders. "But I'm staying close. And if anything feels wrong—"

"Thank you." I'd never be able to repay her.

I drifted loose then, into dreams of Nick painting Trixie's toenails smooth gumball purple, of Corn's gentle laugh, of Julia safe and whole and happy. Tomorrow would come soon enough. Tomorrow we would face the truth.

But tonight, I could rest.

Tonight, someone else was standing guard.

He watched from the shadows. Cops were out front, their faces drawn tight, radios hissing. They thought they were moving in, thought they were in control.

They didn't know shit.

Everything was right on schedule.

She was absolutely falling apart, panic slithering under Her skin, making Her second-guess every creak, every shadow. That was the best part. The waiting. The knowing. Watching it build in Her chest until She could hardly breathe.

Because he was coming.

He was going to teach Her a lesson once and for all. Show Her exactly who was in charge, who always had been.

He moved away from the attic window and squeezed into the large chest. It was half full of blankets. It was pretty comfortable to lie on a few and cover himself beneath the rest. He'd slept in worse places.

Down below, he could hear the detective moving around, getting cozy. Planning to stay the night, no doubt. Fine by him. Let them play guard dog, puff up their chests, tell Her it was all handled.

They weren't as smart as him. Never had been, never would be.

He was about to teach Her the final lesson.

He couldn't wait to finally meet Julia.

CHAPTER 74

I could pick out the undercover cops when I dropped Julia off at school the next morning because I was looking for them. To anyone else, they were faceless parents. I gave her a kiss goodbye and headed out. The drive to Rochester was an endless loop of nothingness: snow-crusted fields, barren trees, the dirty refinery with its steel needles belching black, and the occasional roadside diner whose neon signs blinked with a desperation that matched my mood.

I parked my clunker and stared at the psychiatric institution, all pale brick and sterile windows, trying to muster the energy to go inside. Even under the best of circumstances, visiting Mom felt like stepping into a slow-motion car crash. You saw it coming, knew you couldn't stop it, and so you braced yourself for impact. I needed to talk to her, though. Had to see her face for what might be the last time.

"Tuesday!" she called out the moment I walked into her room. Her voice, shrill with an edge of joy, made me wince. She was sitting on her bed, legs crossed, wearing a robe that might have been white once but now looked more like oatmeal. "Oh, my baby, look at you! Still pretty as a picture, even though you cut off all your hair."

"Hi, Mom." I forced a smile.

"Don't just stand there," she said, patting the spot next to her. "Come sit with your old ma. Tell me what's new. Tell me something good."

"There's not much to tell." I lowered myself onto the bed. The mattress sagged under my weight, and the faint, oversweet smell of the medicine sweating out through her pores filled my nostrils. "Work's fine. Rent's due. You know, the usual."

"You always did have a knack for making life sound like a root canal," she said, chuckling. "Come on, Trixie. Surely you've got something better than that."

"It's Tuesday, Mom," I said, more out of habit than hope. Did it really matter what she called me? I was the reason my sister was dead. "And I'm here to tell you it might be a while before I can visit again."

Her face fell, and for a moment, I caught a glimpse of the woman she used to be. The one who sang along to Aretha Franklin while baking sugar cookies. But just as quickly, she vanished, replaced by the glassy-eyed stare.

"Why?" she asked, her voice small.

I hesitated. There was no way to tell her the truth, that tonight was my last stand, that either I died or Arsen did, but one way or another, it was ending. "I'm traveling," I said finally. "But I'll do my best to come back. I promise."

She nodded, her gaze drifting to the window. The snow outside seemed to hold her attention for a long time. Then, out of nowhere, she said, "How are you sleeping, honey?"

The question hit me like a slap. "What?"

"You used to have those night terrors, remember?" she said, turning back to me. Her eyes were sharper now, clear. "When you were dating that boy. What was he called? The awful one."

My stomach twisted. I didn't offer a name.

"I never liked him," Mom said in a conspiratorial voice. "Told you so, didn't I? But you were head over heels. Young and stupid, like we all were at one time." She shrugged. "And probably he isn't so bad anymore. We all grow up and mellow out."

"I don't want to talk about him," I said in a strangled voice. She was fully convinced that I was Trixie.

Mom tipped her head. "Fair enough," she said. "But he was no good for you. I saw it then, and I remember it now. A mother knows these things, honey. Now could you ask your father to come in here? I need help with that dang leaky faucet again."

I stood abruptly. My chest felt tight, like all the oxygen had been sucked out of the room. I'd come here for a mother who'd left us years ago, one who only lived in my imagination. Well, I'd done my duty by her. I'd given her a chance to say goodbye. "I should go."

"Oh, don't be like that," she said, reaching for my hand. "I'm just trying to help. We all make mistakes. You live, you learn, you move on. Just remember that there's nothing more important than family. Just ask your father."

I pulled away, my skin crawling. "I love you, Mom," I said, heading for the door.

On my way out, a voice crackled over the intercom. "Ms. Tuesday Kenn. Please come to the front desk. Ms. Tuesday Kenn, to the front desk."

A nurse was waiting for me when I got there, her expression one of annoyance. She didn't want to play secretary to visitors. "You have a call," she said, handing me the phone. "A Detective Smith."

My muscles went cold. I took the phone. "It's Tuesday."

"We exhumed Trixie," she said, all of yesterday's warmth gone. "The medical examiner has put a rush on processing the DNA, but the dental and medical records line up with your sister."

I closed my eyes. "Okay. Thanks for letting me know."

"I wasn't done." A pause on the other end of the line. "They line up with your sister except for one thing."

"What's that?" I asked, my grip tightening on the phone.

"The girl in the grave was never pregnant."

CHAPTER 75

"You're wrong," I said. "Or they're wrong. Trixie was definitely pregnant. How accurate is the science on that, anyhow? Don't they just guess by the shape of the pelvic bones?"

Smith exhaled loudly. "The medical examiner was pretty certain."

A flurry of nurses rushed past me, going the opposite direction of Mom's room. "They're wrong," I repeated. "And it doesn't alter tonight's plan, does it?"

"No," Smith said.

I waited for her to try talking me out of it again. She didn't.

◈

Julia bounded out of the school doors with her backpack swinging, her mittened hands waving happily like she hadn't just seen me seven hours earlier. I nearly wept with relief. The police had been watching her all day, but that was no guarantee.

"Hi, Momma!" she chirped, sliding into the passenger seat. Her cheeks were flushed from the cold, her smile wide.

"Hi, baby girl." I ruffled her hair as I pulled away from the curb. "How about we do something fun tonight?"

Her eyes lit up. "Like what?"

"Dinner at Belcamino's and then a movie," I said. "Your pick."

"Really?" Her voice rose with disbelief. "Even though I haven't done my homework yet?"

"Even though you haven't done your homework yet," I confirmed.

◈

Belcamino's was packed, the air thick with the smell of garlic and marinara. Julia devoured her pizza like it was the last meal she'd ever eat. I picked at a plate of spaghetti. Afterward, we went to see *Legends of the Fall* at the Highland Theatre, sharing a big tub of buttered popcorn. Julia was way too young to understand half the film, but she didn't care. She liked the horses and Brad Pitt's hair, and I was grateful for two hours of not having to think.

By the time we returned home, it was late and dark. I hustled Julia upstairs, the old steps creaking under our weight, and sent her straight to bed.

"But I'm not tired!" she protested, her voice sounding muggy from all the dairy she'd eaten.

"It's late." I kissed her forehead. "And if you go right to bed, maybe we'll do something fun this weekend, too."

She grumbled but snuggled under the covers, her eyes already drooping. I left her room with the door cracked, the soft glow of her night-light spilling into the hallway.

I kept all the rest of the house lights on. Every lamp, every overhead bulb, even the garish kitchen fluorescents. Then I poured a glass of bourbon from the emergency bottle I kept hidden in the Cabinet of Lost Hope. I'd never opened the bottle before, but if not tonight, then when?

I dropped into a kitchen chair and raised my glass to the empty spot across from me.

"Here's to you, Nic," I said softly. "Wherever the hell you are."

I drank slowly, savoring the taste. It began to work its caramel magic, popping my joints, relaxing my thoughts. When my glass was empty, I knew it was time to turn off the lights. Just before going to bed, I went up to the attic, opened the wooden box inside my secret room, and took out the paperback-size lockbox I'd been avoiding. I brought it to my bedroom.

Then I slipped into my flannel pajamas and crawled beneath the covers.

Sleep didn't come easily. When it did, it was like falling off a cliff—abrupt and disorienting. But the peace didn't last. Not long after, I was awake again, frozen in place, my body leaden as my eyes darted around the room.

My chest was heavy, my breathing shallow. I couldn't move, couldn't scream.

Someone was whistling "The House of the Rising Sun," the eerie, piercing tune as good as a tranquilizer dart. A cold sweat broke out across my skin, but invisible chains held me fast.

He stood at the foot of my bed, his face half hidden in shadow.

For a minute, I saw Arsen. Older, tanner, fatter, and with a slump to his shoulders because he *had* taken that first shot that night.

But it was worse than that.

"Hello, Trixie," my father said, his voice a low, mocking drawl. "Or should I say *Tuesday*? You've done a great job pretending to be her, I'll give you that much. But a man never forgets his favorite child."

CHAPTER 76

I'd told the lies so long that I had come to believe them myself. It helped that there was a truth at their core. Arsen *had* come to the trailer that night looking for Julia. My father must have come later, showing up for the first time in years, a terrible coincidence. It was their arguing that had woken me. At some point, as near as I could figure, Arsen and my dad started shooting at each other.

Tuesday had died trying to shield Julia, our protector until the very end. Unbalanced by the guilt—I'd been frozen in the bedroom when most of this went down—and unwilling to let Julia and me go into a foster home, I claimed my older sister's identity and moved us to Saint Paul. I took her age, her scholarship, her *future*. It was the only way to get Julia and me out of Lilydale. Wild child Trixie Hendrickson became gifted, stable, eighteen-year-old Tuesday Kenn. We'd already laid the groundwork when I used Tuesday's name at the hospital to give birth to Julia.

I knew we weren't safe, that we were living on borrowed time.

I'd been wrong about who'd been hunting us since that night, was all.

A car's headlights swept across the room, briefly illuminating my father's face. The years hadn't been kind to Daryl Hendrickson, but I could still see the twinkle that'd attracted my mom, the magic that had sometimes lit up our childhoods.

"My sweet Trixie." He took a step around to the side of my bed. "Is it okay if I call you Trixie, *Trixie*?"

My body was locked up tight as a bank vault, but he whistled a little more of the tune to be sure. He tipped his head and studied me, his expression delighted. "You're having one of those fits, aren't you? Just like old times. Wasn't sure if it'd still work." He coughed into his hand. "Arsen told me all about that when I finally tracked him down in Florida after that awful night. Couldn't let a man shoot one of my girls and live, though neither did I want him to get off too easily." He whistled a few more bars.

My heart was thudding so powerfully that I thought I might throw up. "Don't," I whispered, though whether to my dad or my own betraying muscles, I wasn't sure.

He ignored me, settling onto the edge of my bed. "You've done a great job pretending to be Tuesday, just like Nicholas did a great job pretending to be Arsen, six feet in the ground." He grimaced. "Those dumb-shit cops didn't even know I was there. They just assumed your white-trash boyfriend was to blame."

He rubbed his nose. "You know why I was so upset with Arsen that night? It'd come to my attention that he was telling people *he* was the Crying Killer. How much longer until he started acting on that? It was bad enough I was doing it. I couldn't allow a second."

Hot tears leaked out of my eyes. My father had been the serial killer the whole time. It made terrible sense. His temper, the dark closet he kept no matter where we lived. Suddenly, he rolled me over, his hands burning on my lower back. I felt my pajama bottoms being tugged down but still couldn't move. "Yep, he did try it out on you, just like he told me he did. Except it was never an X, like the papers said, at least not the ones I carved. It was always a cross. I wasn't going to let those poor girls meet their end without a blessing."

A shapeless moan drifted out of my mouth. My father let me drop onto my back again.

"Things went south pretty quick after I confronted Arsen at the trailer about his intentions. He got a hot finger and shot your older sister for trying to keep Julia from him. Your friend Nicky jumped in and ate a bullet. I hadn't come for any of that trouble, so I charged out the back. Arsen ran out the front. That's when he saw that the cops had arrived. He skedaddled back inside and must have had just enough time to get his jacket and ID on Nicky and follow me out the rear." Dad shook his head with disbelief, laughing huskily. "Smartest dumb thing that idiot boy ever did in his life. The cops bought it hook, line, and sinker. I guess that's the Lilydale police for you."

He smacked my leg. I couldn't feel it. "Like I said, I finally caught up to Arsen in Florida. He got what was coming to him. But there was still a debt owed to me." He held up his hands like he was framing a marquee. "Trixie Hendrickson, my favorite daughter, the one who'd do anything for her old man." He dropped his hands and glared at me. "Except you didn't, did you? You were just as happy to never see me again as your mom and sister were." His eyes darkened. "So I sought you out, came after the loose end. For a while, you were scrubbed from the face of the earth, the baby along with you. Then I spotted 'Tuesday' in the PI magazine. It was a terrible photo, but I recognized my baby girl right away. Seems like God wants us to be together."

My heart hammered against my ribs, but I still couldn't move. Exactly like every night Dad whistled "The House of the Rising Sun" before beating Mom, exactly like every time Arsen came to the trailer after a bout of drinking, exactly like that devastating final night, when I'd been useless as Tuesday's screams had filled the air.

Dad leaned closer, his breath hot on my face. It smelled like cigarettes and garlic. "Remember how good it was, Trix? When we were a family?"

"No," I choked out.

He reached out to touch my face. His fingers were calloused, familiar in a way that made me want to vomit. "Julia's my blood, and I'm taking her with me. She'll be an orphan after tonight, her dad gator food in Florida and her mom with her wrists slit because she'd gone as crazy as her own ma." His eyes lit up with terrible glee. "Finally, I'll get the family I was owed my whole life. I won't make the same mistakes with Julia that my own parents did with me, or even that I did with you and Tuesday. She'll *never* betray me."

My beautiful, fierce daughter who loved bubble baths and Italian food and singing off-key. Who had Tuesday's nose and my chin and our mother's eyes. Who was the best of all three of us, with none of her father or grandfather in her.

My dad leaned toward me, a straight razor suddenly gleaming in his hand.

"No," I said, low and guttural. "No. No. No!"

Holding tight to the image of Julia, I was able to finally move my arm, bringing the .38 up and out from under the covers. Nic had convinced me to lock it away after The Fracture, and she'd been right. It was too dangerous to have easy access to it when I was unstable. But I'd known I'd need it tonight.

I'd just been wrong about who I'd need it for.

My father's eyes widened. For a split second, he looked like the man who'd cooked Tuesday and me hot brown while weaving stories about the kingdom we lived in.

"You won't shoot me," he said. "You never could stand up for yourself with men. That's the one edge your sister had over you."

The thing was, he was right. Trixie Hendrickson had been a doormat for him and for Arsen. But I wasn't her anymore.

I was Tuesday Kenn—PI, survivor, mother—and I had a daughter to protect.

"People change," I said, and pulled the trigger.

CHAPTER 77

The petite female cop pretending to be Julia was the first one into the room.

We'd made the switch in the movie theater, the officer taking Julia's hat and coat while Julia was whisked off to a safe house.

The cop moved fast, her Glock raised. She paused when her eyes took in the scene: Daryl Hendrickson's body slumped on the floor, a violent splatter of scarlet on the faded wallpaper behind. The acrid smell of gunpowder hung in the air, mixing with the tang of blood.

Smith arrived next, her tailored coat swirling like a cape, her heels talking business to the scuffed hardwood. Her amber eyes swept the room once, twice, and then locked onto me.

I was sitting up in bed, the gun on the blanket where I'd dropped it. I could feel the weight of Smith's gaze like a physical thing, and it took everything I had not to flinch. I'd suspected someone was in the house, had since Julia said she thought she saw Coretta's son going upstairs. And hadn't Liz Bauer mentioned what an excellent hider her brother was? Once I trusted my instincts, I knew exactly what to do.

"Tuesday," Smith said, her voice cool and measured. The words that followed sounded almost like an accusation. "You okay?"

"Peachy," I said, my voice rough and shaky. "Just another typical Friday night."

Smith's lips twitched. She strode past Julia's body double without a word, her eyes lingering on my father's corpse. His head lolled to one side, the hole in his forehead a grotesque punctuation mark to the story he'd thought he could write.

"That's not Arsen Bauer."

"It's my dad," I said.

Her eyes widened. There would be more questions coming. Well, I had them, too. "He must have had a hidey-hole in the attic," Smith said, her tone flat. Her eyes went to my ceiling, where the trap door was open half an inch. "We missed him when we cleared up there." She shook her head, then studied his wound. "You shot him?"

"What tipped you off?" I gestured weakly at the gory mess.

Smith glared at me. "You're not helping yourself."

"He broke into my house," I said, rubbing my arms. "He threatened to kill me. Pulled a straight razor out." I stuck out my chin, daring her to challenge me. "So I shot him."

Smith nodded thoughtfully. "Self-defense," she said, almost to herself.

The sound of radios crackling and boots scuffing filled the apartment, but all I could focus on was the thought that kept looping in my head: *Julia is safe. The killer is dead.*

I'd shot him. Not Arsen. Not the monster from my nightmares.

My *father*.

The word felt foreign. What was a father? Someone who protected you? Someone who taught you right from wrong? Someone who showed up?

He'd done none of those things.

Instead, he'd taught me to be afraid. He'd shown my sister and me that "love" was just another word for "control." He'd beaten our mother, and he'd murdered at least four women.

The horror ended here. In this bedroom. With me.

But god, the weight of it. The impossible weight.

Smith locked eyes with me. I opened my mouth, planning to spit out another cocky joke, but a sob escaped instead. She came over and wrapped her arms around me, humming as she stroked my hair.

EPILOGUE

Mid-February sun sliced through the kitchen window, turning the edge of Julia's curls golden. I was teaching her the secret to a perfect hollandaise—the right balance between lemon and butter, plus slow and steady whisking.

"Momma, it's getting lumpy," she said, her arm moving in frantic circles.

"Easy there, Speed Racer." I steadied her wrist. "Think of it like slow dancing. You want a waltz, not the Running Man."

Her brow furrowed. "What's the Running Man?"

"Never mind." I shook my head. "I'm officially ancient."

Coretta snorted from the kitchen table. "Try being around for two world wars."

Smith—I didn't think I'd ever get comfortable calling her Tayari—just smiled. She'd dressed casually, for her. Cream sweater, matching slacks, a steaming cup of coffee in front of her.

The house smelled like heaven. Toasting English muffins, salty Canadian bacon sizzling on the stovetop, fresh tomatoes I'd splurged on at the grocery store. The kitchen was dressed up for Valentine's Day, the only holiday that managed to push back the gloom of a Minnesota winter. Red paper hearts Julia had cut out hung in the window. A dish of foil-wrapped chocolates sat on the counter. I'd even found a tablecloth with pink and white roses that felt cheerful instead of tacky, a rarity in the Valentine's aisle.

While Coretta and Smith lightly debated the evilness of Saint Paul's snow emergency parking rules, I showed Julia the best way to poach the eggs. The gentle swirl of vinegared water, the way the whites wrapped around the yolk like a silk blanket.

"Perfect," I said as she lifted an egg with a slotted spoon. "Just like that."

Coretta had a hard time staying put while we cooked for her, but that had been the requirement of having her come up for the first meal we'd ever served her. She had to allow herself to be *served*. Same with Smith. I owed both women more than I could ever repay.

We assembled our plates: English muffin on the bottom, then a thick slice of Canadian bacon, followed by a poached egg, Julia's slightly lumpy but perfectly edible hollandaise poured over it all. Oh, and a grilled tomato on the side because vegetables made me feel like a responsible parent.

"Ta-da!" Julia did jazz hands over her creation. "Can we eat in the living room? Please? I wanna watch *Northern Exposure*."

"What do you think, ladies?"

Smith was dousing her eggs with enough pepper to choke a goat. "Sure."

"Fine by me," Coretta said, already halfway to the living room. "Then we don't have to make small talk."

Her son had visited but lasted only a day before she sent him packing. The man Julia had seen going up the attic stairs had been her grandfather. After I told Smith about my father's confession before I shot him, police reopened the original Crying Killer case, exploring the possibility that it'd been Daryl Hendrickson all along. The fact that a trail of murders had followed him the last few places he'd lived lent credence to that theory. Smith gave me regular updates on what they unearthed. It wasn't exactly kosher, but she said it was a fair trade for the help I was giving her. Basically, once I'd reopened Corn's PI agency, I'd taken on the questionable role that he used to play for her department. I looked forward to a long partnership between her and me.

The four of us settled in with our plates, Coretta and Smith on the couch, Julia and me sitting on the floor. On the TV, Dr. Fleischman was complaining about something in Alaska. Julia's plate was already half cleared.

"This is amazing," she said around a mouthful of egg. "Way better than IHOP."

Coretta snorted.

"Chew with your mouth closed, you barbarian," I said. But I was smiling. These were the moments I lived for now. Quiet mornings, teaching her the things my sister and I had had to figure out on our own, making sure she was safe, loved.

◈

After breakfast, Coretta returned to her apartment and Smith left to start her shift.

I cleaned up the meal, freshened my Blackberry lipstick, and bundled Julia and me up against the Minnesota winter. The cemetery was on the outskirts of Saint Paul, peaceful under a blanket of snow. Corn's headstone was simple granite, his name and dates etched deep. Next to him lay my sister. Smith had helped me to fast-track the paperwork that allowed her body to be moved in exchange for me agreeing to regular therapy.

I didn't think she could enforce that deal any more than she could hold me to the weekly coffee meetups we'd been having, but she was right that I needed help. My official diagnosis was post-traumatic stress disorder, though my therapist had added "complicated grief" in the margins. You think? He'd switched me off Haldol, first thing. I was trying Tofranil now. Too early to tell if it was working, but I was hopeful.

I read my sister's new headstone.

Trixie Hendrickson, it said. Beloved Daughter and Sister.

I would be Tuesday, forever, had been for long enough that most days I believed it myself. It was the final gift my sister gave me, the escape plan she'd promised.

Julia knelt to brush snow off Corn's grave.

"I miss him," she said in her high, sweet voice.

"Me too, punkin."

She rested one of the two red roses we'd brought against his headstone and then put the second on my sister's. Julia thought she was visiting her aunt Trixie's grave, not her aunt Tuesday's. Believed she was Tuesday Kenn's daughter, not Trixie Hendrickson's. The lies had kept us together and protected, at least until my dad spotted that article.

My fingers found the raised skin on my lower back beneath my heavy coat. The X Arsen had carved there with a knife, marking me as his, the reason I never took my shirt off with my lovers. It was just a scar now, like the ones inside my head and heart. They'd always be part of me, but maybe they didn't have to define me.

I felt a familiar presence at my shoulder. Nic, my guardian angel, who'd appeared two years ago, when I'd had the mental breakdown at work and needed her to survive. She'd glued me back together, kept me solid enough so that I could keep parenting Julia. Maybe someday I wouldn't need her so close, but that day wasn't here yet. She wrapped her arm around me as I hugged Julia. The three of us stood graveside, our toes growing cold while chickadees argued in the bare branches overhead.

"Hot chocolate?" I asked Julia after a few minutes. "We can stop at that place you like, the one with the mini marshmallows."

Her face lit up. "Café Latte? Can I get whipped cream, too?"

I laughed. "Don't push your luck, kid."

We trudged back to the car, leaving two sets of fresh tracks in the snow. Nic didn't leave any, of course, but I could still feel her arm around me, steady and warm, as we drove away from the people we used to be.

Some lies kept us alive.

Some ghosts kept us whole.

And sometimes the most we could hope for was to be broken in interesting ways.

AFTERWORD

While nearly 8 percent of the US population deals with post-traumatic stress disorder, women are twice as likely to develop it as men.[1] Much of this difference is owed to three factors: the younger age at which girls are exposed to trauma, the type of trauma they experience, and the fact that their trauma is often chronic and appears in primary relationships.[2] In other words, women are not genetically more predisposed to develop PTSD than men; rather, they are forced to live more dangerous lives.

According to a study published by *The New England Journal of Medicine*, 46 percent of women with PTSD experience hallucinations, mostly auditory.[3] The hallucinations can be incredibly confusing and terrifying to the person having them and require compassion from friends, family, and the health care community. The good news is that

---

1 National Center for PTSD, U.S. Department of Veterans Affairs, "PTSD and Women: Research Findings," https://www.ptsd.va.gov/professional/treat/specific/ptsd_research_women.asp.

2 Vivian V. McCutcheon, Carolyn E. Sartor, Nicole E. Pommer, Kathleen K. Bucholz, Elliot C. Nelson, Pamela A. F. Madden, Andrew C. Heath, "Age at Trauma Exposure and PTSD Risk in Young Adult Women," *Journal of Traumatic Stress* 23, no. 6 (October 2010), 2010 Dec;23(6):811-4. doi: 10.1002/jts.20577. PMID: 20963847; PMCID: PMC3121097.

3 Joel Yager, MD, "Hearing Voices in Patients with Trauma," *NEJM Clinician*, March 26, 2020, https://clinician.nejm.org/hearing-voices-patients-trauma-nejm-jw.NA51114.

with the right treatment, PTSD can be made manageable, often resulting in hallucinations disappearing entirely.

If you or someone you know is dealing with PTSD, you are not alone, and there is help available. Here are some resources:

- The Substance Abuse and Mental Health Services Administration (SAMHSA) has a helpline at 1-800-662-HELP (4357) and an online locator for mental health services.
- The Centers for Medicare & Medicaid Services (CMS) has an online tool for finding Medicare providers.
- The US Department of Veterans Affairs (VA) has an online tool for finding VA locations and providers.

ACKNOWLEDGMENTS

My deepest thanks to the wonderful team at Thomas & Mercer, to my agent, and to my writing community for their constant generosity. Most of all, thank you, booksellers, librarians, and readers. You're why these stories exist. I appreciate your willingness to support the dark yet hopeful corners of my imagination.

ABOUT THE AUTHOR

Photo © 2023 Kelly Weaver Photography

Jess Lourey is the Amazon Charts bestselling author of *The Quarry Girls*, *Unspeakable Things*, *Litani*, and *Bloodline*, as well as the Steinbeck and Reed thrillers, the Salem's Cipher novels, and the Murder by Month rom-com mysteries. Lourey writes about secrets, fosters kittens, and travels. She's surpassed a million readers; been short-listed for the Goodreads Choice Awards and the Edgar Award twice each; and won the International Thriller, Anthony, and Minnesota Book Awards. She also has an active reader group on Facebook called Lourey's Literati. For more information, including a link to her TEDx Talk, in which she discusses the surprising inspiration behind her writing career, visit www.jesslourey.com.